THE
MOMENT
BEFORE
DROWNING

THE MOMENT BEFORE DROWNING

A NOVEL

JAMES BRYDON

BROOKLYN, NEW YORK, USA
BALLYDEHOB, CO. CORK, IRELAND

Published by Akashic Books
©2018 James Brydon

ISBN: 978-1-61775-625-2
Library of Congress Control Number: 2017956560

All rights reserved.
First printing

Akashic Books
Brooklyn, New York, USA
Ballydehob, Co. Cork, Ireland
Twitter: @AkashicBooks
Facebook: AkashicBooks
E-mail: info@akashicbooks.com
Website: www.akashicbooks.com

I wish to offer my sincere thanks to Bill and Annette,
as well as to Johnny, Johanna, and everyone at Akashic Books,
for taking the trouble to read this book, believing in it,
and patiently helping make it into something better.

FIRST EVENING

December 12, 1959

I have been back in Sainte-Élisabeth only a few hours when Erwann arrives and batters on my door, his hands oblivious to the splinters, his memory haunted by a girl whose martyred body he cannot leave to the earth. It seems strange to be back in the town of my childhood among the gray stone houses that squat in the gloom beneath their slate roofs. Dominating everything around it, the church spire points up into the louring, falling night. Under a sky hanging pregnant with damp, I feel the trickle of the past seeping back into my mind.

Only two days earlier I had been flown back from Algeria to Paris on a military plane. I stood on the tarmac shivering in the weak sun, staring down at my dust-covered boots and watching twitches and spasms run across my hands. I tried to focus on the washed-out sky, the glitter of North African daylight, waiting for the rough hands of the soldiers who were escorting me to bundle me up the steps and push me through the plane door.

They didn't handcuff me but sat across from me warily, not knowing how to react. Some stared at me with suspicion in their eyes, others jostled and shoved me and spoke loudly of the *fellagha* they had shot and burned. The plane reeked of sweat and oil. One young soldier, a jagged scar running across his neck, looked for a long moment into the depths of my eyes. Then he leaned over and, without taking his gaze off me, slowly released a thread of saliva which spun down and landed on my boots. He spoke in a voice entirely calm, yet imbued with fury.

"It's people like you who are stopping us from ever winning this war. For every one of them we kill, we poison one hundred against us."

Then he turned away and began to write in his journal again, stopping briefly to wipe his mouth with the back of his hand. He didn't even glance up as the plane rattled along the runway and lurched into the air. From the small oval window behind me, I peered down for the last time on the gorges of the Algérois hinterland, great ragged clefts ripped out of the rocks and plunging into realms of shadow between the majesty of the cliffs.

When we landed in Paris the sky was a dull pewter and rain drummed on the tarmac and bounced off the windows. The soldier whose spit had dried in a smear on my boots grabbed hold of my shoulder and forced me out of the plane and onto the soil of my homeland. He stared straight past me and into the mist. There wasn't a flicker of emotion in his face.

"I helped build a primary school out in Kabylia. Kids used to walk for miles to come and learn how to read and write French. Even the kids of the *fellagha* came running down from the mountains to sit in our classroom. We taught them to read La Fontaine and to sing the Marseillaise. I hope they crucify you."

For two days I sat in isolation in a military prison in Paris. I watched the sky lighten and darken in bruised patterns through the reinforced glass window. I watched the same tic pulse across my hands. I stared at the dust of Algeria that lay faintly on my boots. Sleep came only in brief moments and each time I woke I was soaked in sweat, my chest airless and heaving. I couldn't drag myself up from my bunk. I had seen enough prisoners to know the terror of captivity, the walls of the cell looming in front of you wherever you turn. The feeling of being buried. I wondered if I would panic, but I felt only a weird calm. There was nowhere I wanted to go, no life of my own from which I was suddenly severed. Even getting up and walking over to the cell door seemed to require an effort far beyond my strength.

Eventually I was brought into the dark, book-lined office of the examining magistrate. I looked up at him while he spoke but when I left the room five minutes later I couldn't remember his face at all. I just heard the clear tones of his voice resounding with a surprising gentleness in the quiet. He said that the preliminary hearing would take place next Friday, but that I was not required to spend the intervening time in detention.

"Where is your home, Capitaine le Garrec?"

Home? I had stopped renting my apartment in Paris over two years ago. There was only the old house that I grew up in, and which I had not even seen for years.

"Sainte-Élisabeth."

"Then you may return there, although I would ask you not to leave the town and must remind you that, should you fail to present yourself for the preliminary hearing, this may entail further criminal charges."

I nodded and that same afternoon found myself huddled in my army greatcoat at the Gare du Nord, clutching a tiny cloth bag which contained the few rags I had salvaged from Algeria and waiting for a train to take me into the wind-raked fields of Brittany. As the bus from

Saint-Malo wound between the hedgerows, I stared through rain-spattered windows at miles of dead heather turning brown beneath the frost.

Sainte-Élisabeth is what I called home in the dim, forgotten days of my childhood, before disease and old age ate away at my parents while I was too far away to help or even watch. As I walk from the bus stop along familiar, deserted streets the sky seems enormous, bloated, and infinite, billowing over everything. I lose myself in swirls of gray; great, bulbous streaks of darkness; every possible permutation of impending rain. After two years in Algeria I can feel the Breton damp seeping into my body, chilling me, and the ice carried on the wind settling in my blood. Out by the sea, which I can perceive only as a howl frustrated by the rocks, the beam of the lighthouse flashes its warning into the encroaching dark: a fragile blade of light that swings away and is lost, only to return each time and abide in the blindness of the night.

The little house I grew up in gleams white, a miracle of human endeavor dwarfed by the leaden air all around. It seems strange to find it still standing after so many years. It should have been destroyed, broken down, and swallowed up like the past itself, to which it is an eerie monument. The time I lived here no longer exists. It disintegrated in the interrogation chambers of the *service de renseignements* in Algeria. The things I can remember about Sainte-Élisabeth seem alien, as if they had happened to someone else. Fragments of memory embedded in my brain like shrapnel from a bomb.

I open the door and step inside. The air is damp and frozen, but there is order here. Madame Gallier has performed her duties conscientiously. The floors are swept and clean. The grate sparkles. Books stand in order upon the shelves, seemingly untouched. Pots, pans, and plates sit frozen in kitchen cupboards. The circular oak table, around which we ate while the night came ever closer outside, remains where it always was by the kitchen door. There are no cobwebs. There is no soot or dirt. Robert has kept his promise and mowed the lawn and kept the hedges trimmed. There is an imitation of normality here. They have maintained a place where I should be able to live.

I leave the lights off and sit down on the sofa. The faint whiff of mildew floats up from the cushions beneath. I can't remember when I last ate, but I don't have the energy to look for food. I just let the chill breath of the air enfold me and watch the squares of the windows blackening as the daylight evaporates.

It is almost fully dark by the time the thud of blows on my door pulls me shivering out of my torpor. One of those intense nights that seem to flood in off the sea and drown the land is setting in. The sharp cracks of flesh and bone jarring on frozen wood seem amplified in the house's emptiness. For a second, the person staring at me as I open the door is unknown: dark curls of hair framing a tanned face, the chin held at a gently aristocratic angle, expressing the vaguest hint of superiority; a V-necked jumper sitting smartly beneath a tweed jacket; delicate, cultured fingers ending in long nails, like the hands of a guitarist. Then I reconstruct the face as I knew it fifteen years ago: Erwann Ollivier. For a moment he seems lost too. He gazes at me out of the darkness and searches for words. His chest heaves for breath and I realize later that he must have hastened and stumbled across the heather to get here as soon as he found out I had arrived. He must have felt the dead gorse scratch his legs and remembered how, months earlier, those same twigs and thorns had clutched the corpse of a girl murdered and dumped there on a winter's night like this one.

As soon as the recognition flashes in my eyes, he smiles and grips my arm warmly. I turn the lights on in the house. Groping for something familiar, I try to return his smile. Inside, he paces silently, seemingly incapable of giving voice to whatever thoughts had thrust him out into the hostile, wind-lashed evening and driven his legs over the wastes of the heathland to my door.

He has aged. My brain struggles for a second to translate the youthful, unlined face I remember into the careworn, middle-aged man pacing restlessly before me. His jet-black curls are flecked with gray at the temples. The glasses are a little thicker, their glitter hiding the greenish glint of his eyes. The skin of his face seems pulled a little tighter, stretched taut as if it were shrinking. He always appeared weighed down by intellectual preoccupations. Now something heavier is lodged inside him. Something more burdensome and unsettling that exhausts his mind.

I find an old bottle of Calvados in one of the cupboards and give him a couple of shots. Blood rushes to his cheeks and his mouth finds words.

"Jacques . . . I hope you don't mind me intruding like this. I heard you were coming. It was quite a story. Everybody heard . . . I mean, you were always a story here in sleepy Sainte-Élisabeth, even twenty years ago. I remember you being spoken of as a hero. The finest flower of the Resistance! And then you went off to join the police force in Paris. A glorious figure, untainted by the sins of the past, setting out to forge a new dawn! And how did they bring you back? Skulking through the night, practically in chains. What happened in Algeria? I can't believe the things they're saying about you could be true. Whatever did they do to you out there?" There is a softness, a flutter of sorrow in his voice. I don't know what to tell him. The silence stretches out between us.

"It doesn't matter," he says finally. "I came about something else. There's something I need you to do. Because you're the only person who can do it. Everyone else has forgotten." He stops pacing and sits down in front of me. I have the sense that he has rehearsed these words many times in his own mind before uttering them. "But you're going to be here for a while, at least for a few days, and while you are, I want you to investigate a crime for me. It happened last winter, last February, while you were out in Algeria. A girl named Anne-Lise Aurigny. Did you read anything about it?"

I shake my head. Algeria was a vacuum. Nothing in, nothing out. My life was squeezed within the horizons of the hinterland around Algiers: dust scratching my skin and throat; every tree and patch of shade twisting, metamorphosing in front of my eyes to become cover for guerrilla *katibas*. In the basement rooms of al-Mazra'a where the *service de renseignements* did its work, no sound traveled in or out. The detainees' world shrank to the same four walls. Undimmed, lurid lightbulbs and cracked plaster. The screams stayed muffled in the earth. It was part of the technique of interrogation: a suspect must lose, as quickly as possible, whatever links attached him to his own life. In that realm—of family, comrades, home—his struggle made sense. Resistance was meaningful. It shaped his existence. Al-Mazra'a was an exercise in intensive forgetting. Blotting out all connection to the world of memory. Time seemed to distort. A detainee had no sense of how long he had been kept underground. Minutes swelled and stretched. Hours passed like days. There was noth-ing more for him than the few square meters of his cell, the interrogators, and the infinite recesses of his pain.

"I can't investigate any crimes. I'm not a detective anymore. I don't have any authority, and I'm under or-ders to remain in Sainte-Élisabeth until the tribunal. I'm afraid I can't help."

"Jacques, listen . . ."

"I could even be arrested and returned to military prison in Paris."

Erwann smiles and the weariness seeps away from his face. This is how I remember him from when we were students in Paris: vigorous, intense, but with the weight-less intensity of the intellectual whose dramas play out in some abstract realm within his own mind.

"I don't think that you, of all people, can possibly be afraid of getting arrested. The Gestapo didn't stop you joining the Resistance; I can't believe that our bureaucratic and humane police force could stop you from investigat-ing this case. And I need you to find out what happened to Anne-Lise. *Why* something like that happened to her. Not only that: I think you need it too." He gestures around at the cold, immaculate house, at the dead fireplace and the books standing in their useless rows. "What are you going to do in here for the next days, or weeks, or how-ever long it is, while you wait for the French judiciary to prepare its vengeance on you? Work on the technicalities of your defense? Lose yourself in some of the great liter-ary and philosophical classics you admired in your youth? Meditate? Explore the possibilities of individual spiritu-ality? Or just remember the past? Endlessly?"

I can hear the truth in what Erwann says. Everywhere I look, I see the same shadows. The air seems swollen with reproach. It was easier to stare at the walls of my cell. They were closer, blanker. A real prison. One which looks the same to everyone, not one that only I can see.

I want to be able to perceive the Sainte-Élisabeth of my childhood again, the pretty town made to seem tiny by the vast cradle of sea and sky. Yet nothing is innocent anymore. Wherever my gaze rests, the stain of memory falls across it. One moment the world looks pallid and distant, the next it looms in front of me with unbearable intensity.

I know this from Algeria: time seems infinite when you have only the same eternally resurrected memories to accompany you. A few days can stretch out limitlessly. Each hour is a wasteland.

Hours seeming like days. A bare lightbulb glaring at bare walls. Bloodstains only half scrubbed off the plaster. The smell: everything that oozes out of human bodies when they are broken and rotting. There are moments when the screaming that fills the rooms becomes something concrete. Something you can feel. A liquid. It drips into your throat and your chest bulges and heaves. It trickles into your body like poison. You could close your eyes and stop your ears but the cries have already leached into your brain and there they remain, corrosive and eternal, and your dreams are steeped in them.

"Okay. Tell me about Anne-Lise. Who was she?"

"Prosaically: she was a pupil of mine. I taught her philosophy. But that alone doesn't tell you what you need to know, what you'll need to understand to really see what was so uniquely horrible about her death. No, Anne-Lise was, or she seemed to be, something wonderfully *pure*. I know, I know: it sounds idiotically sentimental. But there was something almost otherworldly about her. Just being in the same room as her was, well . . . She had an angelic quality. Ethereal. A kind of strange, luminous perfection that was . . . I don't know. You'll see photographs of her. You can decide for yourself. I'm sure it sounds very far-fetched: the way we transform people through the prism of absence and regret. But she was *brilliant*. No one could deny her that. One of the most gifted students to come through the lycée Jacques Cartier. She was going to prepare the entrance exams for the École normale. Following in our footsteps. Do you remember, Jacques? All those years ago? Some part of it must still live on in your mind, that first excitement upon contemplating the *nature of being*. Anne-Lise thought so beautifully. So clearly . . ."

"And?"

"Somebody killed her. Beat her. Stripped her and strangled her. Then laid her body down on the heather, out on the coast between Sainte-Élisabeth and le Boiledou. That was last winter, just as the snows were leaving."

"Didn't the police investigate?"

"Of course. Capitaine Lafourgue—you've heard of him?"

I nod. Like me, he'd been part of the maquis in the war and had joined the force during the purge. A new, clean generation of police was to be born in order to efface the shame of the past.

"Well, Lafourgue *investigated*, if you can call it that. That is to say: he stamped around for a few days trying to look less drunk than he doubtless was. He may even have deigned to lower his considerable bulk into the heather for a few moments to scrabble around searching for clues. Then, when none turned up, he did what he usually does when there is a criminal to catch: he intimidated and perhaps even arrested a few local tramps. Then he went back to the bar and left Anne-Lise to the worms. That was about ten months ago, and nobody has looked into it since. For so long now there has been only silence. A town forgetting a crime it would prefer to ignore."

He paces restlessly and the muscles in his face tauten slightly, as if he can still feel something toxic chewing at his insides.

"She wasn't just killed, you know . . ." He mutters it into the twilight and the freezing, inky billows rolling in off the sea and enfolding us. "It was more than that. Somebody . . . cut her . . . Somebody who didn't want her to be whole anymore. Somebody who wanted to take some part of her forever . . ."

I can only see the glint of his face reflected on the windowpane. His jaw seems to be gaping, hanging down helplessly, but it could just be the way his reflection is broken up on the shimmering and uneven surface of the glass. Where the light reflects onto his glasses, there is only darkness visible, two black holes punched out of his face.

"Someone from Sainte-Élisabeth," he continues. "Someone still out there, in one of those quiet, unremarkable little houses. Like the ones we grew up in."

He turns and looks at me, suddenly calm.

"I've heard it said that crime intoxicates. That it brings a sense of power, a kind of absolute, tyrannical domination of others. Is that something you've seen, in your pursuit of murderers?" He doesn't wait for an answer. "Out there, in one of the little stone houses you walked past just a few hours ago, someone is drunk on Anne-Lise's blood. When you wander through Sainte-Élisabeth at night, there isn't just darkness. No, you can feel a kind of voracious patience, other atrocities just waiting to come into existence. The darkness has become a cloak, and behind it a predator is hiding, biding his time. Looking for the next chance. The next girl. You need to find whoever did this. Do you understand?"

I can hear the haunting in Erwann's voice. I want to ask him if he can hear a similar haunting in mine. He is unshaven and the dark curls of his hair tumble across his forehead. The skin on his face is drawn like parchment. I touch my own cheek. What can he see in me? Two years in Algeria but it could easily have been twenty. One dead girl whispers perpetually in the cavities of his skull. How many ghosts are shrieking in mine? There is no way to count them. You stop even trying to count. The numbers mean nothing.

"Why me? What makes you think that I can find something that Lafourgue didn't?"

"Lafourgue is an imbecile." His voice twists upward, distorted, as if it's about to snap. Just for a second something breaks in his patience, and then he rediscovers his calm. "He did nothing for Anne-Lise. How could he? This was not the sort of crime he deals with every day. Here we have a man who is most commonly called upon to brutalize some gaping adolescent until he admits that it was indeed he who stole the flowerpots from Madame Lanier's front porch in a moment of youthful high jinks. Perhaps he might even be required to mediate between two farmers, one of whom shot the other's cow over the hedge in a dispute about field boundaries. This he can cope with. I imagine there is even a certain correlation between his mediocrity and the trivial crimes he investigates. But Anne-Lise? This was something altogether different. The reports in the papers feasted on the details: It was calculated. Methodical. Organized. Such incomprehensible wickedness, but with some kind of horrid, rational intelligence behind it. No obvious traces. No witnesses. Meticulously planned and carried out so as to give nothing away, and no hint at all as to why this girl should be chosen to end her days in such darkness."

For a while we sit in silence, and then Erwann speaks again.

"I want you to investigate because I remember you before you were a detective. I remember you as a philosopher. Oh, I'm sure you'll say you weren't and that you were only a student. But you were trained in rigorous thought. In its sublimity and its darkness. Lafourgue's ponderous mind simply could not penetrate whatever subtlety lies at the bottom of this crime. I believe that you will be able to do so."

I just nod. There is no use in trying to explain to Erwann that there is nothing philosophical about crime. That crime is just hunger and rage and poverty. That it's desperation and opportunity. The inevitable, pathological repetition of pain branded into the soul. The slow collapse of an entire society, piece by piece, shred by exhausting shred.

After Algeria, I don't even know what crime is anymore. It should exist in some definable realm of moral failure. It should be something malignant and aberrant that can be identified, tracked, and punished. There must have been a time when crime seemed like something outside of me. Something I could localize, analyze, and counteract.

I want to see it like that again. Now, everything malignant is within me. Let crime be something I prevent and avenge, not what I am.

"Go and see Lafourgue," Erwann says. "I told him that you might want to investigate Anne-Lise for yourself. Whatever you did or didn't do in Algeria, he seems rather impressed by your reputation. He was even eager to meet with you. He'll help you with whatever you want to know."

Outside, the wind lashes the roof and the first drops of rain bounce onto the frozen gorseland and are drunk by the earth.

DAY TWO

I wake up hunched in a chair, my joints stiff with cold. I couldn't bring myself to lie in a strange bed staring up into the dark, waiting for sleep to arrive and bring with it a distorted pulse of memory in dreams. After Erwann left, I stared out into the night, fighting exhaustion until a brittle, fitful oblivion came over me.

When day fully breaks it is nearly nine o'clock and I wander down from the house toward the town. The wind hurtles off the Channel, snapping the leaves and making one great shimmer of the grass. The road winds down to the sea, where the squat gray houses stand next to the waters of the port, bobbing with fishing boats when the tide is high. At low tide, the sludge of the seabed, choked with kelp, stretches as far as the eye can see.

Sainte-Élisabeth clusters around the harbor, and its uneven rows of buildings line the promenade running the length of the town. Everything tends down toward the waters. The sea is both life and death. The fishermen set out upon it each morning in the barely broken dawn and pray they will be among those who come back. Little plaques with dates and names run along the harbor walls. The town has lost many to the violence of the waves; bodies battered by the immensity of the swell, men who breathed their last in the churning tides. The corpses were often never recovered, or washed ashore days later, bloated and algae-ridden, shredded by fish, the skin swollen with salt. People would gather by the harbor, the women dressed in black, the children subdued, to remember those who died in the sea's surges. There was a ritual in the silence of those standing on the promenade, staring out at the great, gray expanse where sea and sky meet. They could accept the violence of the sea. It was the violence of the land which they could never understand—that of poverty, disease, and the slow frustration of existence without horizons.

Toward the end of the promenade is a bar with a cracked blue sign that reads, *A l'abri des flots*. Erwann told me that this was where I would find Lafourgue. As soon as I enter I can see his gray-coated bulk leaning on the bar. I don't need anyone to confirm that this is who I am looking for. Something in his demeanor, an authority that borders upon violence, marks him out as a policeman and sets him apart from the groups of fishermen hunched over dominoes or newspapers. He turns toward me and, standing upright, lifts a single hand and raises it to his temple in mock salute.

"Well, well, well. Jacques le Garrec. A genuine honor. This man," his voice carries across the whole room, in whose dark corners the mutters suddenly fall silent, "this man fought the Germans at home and then he took the war to the Arabs abroad too. Gentlemen, we have a true hero in our midst this fine morning. Monsieur, let me get you a drink." He gestures to a haggard-looking woman behind the bar whose unsteady hand pours two small glasses of a clear liquid. It smells chemical. Scarifying. Lafourgue stands to attention and raises his glass. There is silence in the bar. "To the war that goes on, and to men like Jacques le Garrec, the heroes who fight it. Amen."

There is a sudden, strange silence. Is it unease? Or fear? Lafourgue tips his head back and drinks and the sparse clusters of other early-morning drinkers do like-wise. The tiny drop of liquid that I ingest burns my throat. My mouth feels gummy, as if covered in gasoline. Lafourgue's gaze runs over the silenced bar like the beam of the lighthouse flashing across the land.

"And in what way may I be of service to you?"

He's much older than me, in his midfifties perhaps, and not remotely like the lumbering clodhopper Erwann described. There is something imposing in his very pres-ence. At first glance, his squat fingers clutching the tiny glass and the swollen mass of his cheeks and neck make him look overweight. But as I stand next to him I am aware of an incredible, rocklike solidity. His gray eyes are set deep in his head and gaze out imperturbably from some distant inner realm. His face seems almost square: chiseled and monumental. Yet it is his mouth that draws my attention. Something about the jaws, the teeth, the whole powerful, devouring machinery provokes a nearly constant fascination the entire time I am in his presence.

"I've been asked to look into the case of a girl, Anne-Lise Aurigny, who was killed here last winter. I was told that you investigated the case at the time. Erwann Ollivier said that you might be able to help me."

"Ollivier. The would-be intellectual. Well, look into the case if you want. I'll do whatever I can to help you. I doubt you'll find much, though. It's gone pretty cold by now."

"You should know that I no longer have any police powers and—"

Lafourgue cuts me off with a nod. "No problem. You're among friends here. We'll keep the whole thing very hush-hush." His voice descends to a murmur: "Jesus! They send you out as a soldier to do a job, to fight and kill an enemy: the Arabs. Sneaking little dirt vipers waiting in every hole and under every rock to slither out and attack you. And so you kill them. Like you're supposed to do. Like they told you to and paid you for. Then they string you up for it. Some stunt in the newspapers so that we can pretend it isn't a war at all, and that this isn't happening a thousand times every day."

He heaves himself upright again, his bulk silhouetted against the faint wash of daylight streaming through the terrace doors, and barks across the bar: "This man is a first-class hero. He laid his life on the line to liberate France from Nazi domination and then he did it all over again in Algeria. This is a man who has lived with death bravely, year after year, to save his country. Let us raise a glass in his honor."

The bar is now eerily quiet. Men put down their crosswords and playing cards and reach obediently for their glasses. They drink meekly, and then stare down at their hands waiting for the next order. Lafourgue exhales contentedly.

"Listen," he says, "by all means look into the case. Poke around in the files, put the wind up a few local degenerates, let me know if you need a bit of pressure applied on a suspect." He grins and bunches his hand into a fist. "But you won't get anywhere. The crime scene, the whole trail leading out from the victim, her past, it all leads nowhere. You know why? Because the girl was a whore. A filthy little bitch dragging that perpetual itch of hers all over the countryside, letting her whore's reek go floating all around and drawing the attention of every man passing within a mile of her. Most times, you can't catch the killer of a creature like that. There's no pattern to her existence. No motive. No history. She just got too close to the wrong guy, God knows who he was, some prowler passing through who toyed with her and killed her."

"Was there evidence of sexual contact before death?"

Lafourgue shakes his head. "Not this time. But your man didn't leave *any* traces. There's nothing left for you to find." He downs a final gulp of the clear alcohol and reaches for his hat. "Come on. I'll drive you to the police station and you can go through whatever files you want. Then we'll go and talk to André. Dr. Roussillon, that is. He's the doc who did the autopsy. There are some peculiar details that you'll need to hear, and André can explain them so much better than me."

Lafourgue's office is chaos, with sheaves of papers heaped on the desk, filing cabinets open, and an old shirt lying creased in one corner. He hands me a thin manila file containing a handful of photographs and a few paragraphs of typewritten notes and leaves me alone. Who was Anne-Lise: Erwann's ethereal being or Lafourgue's whore?

The pictures are clear, forensic. A close-up of her face. Or what used to be her face. The hair is still her—strands of glitter falling about her shoulders. The rest isn't anything. A huge tear runs from the hairline down the cheek. The head looks split in half. I can see where the eyes were, but now they are just swollen lumps of flesh, gummed shut. Sightless. She must have died blind, in agony and darkness, feeling some predatory fury destroying her face. The jaw hangs loose, cracked on one side. Those teeth still left in her mouth jut horribly, knocked into queasy angles. Her top lip is split right up to the nose so that her mouth looks like one more shapeless hole torn into her head. Erwann said she was beautiful. By the time she died, she wasn't even human.

Another photo, this one from where she was left. Claws of winter heather stretching out toward the sea. Anne-Lise lies on top of them, white—pure, bone-white— against the knotty fingers of gorse clutching at the frozen land and waiting for spring to live again. For Anne-Lise, this is the end. She's been stripped. Her clothes were never found. The killer either destroyed them or kept them, hid them away in some secret recess as a shining and unrelinquishable prize. He wanted Anne-Lise to be found naked. One hand lies across her breast, like a gesture of modesty or a vain hope of protecting her body. The other hand is flung outward and seems to scratch at the ground. Desperation? Or ecstasy? A parody of pleasure. In death she mimes both chastity and wantonness. A brutalized girl with torn flesh where her face used to be, abandoned to the insects and the frost to fight over her remains.

According to Lafourgue's brief notes, there were three suspects, all of whom he saw as quite likely perpetrators.

First picture: a man in his thirties, his dull eyes staring vacantly over the photographer's shoulder. Gray stubble roughens his skin in uneven patches. His hair springs up in clumps. Streaks of dirt smudge both cheeks. Julien Kerbac, a down-and-out who roamed the land from Saint-Malo along the coast to Saint-Cast, bunking in cowsheds and ditches. A haggard drifter at home in the wilderness. Lafourgue seemed to have picked him out because of a history of violence: drunken brawls, erratic behavior, and verbal abuse. Once he got high on paint thinner and exposed himself to a local farm girl. I can see no evidence of a connection between him and Anne-Lise. He was just one of the usual suspects.

Second picture: a boy of around eighteen, eyes exploding into the camera, radiant with hatred. He stares so intensely that the glare suffuses the whole picture. His hair is jet-black, so smooth it's almost liquid, gushing down his cheeks and falling around his neck. The high cheekbones appear to stretch the skin upward, making it unbearably translucent and frail. Lafourgue's painstaking script reads as follows:

> Sasha (Aleksandr) Kurmakin, b. 1940, son of Russian émigrés who escaped the Communist menace. Both parents politically unaffiliated and no known associates. Clean records. Kurmakin himself a school dropout despite exceptionally high grades. Member of Communist Party as of '57. Actively involved in distribution of pro-Russian propaganda. Spotted several times in Communist-backed demos against the army's defense of the colonies. Known agitator with links to various leftist and militant groups. Romantically and almost certainly sexually connected to victim. Possible motives for murder include jealousy, some sort of sexually deviant violence growing out of control and leading to death, anarchic experimentation with crime.

Third picture: a man in his late forties, smiling like this isn't a mug shot but a portrait. Even so, the smile appears a little wan, slightly contemptuous: courteous, but letting the suggestion appear in the strained lines at the corners of the mouth that he has other places to be. His hair is smooth and parted in the center. There is a refinement about the narrow, delicate features, but something cold as well. The eyes glint like glass. Two dead pools with shimmering reflections. Lafourgue's notes read as follows:

> *Christian de la Hallière, 48, direct descendant of Knights Templar. Owner of run-down Château de la Hallière about 2 km west of Sainte-Élisabeth. Family fortune squandered long ago. Joined the Légion des Volontaires Français contre le Bolchévisme in '41 as a Fascist of long-standing conviction. Fought on the Eastern Front '41–'42, and later in Poland as part of the Division Charlemagne of the Wehrmacht. Exile in Tunisia after the war. Returned to France in 1947 after the amnesty to find "the land I fought for overrun by the Jews and Communists I defended it against." Well known to Anne-Lise although the nature of the relationship is not clear. C de la H denies sexual contact.*

Nowhere in Lafourgue's notes is there any mention of tangible evidence: fibers, fingerprints, witnesses. Motives or leads are sketchy at best, if not completely absent. There is nothing here that could lead back to whoever reduced Anne-Lise's face to torn flesh and dumped her on the heather. Whatever investigation he undertook, it ended in blankness.

I return the file to Lafourgue.

"I'm sure you'll want to talk to André now," he says.

The morgue is an old stone building with tiled walls, and Lafourgue leads us down into the basement. As we descend the stairs, my chest heaves and contracts. The air is being squeezed out of my lungs. Cold steps leading downward, out of the world of light. The tramp of feet in unison.

At al-Mazra'a, the detainees are taken straight down into the mazy warren of basement rooms, where dingy corridors run in all directions. Bulbs glare on the ceiling but seem to emit very little light. The detainees follow us through the warren and at first their steps match ours. Then you start to hear it: the pace slowing, shuffling, feet desperately trying to prolong this walk. As soon as they step into the warren, they begin to forget the world. Everything shrinks to this long parade through the labyrinth, manacled between two or three soldiers. No one knows what lies at the end of it. Some look around, eyes flitting from side to side. Others just stare at the ground. Perhaps in their heads they are praying. Sometimes their mouths move mechanically, asking Allah to clear their minds and make their bodies ready.

"Are you okay? Le Garrec . . . ?" The words sound far away. Lafourgue is standing at the bottom of the stairs talking to a man in long black rubber gloves and a white smock. I force myself to step down to meet them. Three metal autopsy tables, scrubbed down and gleaming, stand in the center of the room.

There is always some blood left on the chairs, on the walls, on the floor. A new detainee will see it the moment he comes in: ghostly rust-brown imprints leaching into the plaster and worming into the pores in the stones. The final traces of the vanished. That molecular evidence remains in the secrecy of the interrogation rooms, tiny flecks of memory preserved in the engulfing wave of a war.

On one of the tables lies a body covered by a sheet. This is how the detainees at al-Mazra'a finished their existence: shapeless lumps under tarpaulin in the hangars. Some of them were lucky enough to die believing that Allah would gather them in, their minds bathed in radiance before we brought darkness to them. A few hours of respite. Then came the next detainee.

Dr. Roussillon straightens his bow tie, nods professionally at me, and says, "Florian tells me you want to know about Anne-Lise Aurigny. Well, I'll tell you what I can. The wounds and the mutilations were unusual enough to stay in my memory, even this long after the fact."

Lafourgue winks and saunters off to one of the autopsy tables. Pulling back the sheet, he squints at the cadaver's bluing flesh like a connoisseur.

"Lafourgue showed me the photographs. It looks as if Anne-Lise was beaten viciously, and at length. Was that the cause of death?"

"No. As you say, she was severely beaten and for a long time—I would say at least a couple of minutes. Both cheekbones were smashed; the jaw was crushed into several pieces. The retina in one eye was completely detached and the other eye was basically jelly. If she'd been left alive, she would have been virtually unrecognizable."

"Was any kind of weapon used to beat her?"

Roussillon frowns. "I think so. Judging by the way the flesh tore, I'd say something heavy and uneven. He hit her so relentlessly that she must have been knocked unconscious."

"But she didn't die like that?"

"No. He left her for a while. Then he strangled her. With his hands this time. That surprised me. It would have been safer to use a rope. Hands leave traces."

"Would she have felt anything by then?"

Roussillon shakes his head.

"Lafourgue said there was no evidence on the body. That seems unusual for what would appear to be such a violent crime."

Roussillon nods and pushes his white hair back from his brow. "There was certainly a period of frenzy, at least when the beating took place. Although even then he didn't hit her with his fists—that could have left incriminating scars. Perhaps he also strangled her in a frenzy, I don't know. But what he did next was very calm. He removed and hid or destroyed her clothes. He washed the body inch by inch: her hair, her hands. He cut her nails. He took his time and scrubbed away all traces quite methodically. From the way he reacted to the murder—no shock, no panic, a total control of the situation—we thought it must be someone who had killed before."

Lafourgue's voice cuts across the room: "We looked for similar unsolved murders in Brittany in the last five years but nothing obvious stood out. If he has killed before, it was either farther away, long ago, or else he hid the body so well it was never found."

"The strangest part is the final act of mutilation, though," Roussillon continues. "It was made postmortem. *Hours* postmortem. He must have kept her body for at least six hours, cleaning it impeccably to erase whatever it could tell us about him. Then, at some point, he took something like a scalpel and cut a hole in her side about four centimeters wide and three deep."

"There's no reason for it," Lafourgue says. "Nothing logical. She'd been dead for hours. It might be some kind of ritual. Something tribal brought over by jungle Negroes or some Muslim barbarism called for in the Koran. You'd know more about that than us. We didn't manage to turn anything up, though. Maybe you'll have more luck."

"What about afterward? Has anything similar been reported since?"

"No. Not as far as I know." Lafourgue picks up the sheet once again then lets it fall over the corpse's ashen face. "What would you expect?"

"I don't know," I respond. "But I'm not sure the murderer had killed before. The fury of the beating seems spontaneous. It took him by surprise to feel so much bile clogging his insides. That initial violence was a shock: a canker bursting. But the way he responded to the crime is telling. The almost contemplative mastery of the situation—it's like a wave of power. He wasn't horrified by what he'd done. He was fascinated. Exhilarated. Rage drove him to crime, but rather than appalling him, it thrilled him. I think you should look for similar crimes committed afterward too. There's a kind of transition here, as he feels Anne-Lise's last breath shudder in her throat. Something new is born. I'm not sure he can go back now."

Lafourgue shrugs. "I'll look into it. Check with a few buddies that nothing's come up. Whatever you want."

"Killing isn't just an action. It's a way of life. An art."

Lafourgue looks at me oddly. "I'll follow it up."

The air in the morgue seems thin and oxygenless. I feel trapped underground.

Killing is a way of life.

I arrive at al-Mazra'a in August 1957, with the service de renseignements under army jurisdiction and the green uniform feeling strange to me and scratching my skin. Al-Mazra'a is an old agricultural complex, silos turned into soldiers' quarters and grain cellars into cells. The jeep bounces on the hard dirt road and, above us, the sky seems enormous, a vast dome of turquoise spiraling in concentric waves. It feels like standing in a great mosque, dwarfed by the gleaming, ethereal vault. I can see why so many dreamers stopped here, enchanted by the blue fire glowing majestically above them, drunk on the air it warmed.

I am sent immediately to report to Lieutenant-Colonel Lambert. Whenever I've heard his name mentioned, it is with a kind of awe. I stand outside his office for a long time, waiting for him to summon me. Finally he comes out and, without turning around, beckons me to follow. His gray hair is shaved close to his skull. His blue eyes blaze and demand my attention with a kind of magnetic force. The features of his face are drawn, thin, severe. Despite having been in Algeria for years, his skin is pale, as if immune to the sunlight. He moves with a rigid, unbending power and doesn't once look behind to see whether I have followed his order or not.

Out in the full sun, behind an old hangar, French soldiers are standing beside three Arabs kneeling on the earth and staring blankly at the ground in front of them. They don't look up as we approach. Lambert nods to the soldiers and his fingers reach down to his belt, flick open a stud, and take out a pistol. He beckons to me, again without looking, and presses the gun into my hand. He is small, but his fingers are so hard I can barely distinguish between them and the butt of the gun. There is an incredible concentration of sinew in his movements, something coiled and expectant.

He points to the first man kneeling down on the path, who seems no more than eighteen, with wispy stubble drawn in uneven lines across his cheeks. His jaw trembles where a tic pulls the skin in quick jerks. I can't see his eyes.

"Shoot him," Lambert says.

I don't move.

"What is wrong with you, capitaine?" He leans on the last word. I had been warned that the army were contemptuous of the police ranks kept by those drafted into the service de renseignements. "Do you understand French? Shoot that man." The pistol feels impossibly heavy in my hand, as if I couldn't lift it even if I tried. Lambert stands just in front of me and I can smell the sweat rolling off his shirt. One of my legs begins to shake. In three years in the Resistance and ten in the police, I don't remember my body shaking like this, with such uncontrollable insistence.

"Sir, I can't shoot that man. He is unarmed and—"

"Capitaine, I could not care less what you think. You were given *a direct order by a superior officer to shoot that man, and you are now disobeying that order. Shoot him."*

The heat is unbearable, as if the air were on fire.

"Sir, it would be a crime to shoot an unarmed and defenseless man."

"Capitaine, this man is a terrorist who protects members of the FLN. And if he isn't, then one of the others here is. I need to know what they know. If I don't find it out, French soldiers will be killed. Do you understand? Now shoot him in the head."

I'm not sure how long I stand there. The air seems to be burning my throat. My mind races, searching for words, but there is only emptiness and silence. At some point, Lambert takes the gun out of my hand, walks over to the boy kneeling on the ground, and shoots him through the back of the neck. The body jackknifes and slumps to the ground. The head lolls back. The eyes are wide open in shock. Lambert gestures toward the other two men, still kneeling in the dust. One of them glances up quickly at the body, and then turns away almost immediately. Sweat is pouring down his face but he seems to be shivering at the same time.

Lambert's voice is quiet and even: "Take them back to the warren and find out what they know." He turns to me. "Where do you think you are, capitaine? In some Maghrebi prison station? You aren't here to investigate according to the law. We are the law."

"Colonel Lesage told me—"

"Lesage likes to pretend he has clean hands. He sends me recruits like you doped on propaganda and lies. He wants to pretend that this isn't a total war, but it is. The government likes to hear his story—it's good politics and it plays well with civilians—but it's a myth. The fellagha are in every house and every field. They worm into every crack and every tiny space. We have to burn it all down if we want to eradicate them. The fellagha are a disease. We either destroy the entire habitat of the microbes or the plague will kill us all."

Behind Lambert, the youth's body lies sprawled in the sun. A great wellspring of blood, wine-dark, has pooled around his shoulders and traced a circle around his head.

"Capitaine, you now need to forget whatever Lesage promised you. You are here to save French lives. This is what the service does. We do it so that as few French soldiers as possible are flown home in tiny pieces, or with their tongues cut out, or charred beyond recognition, or castrated. Because that is what these people"—he cocks his head toward the corpse—*"will do. Remember where you are. Perhaps, before now, you failed to properly appreciate the nature of your mission. Next time you disobey a direct order, I may well have to shoot you too. If that is what is necessary in order to protect France, then that is what I shall do. Lesage will not be able to save you. Do you understand?"*

My throat is coated with dust. Words can't get through. I just nod. Lambert points in the direction of the accommodation block. White lime-scaled farmhouses. The glint of the sun that comes bouncing off them is blinding, like a scimitar blade sawing at my eyes.

"When you walk back out of there," he says, "you come out a soldier. Pas un flic. Now get lost."

Somehow, the green army bag has found its way into my hand and my feet have started to move. The earth crunches beneath my steps, dusty on top but baked hard beneath.

Lafourgue's face floats next to mine. "I said, is there anything else you want to know here?"

"No. But I want to see where the body was left. Can you take me there?"

"No problem. It's not far outside Sainte-Élisabeth. On the coast road. It's a nice drive."

Lafourgue and I sit in silence as the car, swaying to and fro, chews up the road in front of us. On our left, stubble fields stretch out grayly. Stunted roots of corn poke through the earth like tiny, useless limbs. Grass dissolves into mud. On our right, the heathland tumbles down toward the cliffs. Brown clumps of gorse are bunched like fists, clutching tightly at their thorns. Behind them, the sea appears swollen, writhing glassy and pregnant in the bays.

We are about two kilometers out of Sainte-Élisabeth when Lafourgue swings the car into a sandy lay-by and says, "This is it." As we walk back up the road, the wind bites at our faces. It carries the ice from the atmosphere and the dank leaching off the sea. Over on the horizon, a pale band is pushed back by the blackness of the sky.

Lafourgue said the killer came out of nowhere and vanished again. There was no connection between him and Anne-Lise. The crime was tangential to her. A wanderer, a predator, suddenly appeared from out of the night and found her in his field of vision. With no fingerprints, footprints, fibers, or witnesses to lead back to him, he simply melted back among the shadows, returned to invisibility, and left us staring vainly at empty signs. There is nothing to investigate: a brutal crime and a trail that goes nowhere.

I have to believe there is something else here: something logical, a crime that flows out of who Anne-Lise was, or what she was to somebody else. Something of the past that is retained and remembered in the present.

Night is closing in. Lafourgue cuts into the heather. As he strides over it, his feet stamp and sink into the saturated earth. He points down to a piece of ground much like another.

"Here. This is where the body was left."

The fractured line of the cliffs snakes against the sea. The rocks glow white in the failing light. Over on the headland, the lighthouse stands blackly against the inky sky. The beacon hasn't yet been switched on.

Lafourgue shrugs. "Why dump her here? There's nothing around. She must have been killed miles away and then brought here. Why not bury her somewhere? Hide the body. Hope enough time passes for everyone to forget and stop looking for her."

Gorse cracks beneath my feet. Thorns prick at my ankles. There is nothing to see here.

"Had enough?" Lafourgue asks.

I shake my head. The nothingness of it. Cleanliness. Order. The body wiped clean and purified. Traceless. That very nothingness becomes something to look at. No tracks or prints. Wasn't that a sign in itself? The absence of information shrieks out and becomes something to guide us. An indication of a methodical cunning capable of suppressing all unwanted data given by a corpse. This isn't the work of a vagrant or a violent, befuddled opportunist. It reeks of intelligence.

Nothing here is unplanned. Everything has meaning.

The heathland isn't a dumping ground. It's a temple. The place was carefully chosen. This is the spot where she needed to lie. Here is where the killer wished not to dispose of but to display her body. He arranged it so that she was nestled in the heather, the hibernating plants miming death and clutching her in their sleeping grip, and the whiteness of her body lay framed by the chalky expanse of the rocks and the howl of the sea.

Is it not all the product of a particular kind of order? A glinting, pathological precision?

But not just precision: something like art. The cadaver offset by the gray, eternal heave of the sea. The heather imitating decay. Flesh returning to earth. The body surrendering to one final contortion as rigor mortis set in, fixing Anne-Lise forever in that ambiguous pose that was both chaste and wanton. It radiates an eerie symbolism, like a medieval painting; something darkly allegorical; a mystery resistant to understanding: the too-nourished flesh blanched lily-white in death, and the hole in her flank like the spear wound in the side of Christ crucified.

The pale band on the horizon has been squeezed to the faintest ribbon of glitter where sea touches sky. The lighthouse beacon has been switched on and its artificial brightness sweeps across the earth. Then the frail beam is flung out into the immensity of the night.

Lafourgue grabs my elbow and steers me back toward the road. The first drops of rain are beginning to crystalize in the air swollen with spindrift and burst fatly on the car roof.

"I'll lend you a car, so you can start to make your own investigations tomorrow," he says. "For now, let it go. I'll take you home."

I am fully expecting the knock on my door that tells me Erwann has arrived. He appears in a flood of icy water dripping off his skin and soaking his clothes. He shudders by the fire in the grate as I tell him what I saw today and explain that there is nothing in Lafourgue's case file that suggests a direction for the investigation.

"Lafourgue is an idiot," Erwann says. "A hopeless yokel bumped up to the rank of police inspector simply because he hurled a few bombs at unarmed German supply trains during the war. In some spurious attempt at moral regeneration, we have populated important social positions with dismal little opportunists quite incapable of living up to the dignity of their roles. Lafourgue is a drunk and a bully. Of course he would be incapable of grappling with a crime like this. Please don't let that put you off investigating. You can't imagine the relief I felt when I heard you were coming back to Sainte-Élisabeth and I realized there would be someone here with the ability to offer justice to Anne-Lise."

Once again, I see Lafourgue's cold, gray eyes and the powerful frame of his jaws. He is certainly a bully, but I did not sense any of the stupidity Erwann mentions. There is something measured and deliberate in his every gesture, a calculated force that is the antithesis of stupidity.

"Lafourgue seems to have focused on an ex-Nazi called Christian de la Hallière and Anne-Lise's boyfriend, Sasha Kurmakin, a child of refugees. Did you know them?"

"A little. I warned Anne-Lise about them both. De la Hallière isn't an ex-Nazi at all: he's a pure, unreconstructed Fascist. He walked through hell on the Eastern Front, and all because he believed so much in Hitler's ideals of a *judenrein* and *kommunistenrein* Europe. He came through it minus three toes lost to frostbite but with his convictions strengthened and an encyclopedia of depravity and suffering stamped into his brain. Kurmakin is different. He's just a child. Anne-Lise knew that. She was just dallying with him. Playing at being a normal teenager. He was . . . *picturesque*. She couldn't really take him seriously."

"So you don't see him as dangerous then?"

"It depends what you mean by dangerous. Imagine that you give a precious object—something gorgeous but fragile, breakable—to a child. Now, the child doesn't *want* to break it. In fact, he's fascinated by it. Captivated by its shimmering magic. He feels proud to hold it, like that makes him the owner of it. It gives him a sense of power, an illusion of his own specialness. The problem is that he's not special. He's a stupid, clumsy child. He doesn't mean to do any harm, but he can't escape his infantile crassness, so he smashes the precious object without being fully aware of what he's doing. By the time he looks down and sees the shards, it's too late. In that sense, Kurmakin is dangerous." Erwann's tone is condescending, but there are flecks of venom in his words.

"Since there's nothing to follow up from the discovery of the body, I'll start tomorrow by going to Anne-Lise's house and talking to her family. Lafourgue thinks it's all a waste of time."

"You don't agree."

"I don't know. The way the body was left, and that peculiar wound in her side . . . It all feels so *personal*. There are so many layers of meaning. Symbols that need to be decoded. The question is whether Anne-Lise could have been anyone—a blank slate for a murderer's pathology—or whether it had to be *her* body he did those things to. I'll start with her. Who she was. What she might have been to someone else. That's the only starting point I have."

How else can I look at the case? After all this time, the only thing to go on is Anne-Lise herself. Who she was. Why someone would have wanted to hurt her. The wounds feel personal, but perhaps only because that is how I need to perceive them, otherwise I can never penetrate the mystery of what happened and Anne-Lise's death will fade and be forgotten.

But already, I know I am not simply reading events but interpreting them too. Changing them. Making them into what I need them to be.

It's like the *service de renseignements*. Algerians are brought in, terrorists, sympathizers, and bystanders all jumbled together, and we make them into the sources of our information. *All of them.* They all end up giving information: silence is as suspicious as speech. Whether they say anything or not doesn't matter. Silence can be a proof of guilt just as much as admission. We don't discover guilt; we invent it. We have the means to turn everything they do and everything they are into information. We find things that they might be saying, things that aren't necessarily true or untrue. Things that don't exist but which we make into realities, and which spread virally until the idea of truth is long forgotten and the methods of the *service* are all that remains.

Erwann stares at me sorrowfully. His green eyes dilate, like he's trying to see into me.

"Whatever made you decide to go to Algeria? You must have known that it was a lost cause. You certainly never believed that we had any right to the land. Everything that we plundered needs, eventually, to be returned. However many French people were implanted there, they were only ever foreign bodies. Something toxic grafted on with violence. Infection. Sooner or later, the lymphocytes will come. Joining the police: that was something I could understand. You were a hero back in '45, and what philosopher doesn't secretly share Marx's dream of changing the world? Yes, the police must have been exciting for you. But the Algérois? Whatever were you hoping to find there?"

"It was Lesage. You remember?"

He nods. René Lesage. He'd graduated from the École Polytechnique with one of the best scores of the past decade. When I met him he was only in his late twenties but already almost completely bald. His eyes were soft though his voice was hard and cold. He ran a cell of the maquis working throughout northern France. Arrested by the Germans in '43, he'd spent four nights in the Nazi headquarters at the Hôtel Aurore. Whatever he lived through in those four days, he never told anyone, although he managed not to talk. When he was released, one of his eyes was so badly damaged that his world forever more looked drenched in fog and snow.

When I saw him again, in early '57, he wore a patch over it, making him look sinister, like an incarnation of disease or suffering. His good eye still gazed softly but his skin seemed yellowed and liver spots ran prematurely across his hands and up his arms. He'd been in Algeria since the beginning, drafted there in '45 after the repression in Sétif left dozens dead and injured. He contacted me and invited me to his office on the avenue Foch. By then, Algiers was in lockdown. Algerian women with homemade weapons under burkas or in bags were walking into European cafés and leaving behind bombs which detonated in hails of glass, plaster, and torn flesh. The French were combing the city block by block, pulling Arabs out of their homes, making seizures and arrests. It was a display of power. The more innocent people got hurt, the more effective the message. There were barricades and searches on the streets. Women waited in line for hours after buying groceries to be searched before they could go back home. Out in the countryside, French military personnel who had just returned from the humiliation of Indochina read a few pages of Mao, repeated obediently that the insurgent exists within his own community like a fish in water, then set about destroying the very fabric of that habitat.

Lesage was furious, eaten up by a rage that simmered in every word he spoke. He saw Sétif as an idiotic blunder that had managed to turn a straightforward protest for independence into a massacre and thus into the spark for a war. He never once referred to the conflict as maintaining order: like Lambert, he called it a total war. No front. No designated battle zones or no-man's-land. The war was everywhere. On every street corner. Every woman and child was a potential combatant. He told me that he needed information from people who knew how to gather it.

"If you don't go," he told me, "then there will be someone else in your place. Someone else whom I did not handpick for the assignment. Someone not ennobled by the long fight in the shadows that we undertook in the Resistance. This person will probably be someone more brutal than you, more unenlightened, more sadistic, someone aroused by the possibility of inflicting pain and abjection upon other human beings. I cannot sit here and lie to you, Jacques. What the *service de renseignements* does is ugly. But only from the inside can we prevent it from becoming an abomination. We can control that ugliness so that it is purposeful and necessary. It is a sacrifice . . ." His yellowed fingers reached out and gently tapped the black patch under which his damaged eye saw only static. "In the Resistance we sacrificed our bodies. Here, we are more likely to lose our souls. I wish it were otherwise, and that we could obtain information without becoming steeped in blood and torment. I need to find men for whom the line between necessary force and hideous cruelty is absolute. This is what you can give to me."

Erwann shakes his head in frustration. "You can't possibly have believed that!"

"Why not? The idea of sacrifice made sense to me. I could remember what it was like to live under occupation, thinking that you had nothing left to lose. I imagined I could understand what the Algerians thought."

"And when you were there? Did you still think so?"

"No. I felt like an alien. Or, perhaps, like exactly what I was: a colonialist. Even thinking the way I had been, like it was my responsibility to help those poor people whose land we were occupying, began to seem appalling. Because isn't that exactly what a colonialist would think?"

Erwann walks over and stands next to me. The clock in the dining room sounds a solitary note. One o'clock. Somehow, at al-Mazra'a, there was always a glint of starlight to thin out the darkness. Here, the sky is forever drenched with rain; clouds block out the sidereal glow.

Erwann puts a hand upon my shoulder. "This isn't your fault, you know: this horrible crime that you've been accused of. You mustn't feel that you have to take the blame for it to atone for having been there. You must fight against the accusations and clear your name. It was a war, that's what you said, and atrocities happen in wars. I imagine you did everything you could to stop such barbarism from taking place. Don't allow the guilt that you feel about having served in Algeria to force you to take the blame for a crime of which I have no doubt you are innocent . . . I can see they polluted your mind with the violence of Algeria. But at least fight so that they don't destroy your name as well."

His hand lies softly on my shoulder. I cannot feel any conviction in the grip.

DAY THREE

I have already been awake for hours when the first glow of dawn begins to frost the blackness. It glimmers faintly, a ghostly sheen in the distance. I slept for a while. Then I was kneeling next to the body of a teenage Algerian girl. Blood was pooling around her. Filthy red-black blood. Gummy and insistent, it beat against my legs in waves. I wanted to stand up and get away but my muscles wouldn't respond. My trousers were sodden with gore. I wanted to wipe them though I couldn't bear to touch them.

I awoke, my lungs heaving, gasping for air.

Erwann didn't leave last night. I find him asleep in an armchair, curled up to fend off the cold. Perhaps he couldn't face the trek back across the lightless heath. Perhaps there is something intolerable in his isolation, something that gnaws at him in the long, empty hours and means that he would prefer to sleep here, knowing there is someone else present. Yet in sleep, the years seem to peel away from him. The lines wrinkling his eyes recede. I could envy him what looks like peace.

I close the door quietly behind me, leaving him to whatever dreams are flickering in his mind.

Dawn burns softly in the air. Standing on the grass in front of my house is a gray Citroën with a note from Lafourgue stuck under the windshield wipers. It reads: *keys in glove compartment.* I pull the choke and the car coughs to life. It hums along the corniche down toward the center of Sainte-Élisabeth. Mudflats stretch out for miles where the low tide has drawn the sea almost out of sight. It looks like a moonscape where the waters have been sucked away. Green streaks of algae run in oily shimmers across the uncovered seabed. Avocets strut across the mud, pecking at worm casts. Gulls circle against the leaden skies, filling the air with their chatter.

It seems an eternity since I last saw these things. Dried stalks of barley in winter. Rows of hawthorn. Crests of sand grass pricking the tops of the dunes.

Home.

Erwann called it camouflage; a murderer lurks behind it and waits.

I need to find out who Anne-Lise was. To pull her out of the void into which death has cast her. I want her to live again, faintly, just for a few days, beneath my gaze.

Her mother lives on the rue de la Grande Baie at the northern edge of town where the road curls between the laurel trees and down toward the shore. The house is neat; unremarkable; whitewashed. Blue shutters pulled to. A gray slate roof blending into the greater gray all around.

The tongue of the bell clacks gratingly in the early-morning quiet. There is silence inside, then a shuffling and scrabbling that seems to last for long minutes. A woman in her midforties answers the door. Her eyes are blurry, her hair faded blond, graying at the edges. Her skin is creased around the eyes, stamped with the faint scars of her past. She shudders as the wind off the sea lashes her flesh and she hugs her dressing gown tighter around her sides. She looks puzzled, like she's groping for an answer, and I realize that we have met before.

"Sarah? I'm Capitaine le Garrec. I came into your bar yesterday with Lafourgue. You served us. I don't know if Lafourgue told you, but I would like to investigate Anne-Lise's death. I know that the police didn't find much last time, but I want to try again. I know that it could be painful for you, to rake over the past, but—"

She cuts me off. "Come in. It's a mess. Will that bother you?" She fumbles inside, trying to clear some space on the sofa. Flushed, she gathers three empty wine bottles, a jumble of bills and scrap envelopes, and a functional plain white bra. She mumbles something about not having guests often. She doesn't sit down herself, but stands over by the window, still hugging her sides, gazing out into the mist shrouding the sea.

"May I ask you about the day Anne-Lise disappeared?"

She nods. "Anne-Lise. Yes. Okay." Her voice sounds far away. "Would it . . . Would it be too early to offer you a little drink? It is quite early, isn't it, but . . . perhaps you'll take a little cognac?" Her hand shakes slightly where it holds the folds of her dressing gown together.

"By all means."

"Thank you," she says quietly. She returns with two large half-filled glasses and places one in front of me. The sweet disinfectant odor wafting from it makes me nauseous. Sarah gulps hers and pinkness floods her cheeks. Her eyes widen and glitter. Her hands lie still.

"What would you like to know?"

"The day Anne-Lise went missing, it was the sixteenth of February, a Monday, I think. Tell me what you can remember about that day."

"I couldn't forget any of it. I don't know how much it will help you, though. She had gone to school, as usual, to Saint-Malo. You know that she went to the lycée Jacques

Cartier there? She wanted to do the *classes prépa*, you know, for the École normale. She was always a clever girl. Afterward, people kept saying how she'd had a bright future ahead of her . . ." Her eyes seem drawn to the mist that is now rising, floating over the fence, crawling through the garden. With a start, she lifts her empty glass.

"Where are my manners? It must be time for a refill. Would you . . . ?" Seeing the full glass in front of me, she doesn't even bother to finish the question. As she wanders back into the lounge, she totters a little.

"It seems pointless now to go back over it. Nothing happened that day. She went to school on the bus, like she always did. I didn't see her. She left in the dark. She never came home."

"When did you report her missing?"

"That evening. About ten o'clock. She never would have stayed out that late. Sometimes she stayed with a friend. But I always knew where. She told me she'd be away for a day or two. This time, nobody knew where she was. I knew that something was wrong. But I didn't think that . . . you know."

"Did she seem to be in any kind of trouble? Was she anxious? Scared?"

"Not then. A few weeks before, she'd been crying her eyes out over something. That wasn't like her. She'd never done that before."

"A boy?"

"I don't think so. She didn't really need to care about boys. They came running after her all the time, even if she paid them no attention. I don't know what made her cry like that. For a while she couldn't even concentrate at school. I don't think she'd ever got lower than 17 for any work she did, and all of a sudden she was lucky to be getting 11 or 12. But with time, she seemed to snap out of it."

"When was that?"

"Just after Christmas. Though everything seemed fine again. Until . . ." She stops her mouth with another slug of cognac.

"Would you mind if I asked you for two things? Firstly, I'd like to look at any of her possessions that you still have. I want to see if there's anything among her belongings that can help me to reconstruct the last weeks of her life."

"Why not? Look around her room, if you like. I haven't touched it since then. I kept meaning to, but . . ." She gestures around at the dirty glasses, the strewn papers, then the clothes lying around the living room. "There's always something else to do, or not do, instead."

"Thank you. Secondly, do you think you could give me a picture of Anne-Lise? Something that reminds you of her as she seemed to you? I'll return it to you when I've finished my investigations."

For a second, I catch a flash of mistrust in Sarah's eyes. Then she nods slowly. "I suppose so. Will it help?"

"I want to see her as she was. To have a sense of her identity and how other people saw her." Not just as a corpse laid out upon the gorse in some hideous staged gesture, her hands clutching at herself and at the frozen earth.

I hear Sarah's hands rifle among piles of paper, then she returns with a creased little sepia-tinted square.

"I'm sorry," she says. "I should have taken better care of it. It was shot at the start of the school year. I noted that on the back." In careful script, it reads: *septembre cinquante-huit*. "I just threw it in a drawer somewhere and forgot about it. How was I supposed to know that there wouldn't be others?"

She closes her eyes and her body shivers, her scrawny hip bones jutting against the thinness of her dressing gown. It feels indecent to see her like this, so I look at the photograph instead. Anne-Lise stares coolly past my shoulder. Her hair tumbles in light waves. Even the crinkled sepia can't take away the glow of her skin. Her mouth is pursed a little. I glimpse boredom in the glassy depths of her eyes. She looks like a girl waiting for a better future to come and efface the present. She, too, couldn't know that this image would fix her forever, and that all she was in the flash of the photographer's bulb is all she would ever be.

"May I take it?" I press it into the warmth of my pocket. It sits there like a relic, a charm: a tiny piece of the past in which I will try to lose myself. I will reconstruct memories of Anne-Lise to fight against my own memories of al-Mazra'a. Perhaps this dead girl left to freeze on the Breton heathland can shield me from the other dead girl, down in the basement of the *service de renseignements*, her blood pooling around my knees.

"Anne-Lise's room is just at the top of the stairs," Sarah says. Her fingers clutch the empty glass tightly, her bones visible beneath the skin. "Everything is just as she left it. Take as much time as you want."

The bed in Anne-Lise's room is unmade, piles of books lie on the desk, and drawers hang half-open. There are houses like this in Algeria: chairs left askew or toppled around tables set for dinner, clothes laid out ready to be worn. The sudden suspension of life is uncanny. Absence shrieks out in rooms that anticipate their inhabitants' return.

As I search her things, running through those habitual

actions brings back the time when I was a policeman. I cover her room quickly but methodically, and my hands move skilfully. For a moment I am back in the *brigade criminelle*, a detective, and Algeria is just a blank space on a map. I check Anne-Lise's wardrobe, searching for a hint of something unusual in her life: rips, stains, anything hidden in pockets or linings, clothes that don't look like hers or look as if they may have been a gift. Then I turn to her desk, where scrawled notes for a school assignment still lie, alongside books left open on pages she was reading. The title remains, in blue ink faded by months of sunlight streaming across her desk, for an essay to remain unwritten: *Is it possible to speak of a philosophical treatment of love in the work of Baudelaire?* These words, from the poet's notebooks, were in her head as she walked through her last days:

> In love, as in almost all human affairs, the "entente cordiale" is the result of misunderstanding. This misunderstanding is pleasure. The man cries out: "Oh, my angel!" The woman coos: "Mamma! Mamma!" And the two imbeciles are persuaded that they are thinking in concert. The insuperable gulf, which bars communication, remains unbridged.

And then, farther down:

> I believe that I already wrote in my notes that love bears a strong resemblance to torture or to a surgical operation. But this idea may be developed in the bitterest of fashions. Even if the two lovers are infatuated and full of reciprocal desire, one of them will always be calmer or less possessed than the other. This one is the operator, or the torturer; the other one is the subject, the victim. Do you hear these sighs,

*preludes to a tragedy of dishonor, these groans, these cries,
these death rattles? Who has not offered them, and who has
not irresistibly extorted them? And what do you find that is
worse in interrogation carried out by meticulous torturers?
These rolling sleepwalker's eyes, these limbs whose muscles
protrude and stiffen as if subjected to a galvanic battery,
drunkenness, delirium, opium, in their wildest effects, do
not yield such terrible results, such strange specimens. And
the human face, which Ovid believed fashioned to reflect the
stars, now speaks only through an expression of insane feroc-
ity or relaxes in a sort of death. For, without doubt, I would
think it a sacrilege to apply the word "ecstasy" to this kind of
decomposition.*

*Terrifying game, in which one of the players must inevi-
tably lose control of himself!*

I flick through a very fine edition of Les Fleurs du mal:
gilt-edged, bound in Moroccan leather. A gift? There is
no inscription in the front. I go through Anne-Lise's piles
of notes line by line. In the margin of one page, she has
scribbled: J'ai peur de l'araignée. Her school notes are neat,
crystalline, thorough. They cover page after page. Then,
suddenly, around Christmas, the handwriting trembles
and meanders. It looks like the onset of a nerve disease.
Her notes thin out. For a few weeks, Anne-Lise loses
control. Then, after the new year, as the snows of 1958
drift into 1959, as suddenly as it appears, the confusion
subsides. She seems herself again: alert, bright, her mind
turning elegantly and precisely. Then, after the fifteenth
of February, there is nothing more. Blank paper. White
upon white. Like another fall of snow coming down and
wiping out Anne-Lise's voice forever.

At the back of one of her desk drawers a scrap of paper catches my eye. A torn corner of an exercise book, it has been carefully folded and preserved—hidden, even— beneath her other papers. It reads:

DEATH PAUSE PEACE LONG YOURS
5 14 4 21 9   23 18 17 2 20   4 1 12 13 1   13 21 8 19 ?

I stare at it for a while, but nothing clicks. Something about the words nags at me. I put the paper carefully into my pocket. Outside Anne-Lise's window, the sun has started to glow weakly, vaporizing the mist. The quiet of her room is eerie. It's not like a shrine, but like a denial. Sarah isn't trying to embalm and preserve the past, she's trying to *forget* the present. The edges of Anne-Lise's photograph feel rough in my pocket. Her room feels tragic, drenched with loss. Everything seems desolate and foreboding: clothes hanging unworn in the wardrobe, books gathering dust on the shelves, the path across the lawn and out into the tree-lined road where she must have set off, one day in February, for the last time. She probably barely noticed these things, which were merely the backdrop to a life she couldn't wait to cast off. She saw herself in Paris, reading philosophy, far from Sainte-Élisabeth.

A final thing draws my attention. Next to the title of the essay she will never finish, she has written a name: *Anneliese Aurigny.*

Downstairs, Sarah has bustled about, perhaps trying to restore order to the sitting room. Dirty clothes and discarded crockery have disappeared. Sarah sits by the window, her legs curled beneath her and a glass of cognac gleaming in her hand. Her eyes are bleary again, as if the rush of the alcohol has worn off and she can now start to feel its familiar corrosiveness scraping her insides. She looks up expectantly.

"Who was Anne-Lise's best friend? If I wanted to get more information about her—who she was, her contacts, friends, where she used to go—who would I go to?"

"Mathilde Blanchard. Have you heard of her?"

I shake my head.

"She's got a bit of a reputation around here. She couldn't have been more different from Anne-Lise. She's been drunk in my bar more times than I can remember. Spent the night on a tarpaulin in the back or left on the arm of some stranger, I don't know who and I doubt she did either, a good dozen times. The Blanchards adopted her, but they didn't really know what to do with her. Who would?"

"Why did Anne-Lise like her so much?"

"I don't know. Maybe they both felt like outsiders here."

"Does the expression 'the spider' mean anything to you? I found it among Anne-Lise's notes."

Sarah stares vacantly. "I've never heard it. She didn't really say all that much to me, though. Not about what really mattered to her. Just her age, I suppose. I'm sorry . . . I see I'm not being much help."

"There's another thing. It might be nothing, but I noticed that Anne-Lise had written her name in an essay as *Anneliese*. Was that also a nickname?"

"No." Her face is suddenly white. "Anneliese was her real name." She glances at the empty glass ballooning in her hand, lurches upright, and pours herself another drink. This time, she doesn't even bother to offer me one. "Anneliese is the name that Otto and I—that her father and I—gave her when she was born. That was in 1941."

"Otto. So he . . . ?"

"You can judge us if you want. Everyone else has. They judged me back then and they're still doing it now. There was such . . . *malice.* Such hatred. Just because Otto was German. He wasn't a Nazi. He wasn't even a soldier. He was just an engineer. He didn't fight or kill anyone. He defused bombs. He tried to stop people getting hurt."

"Where is he now?"

"I don't know. Back in Germany, I think. We haven't spoken in more than fifteen years. I wanted him to stay here but he couldn't live with the hatred. He was a gentle man. A pacifist. War scared and sickened him, but then the peace did too."

"So everybody here knew that Anne-Lise was the daughter of a German?"

"Of course they knew. Everyone here knows everything."

And Anne-Lise grew up surrounded by hatred. A foreign body left by the retreating occupier. A reminder of France's torment and shame.

"Did Lafourgue know?"

"Of course he knew." Breathing hard, she stares down at her hands. Her throat seems to be constricting.

At no point do Lafourgue's case notes mention the fact that Anne-Lise was half-German, yet who knows what resentments might have festered behind the gray stone walls of Sainte-Élisabeth; humiliations choked back for years; loss decaying into obsession?

"Do you know the one thing that has given me pleasure in my life?" Sarah asks calmly. "Watching Anne-Lise grow up. I was terrified of how her life would be. How she'd have to skulk about with her head down, apologizing for what she was. That's why I changed her name to Anne-Lise. To try to help her hide. When she was young,

I always had the impression that everyone was just waiting, waiting and waiting, to see what kind of monstrosity
would emerge from her as she got older. But she was a
beautiful child. Clever and so assured. She wasn't like
me. She didn't need to hide. She even started calling
herself Anneliese and thought about changing her name
back officially. She said that it was who she really was.
She learned German in school at a time when no one else
wanted to. She read all kinds of German literature. She
couldn't understand how I had never learned to speak it."

Sarah stares blankly into the mist outside and her gaze
wanders among the nothingness. "I think she pitied me."
It is almost a whisper. She peers at the whiteness outside.
She fills her glass again wearily. She knows it's no use.
Her memories are more abiding than the anesthesia. She
can't forget what has been branded in her mind. Even if
her brain doesn't recall, her body will. Hands shaking.
Cheeks flushed red. Head swimming.

"Lafourgue seems to have considered a man named
Christian de la Hallière as a suspect. He was a Nazi,
and may even still be one, from what I've been told. Lafourgue certainly thought he was potentially dangerous.
Did Anne-Lise have any contact with him, as far as you
know?"

"Yes, she did. But he disgusted her. He was a Nazi to
his very marrow. The whole thing excited him: the pa-
rades, the bullying and killing of the weak, all of it. So
he spent a lot of time with the Germans during the occupation. Before he joined up, that is, and went to fight
in Russia. Anne-Lise wanted to find out who her father
was. Where she really came from. She wanted to know if
Christian had known Otto during the war."

"Had he?"

"Barely. He probably would have despised Otto anyway, if he even noticed him at all. Seen him as servant class. The Germans he admired were Prussian aristocrats who could trace their ancestors back for generations. Otto was a farm boy from the Hunsrück. He was an excellent engineer, though. But he had a Jew somewhere in his background, so they put him on bomb detail. It was an efficient solution, I suppose. He either saved German lives or got killed. Either way, they won."

"Did Anne-Lise spend much time with de la Hallière?"

"I don't think so." Tiredness suddenly seems to flood through her. Her skin blanches. "Maybe I'm wrong, though. There's a lot about her life that I probably don't know, and that I perhaps don't really want to know either . . . But you'll need to find it out, won't you, if you're going to catch the person who . . ." Her voice trails off.

"What about her boyfriend, a Soviet, Sasha Kurmakin? Lafourgue mentioned him as a possible suspect too."

Sarah's eyes blaze. Life pulses through her again. "What nonsense. Sasha is the kindest boy you can imagine. He would never have hurt Anne-Lise or anyone else. He's just a little bit different, that's all. Just like Anne-Lise was. When Lafourgue investigates someone . . ." She pauses, and her mouth twitches.

"What?"

"It doesn't always mean that they're a suspect. Sometimes it's just someone Lafourgue wants to have power over for a while. Interrogating people and imprisoning them are his ways of settling scores. Or of keeping himself entertained. An investigation like this gives him ways to hurt people he doesn't like. I'm not really sure that he ever actually looked into Anne-Lise's death at all. He never—not even once—found anything . . ."

I want to ask Sarah if she has any idea why Anne-Lise was mutilated, but I think better of it at the sight of her trying to drown in cognac, her hands twitching, her head tilted toward the mist and recalling something that no chemical will ever efface.

I thank her for her time and let myself out.

The Château de la Hallière lies on the coast road that winds west out of Sainte-Élisabeth, snaking between the heather and the shifting masses of the dunes. The sea gleams gray, dissolving into white froth where it batters the rocks. Spindrift glitters in the air, torn by the wind from the foaming tips of the waves. The car jolts along the corniche and shakes under the assaults of the gale. Windows rattle. The air is a maelstrom.

The château itself sits hunched on the side of a wooded slope, overlooking the bridge that crosses the estuary at the baie des Grèves Rocheuses. With the tide out, the glaucous, waterlogged sands stretch out into the distance. It looks desolate, like the wind-scarred soil of some alien planet. The slate roof and stone walls of the château sit in the shadows above the river mouth. Toward the eastern end, the roof has begun to collapse. Emptiness gapes between cracked slates. Timber joists poke out like the sudden eruption of bone through skin. Moss clings to the stones in green and brown clumps. Around the windows, rotten wood splinters in the air sodden with salt.

The bellpull is soaked through. Black mold crawls right up its length. The bell clangs dully, sending a cackling horde of gulls that were prowling in the estuary's mud swarming up into the air. The woman who opens the door has deep liquid-brown eyes. Skin tan as oak, soaked with the sun of the Levant. The world goes fuzzy before my eyes.

Her eyes are still open. They stare vacantly as if she were in the grip of a nightmare haunting this, her final and infinite sleep. I reach out to close them and find that her skin is warm. It shocks me. A tiny electrical prickle. As if the sun of the Maghreb were still infused in her body. With her eyes shut, she seems to slip away. Her face becomes an immaculate mask. The strained, twisted lines that suddenly appeared at al-Mazra'a fade. As life ebbs out of her, so too do her griefs. Death erases the memory of these last few days and this basement that became her whole world. She looks like what she is: a child.

The first trickle of blood washes gently against my knees.

"How can I help you?" The woman's voice is muted and distant. Her lips are dusky. Golden bracelets clack at her wrists. Only a whisper of some diaphanous fabric separates her body from the lacerations of the wind. She shivers and the points of her nipples stand out against the jet-black shimmering veil that barely covers her body.

"Would you ask Christian de la Hallière whether he would be prepared to see Capitaine le Garrec? I'm investigating the murder of Anne-Lise Aurigny. I believe that she and M. de la Hallière were acquainted."

The woman nods and the dark squiggles of her hair bounce and gleam. She invites me to step inside and I watch her shimmering parabolas disappear down a murky corridor. A faint smell of putrefaction floats on the air. An electric light buzzes overhead. The paintwork has long since faded to gray and its mildew-bespattered, flaky surface creeps along the walls in abstract patterns.

The woman returns, and in her hand is a newspaper cutting. "Two things," she says. "Firstly, M. de la Hallière asks whether you are here in an official capacity."

"No. I have no official powers."

"Good. M. de la Hallière said that these things are always more interesting when they are personal. Secondly, he asked me to show you this." She holds up the torn article. "He would like to know whether it is about you."

She hands me the crinkled paper. The headline says: "RESISTANCE HERO TURNED WAR CRIMINAL?" Next to it is a grainy image of a man with close-cropped hair and dead eyes. The picture was taken by the army just before I left for Algeria. I can't recognize the person fixed in those yellow-brown smudges. The text tells a story to match the face:

> *A former Resistance fighter has been sent home from Algeria under the shadow of a heinous crime.*
>
> *Yesterday morning, Capitaine Jacques le Garrec was returned to France on a military plane after two years of service. Le Garrec, 41, who grew up here in northern Brittany and attended school in Dinard, was ignominiously repatriated after details of a horrific crime, in which he is suspected of involvement, created a scandal in Algeria and sent shockwaves throughout France too.*
>
> *Le Garrec went to Algeria with a distinguished Resistance record behind him, having joined the maquis in 1941 and played a valuable role in the group Patrie et Liberté right up until the Liberation. He participated in four missions to sabotage trains stocked with Nazi matériel and wrote many inspiring editorials for the clandestine newspaper* La Lutte *which urged his compatriots to fight openly against the oppressor in the name of humanity.*
>
> *These impressive credentials won him a place in the* brigade criminelle *in Paris where, by all accounts, he served diligently and with moral purpose for well over a decade.*

However, even before reports of the Algerian atrocity, there had been evidence that not all was well with le Garrec. A fellow student, who studied philosophy with him at the École Normale Supérieure, recalls him as a highly competent thinker, but one ineluctably drawn to the darkness. Nihilism fascinated him, it seems: he studied not only Nietzsche but also the Nazi Martin Heidegger. Then, after the war, he grew interested in so-called existentialism.

Readers of this paper will surely recognize that existentialism is just the latest name given to a current of dangerous nihilism that has stalked Europe for decades now, and which contends that human life is meaningless and without value. Perhaps this faddish pessimism ate further away at le Garrec, rendering him incapable of ethical judgment.

What is certain is that on the thirteenth of September, 1959, he was stationed with the French army in Algeria as part of the service de renseignements. At around ten o'clock on this morning, Capitaine le Garrec presented himself at a local police station and asked, in passable Arabic, to speak to an officer. In the back of his jeep, wrapped in tarpaulin, was the body of Amira Khadra, a 19-year-old Algerian girl. She had been brutalized and then shot in the head.

Le Garrec neither took nor refused responsibility for the crime. Curiously, he asked for the local police to investigate the matter, but then failed to provide any account whatsoever of his own actions or his relationship to the girl. He even went so far as to refuse to explain where the body had come from. However, there seems little doubt that the girl had been detained by the intelligence services and Capitaine le Garrec had been responsible for her at the time of her death.

Le Garrec has since been escorted back to France and must attend the preliminary hearing of an army tribunal this coming Friday. Thus far, no comments have been forthcom-

*ing, either from le Garrec or from the army, and so we must
wait until the hearing before the first veils of mystery can be
lifted from this grisly affair.*

I hand the article back with a nod.

"Christian will be pleased to receive you," the woman
says. "Please follow me." She escorts me into a vaulted
living room whose only source of light is a fire leaping in
the grate. With each gust of wind that swirls down from
the chimney, the flames scatter and dance, sending shadows lurching across the walls.

De la Hallière himself is seated in an armchair, allowing the light of the flames to glow on his cheeks
and throw his eyes into gloom. His chestnut hair falls
smoothly down from a parting in the center of his head
and floats gently around his face. His skin is pinched and
runs taut over the cheekbones. A thin scar burns sharply
above his left eye.

"M. le Garrec, what fortuitous wind blows you in
this direction, I wonder." He doesn't get up. "One gets
so used to being the *only* war criminal in one's neck of the
woods. How terribly exciting to meet another. Do *please*
take a seat, and I shall ring for Aïcha to bring some re-
freshments." His fingers tug idly at a frayed cord beside
the fire. The Levantine woman reappears, with that same
chiffony film of black clinging to her skin and whispering
around the sway of her body as she walks.

"Fetch me a brandy and some cigarettes, and whatever
M. le Garrec would like."

"Just a cigarette. Thank you."

As Aïcha busies herself at a sideboard, de la Hallière
cuts her off. "Wait a moment. Aïcha, come back here. M.
le Garrec, would you like her to *crawl* over there to fetch

you your cigarettes? She will, if you would prefer. This will also afford you the opportunity to inspect her hind-quarters, which have the voluptuous fullness typical of Maghrebi women."

Aïcha says nothing, though her eyelids fold and her gaze drops to the floor.

"Would you prefer that?"

"No."

"In that case, Aïcha, please proceed with your task." He leans back. "Do you know, M. le Garrec, *why* she will crawl over to that fine piece of Louis XVI furniture for you, should you so desire? Let me enlighten you: it is a sign of the inherent baseness of the race to which she belongs."

"Perhaps it's just the state of powerlessness that you hold her in. A foreigner here with no contacts and no-where else to go."

"What an absurd notion! Allow me to explain the matter to you from a pathological perspective. In the Nietzschean sense, I mean."

Aïcha floats between us and, bending down, cups a lighted match between her hands. As I lean in toward it, the oily perfume of her skin trickles down my throat. Her hair wafts around my face, glowing black. The taste of licorice tingles on my tongue. De la Hallière waves a hand at her and she is dismissed.

"You, le Garrec, with your name suggestive of fine Breton ancestry, would surely not countenance abasing yourself in this manner. Perhaps you attribute this to some personal nobility, or to a cultural penchant for resistance nurtured through years of opposition to the ghastly Jacobin centralism of the Republic. You would be wrong, however. Because a new substance has been discovered—you may have heard of it—DNA. Apparently it contains all of the information about each of us, and what we shall become. When it has been fully researched, I have no doubt that it will revolutionize our understanding of the different races. This tiresome liberal relativism called *equality* which seems to have grown out of the ashes of Auschwitz will be exposed for the Negro-Jewish propaganda that it in fact is."

Fumes from the cigarette snake before my eyes. I haven't smoked since Algeria. For a second, I feel the burning air of Africa once again.

"M. de la Hallière, I didn't come here to discuss the racial characteristics of your housekeeper. I came to ask you about the murder of Anne-Lise Aurigny."

"Housekeeper?" He smirks. "My dear fellow, let us not take refuge in euphemisms. We have both seen the horrors and the glories of war close up, you in Algeria and me on the Ostfront. What an extraordinary place—hell is not fire, le Garrec, it is ice, boundless wastes of ice . . ." His eyes glaze for a second, then he shakes his head. "Let us call things by their proper names. Is that not a divine and necessary task? Aïcha is my *slave*. Come, come." He waves away whatever objection I am supposed to make. "We can do better than to rehash that dismal little fiction about democracy and social progress that has become so dear to the newspaper-reading, enfranchised masses in recent decades. I know, I know: they work for fewer hours, have disposable income to spend on cultural activities such as books and the cinema, temper their sexual impulses with birth control and thus manage the size of their families. It is all very touching, how the working masses have grown their own little souls. But none of this masks the reality of the DNA. Aïcha is a born slave, and I have provided her with the circumstances in which she may fulfill that vocation. She does my bidding entirely, self-abnegatingly. A society does not have to allow or even avow slavery in order for it to exist. I am quite sure, capitaine, that the dead girl in the back of your jeep learned, perhaps in very great pain, what it feels like to be a slave over those last days of her existence. Perhaps she thought life was different. She had been *educated* in some Europeanized school. *Emancipated* from Muslim traditions. Then the war came and she died with the taste of her slavery upon her tongue. That is how it should be."

He swills some brandy around in his mouth. "Actually, Aïcha has some European blood in her. A Polish grandmother, I believe. Normally I would be suspicious of crossbreeding, but here it has been curiously successful. I would give her 16 out of 20, a rare score indeed." He smiles weakly. "I met her in Morocco after the war. France wasn't a safe place for those of us who'd seen something glorious in fascism, so I had to find somewhere else to live. I can't remember exactly what I promised her if she came back with me. Marriage, perhaps. Jewels. The gilded life of a chatelaine. Sumptuous soirées where she could wear elbow-length gloves and be admired by members of the Légion d'Honneur and the cream of high society." He glances at the mildewed walls floating in the dimness and chuckles. "Ultimately, she's just a slave. How else could her story end?"

"Monsieur, I would like to ask you about Anne-Lise. How well did you know her?"

He exhales lazily, allowing plumes of smoke to drift and wreathe in the air around his face.

"I feel that it would be rather indecorous to give away any particulars of my relationship with Anne-Lise. Surely you could not expect a gentleman to be so indiscreet."

"Then why do you think she was mutilated?"

For the first time, a quiver runs across his face. "*Mutilated . . .*" He runs the word around in his mouth like a connoisseur. "I'm not sure she was mutilated. Someone cut a piece out of her. But that may have been a gesture of love. We wish to cling to those things that we love. Mutilation sounds so terribly vague and destructive. I'm not sure the killer saw it like that."

"Were you aware that Lafourgue considered you one of the chief suspects?"

"My dear fellow, whenever a crime is committed in these parts, I am invariably one of the chief suspects. Fascist leanings make one a suspect by default. I do remember that he seated his considerable posterior upon that very chair a few months ago and fired off some rather inconsequential questions at me. I don't recall how I replied, and I'm not sure that I was aware of being any more a suspect than I normally am whenever someone casts off the chains of convention and takes pleasure in the free expression of criminal impulses."

"Lafourgue considered you a man of pathologically violent and fundamentally sociopathic tendencies. Did you ever fantasize about hurting Anne-Lise?"

De la Hallière sighs. "Who doesn't have violent fantasies? Our democratic modernity seems to demand them. How often—when I see some local politician making speeches promising a brighter tomorrow, sick pay for the workingman, improved education for workers' children—how often does it fill me with a kind of rage? A righteous fury grips me as I watch this lackluster demagogue empowering the basest subspecies that exists among us, out of which no flower of nobility or art could ever bloom.

Perhaps you have felt it too? I long to grab my riding crop and stride over to the fellow! The air seems to scream at me: *Thrash him! Thrash this enemy of lineage and of roses!* I long to see the horsewhip draw blood from his back! To see him writhing on the ground, howling his impotence and agony like the ape that he is!" He stops dead. "Is that a sociopathic fantasy? If so, then perhaps what Lafourgue says about me is correct. Is that what you were looking for?"

Inside the crumbling château, I have lost all sense of time. There are no windows in the hall and de la Hallière's voice trickles through the gloom. He enjoys being questioned.

"Do you think Anne-Lise was killed out of love?"

He purses his lips as if searching for a word or the memory of a taste. "Can you imagine what the Ostfront was like? I joined the Wehrmacht and that's where they sent us. It didn't take long out there to know it had all gone bad. We went not to fight, but to die for an ideal. The ground was like iron underfoot. The wind was like a perpetual assault. Icy claws ripping at your skin. Eventually it was a total rout. No more matériel. No more orders. I don't even know how many kilometers we'd retreated but the space just seemed endless. Nobody was under any illusions. The war was being lost here. Fascism died in the wastes of that winter. As it did, some members of the division seemed to have a change of heart. *Kein Krieg mehr!* They wanted us to leave the Russkies alone. I mean those skinny, starving peasants whose miserable settlements we were passing as we fell back. All that bourgeois democratic Frenchness came flooding back into them.

"One day, we came across a peasant girl lying beside the road. Something had crushed her foot to the point where there was no foot left, just a kind of crimson lump browning and blackening in the freezing air. She didn't look up as we passed and she didn't cry for help. She just stared vacantly into the sky. As I got closer to her, I could see that the ice had frozen the pulp of her foot and stuck it to the stony surface of the road. I heard some voices saying that we should try to free her and get her to a settlement nearby. That would have been *heroic*, I suppose, what with the Russians so close behind us.

"I stared at the girl's face for a while. Her skin was bone-white. She seemed to look past me. I suppose I could have just let her die.

"I shot her in the eye. Her body was so cold that the blood could hardly squeeze out of the socket. Behind me, I could hear the outrage of bourgeois, democratic voices.

"Now, I suppose that whoever killed Anne-Lise did it for the same reason that I put a bullet into that Russian peasant's skull. Oh, not to see those looks of sickened horror on the faces of some of my companions. Men who, only recently, had been slaughtering Russians in the service of a regime explicitly geared toward the extermination of a certain portion of the human race. Not that I didn't savor those reproachful stares from men whose mythical *humanity* had now come flooding back in defeat.

"No, I shot that girl because it was a crime. We knew it was a crime. The war was over and there was no power to sanction the violence anymore. If it had been an order, it would have been merely pointless. It was a crime, and crime is one of the highest pleasures that can be experienced. We may claim to abhor war, in this sanitized century we inhabit, but the conflicts we have fought have pushed brutality and depravity to hitherto unseen levels. War allows us to taste the pure narcotic of crime.

"Just for a second, as I watched the girl's body twitching, I felt my own individual desires surging forward, writing themselves onto the world in defiance of the crushing uniformity of a socially useful morality. Life, M. le Garrec, so quickly becomes a net. All we experience is the perpetual nullification of the drives. This is, I suppose, the price we must pay for participation in society. That is: to go to work in bleary-eyed stupor, to read the newspapers and develop personal opinions about current affairs, and, once every few years, to mark our cross on a ballot paper, as if that were a sign or guarantee of equality.

"Now, I have no idea who killed Anne-Lise. All I can say is that it was not me. But whoever did it lived more intensely in those few tormented hours that were Anne-Lise's last on earth than in the rest of his pallid existence. I am deeply saddened by Anne-Lise's death. For such a low-born thing, she was surprisingly touched by the spirit of aristocracy. But more than that, I envy her killer the unadulterated exhilaration which exists, and can only exist, when all social convention falls away and we wallow in the crimes that lurk within us all in the form of desire and the eerie whispers of our dreams."

By the time I leave the château, darkness has fallen. The forests are just swaying shadows. From the estuary, the murmur of the sea rises into the night.

I left de la Hallière in a frenzied state, his lips flecked with spittle as he denounced the Reds and the Jews who had overrun France since the war's end. He could have gone on long into the night, barely listening to my questions, delivering his endless tirades into the echoing vaults.

The coast road is deserted. The headlights skim the gorse, picking out the tips of the grass. The sea, invisible as its darkness melts into that of the sky, is just a hiss where it froths at the base of the cliffs.

I try to sift everything I heard today. Something nags at me and makes my gaze twitch uneasily. Something isn't quite right. I try to recollect the substance of my conversation with de la Hallière. Is there a significant detail lying just behind something he told me?

But it isn't de la Hallière whose words flutter uneasily in my brain. It is *Sarah*. Her talk of hatred and malice. Her hands shaking. I think back again queasily to our interview. What did she mean?

I finally track Lafourgue down on the jetty, sharing a bottle of local brandy with some other policemen as they gaze out into the freezing night. He beckons me to sit beside him and nods when I ask him to tell me about what happened to Sarah during the war.

He says that she was in her twenties at the time of the defeat and nothing like her luminous, self-possessed daughter. She left school without her baccalaureate, having dreamed her way through her education, and battled only half-heartedly to get her marks into double figures. She drifted into waitressing at A l'abri des flots, where she would wipe the tables down, shivering in her white blouse in the breaking dawn. She carried cups of thick coffee or shots of spirits to the fishermen in the half-light before they went out to sea.

Lafourgue says that people argued afterward about exactly what happened during the war. Some tried to defend Sarah, and said that when the Germans came in she served them reluctantly, watering down the spirits and making sure that the beers she served were flat. Others said she suddenly came to life. Her cheeks were redder than usual, her eyes brighter, her steps a little quicker, the roll of her hips a little more pronounced. She enjoyed serving the Germans, who called her *Fräulein* very correctly and, just occasionally, *Liebling*. They made her feel important. They made the fishermen, who had ignored her for so long, sit outside on the freezing terrace while she busied herself inside, her cheeks pink with anticipation, a couple of buttons of her crisp, white work blouse hanging undone, revealing her tight, white chest heaving beneath.

And Lafourgue? What does he remember?

He shrugs. The Nazis weren't like the French soldiers, he says. They could make you feel afraid. And what is more hypnotic than fear?

Otto Steiner was just a face in the crowd. A nonentity. A good match for Sarah, Lafourgue says. Only in his midtwenties, he already had a face going pudgy around the jowls. His eyes were brown and wide and trusting. Sarah used to sit cocooned in their kindness. Lafourgue could see fear flickering in them.

"Sarah said he was part Jewish, and that's why he was allocated to bomb disposal."

Lafourgue shakes his head. Otto was simply too feeble to serve in the regular army. He had chronic problems with breathlessness and fatigue. Sarah preferred to think of him as a gallant victim of persecution rather than seeing him for what he really was: a runt. And why wouldn't she? She spent the war years in considerable comfort. While the fishermen sat outside at their tables sipping ersatz coffee made from barley, she nestled indoors by the fire, tingling from caffeine and tobacco. She wore stockings and felt the coastal winds rip through her hair as Otto's car, for which he always had fuel, sped along the corniche past the trudging locals.

The war years were good to her. The malevolent looks she got didn't make her feel guilty. It was naked jealousy. As the winter of 1940 mellowed into the spring of 1941, Sarah carried her burgeoning stomach with pride. She and Otto christened the baby Anneliese in the church at Sainte-Élisabeth on July 14, 1941.

Lafourgue stares out to the sea. People here know how to wait, he says. They don't forget.

By the summer of 1944 the last Nazis had pulled out of Brittany. The local committee for *épuration* had already been set up, headed by a local schoolteacher, Gilles Grégoire, whose clandestine poems had been published by Éditions de Minuit. Later, in 1945, he would resign from his position in disgust after discovering that the graves of five militiamen, tried and shot in the neighboring village of le Guildo, had been dug before the judicial proceedings even began. In 1944 he was still calling for justice and calm in the process of rebuilding the country.

Sarah and Otto kept the curtains in their house drawn and held their hands over Anneliese's mouth to stop her crying, hoping that their very existence would be forgotten.

It wasn't. On October 14, 1944, three fishermen who had often sat outside on the terrace of A l'abri des flots watching Sarah bathed in firelight, her laughter visible but inaudible through the thick glass, kicked the door of her house off its hinges and walked inside. The oldest, Marius Martin, was twenty; the youngest, Jean Goff, was just sixteen.

Martin had a boat hook with him, which he used to splinter the wooden doorframe. Then, as he stepped inside, he brought it down on Otto's head when he stood up to protect Anneliese. Sarah heard wood crunch into his skull before he sank into darkness. Goff grabbed her and forced her onto the ground with her face pressed into the floor. He lay on top of her, pinning her arms to her sides. He could feel her buttocks rubbing furiously against him as she squirmed. It made him laugh. He loosened his grip a little so that she could writhe even more.

Martin walked over to where Anneliese was sitting silently and picked her up. As soon as he had her in his hands, he realized that he had no idea what to do with her. He lifted her above his head.

On the floor, Sarah shrieked.

"The child is a curse," Martin said. He twirled her around in the air above his head. Anneliese smiled; her little brown eyes shone. Martin looked at her. For a few seconds, there was calm. Martin stared at Anneliese's translucent skin and the blond shimmer of her hair, and then he put her down.

"It's the mother we want," he said. "Bring her outside."

The three fishermen dragged Sarah out into the street by her hair. She saw none of it. As soon as they put Anneliese down, she closed her eyes and surrendered herself to them. Goff carried a chair out into the street and bound her hands and feet to it. Across the rue de la Grande Baie, faces began to appear in windows. Some wandered into their gardens for a better view. Martin pulled a razor from his pocket and began to hack, slice, and pull at Sarah's hair. It came out in thick clumps in his hands. He tried to throw it down onto the ground but it stuck to his sweating fingers.

Goff called out to the watching neighbors: "Punished for screwing the enemy! She rutted all through the dark years! Now it's coming back to her!"

Sarah felt the razor burn where it scraped her scalp. She felt her skin burn where the blade dug in. She felt her scalp on fire where her hair was torn out at the roots. Martin stood back to look at her. Blood was running down her face in grimy trickles. It stuck the hairs to her cheeks and neck. Gashes and grazes crisscrossed her scalp. Her hair poked out only in intermittent tufts. Her eyes were still closed.

Goff took the cardboard sign that he had daubed with tar and hung it round Sarah's neck. In uneven capital letters it said: *CETTE PUTE BAISE LES CHLEUHS*—*this whore fucks the Boche*.

"Turn her around," Martin said, "so that everyone can see the sign." Behind them, anxious, racing footfalls echoed in the street. Grégoire, his face flushed and his heart pounding, came waddling toward them. He wiped the sweat off his brow and the steam from his glasses and, peering through the newly clean lenses, examined the body tied to the chair and the condemnation around its neck.

"What are you doing?" he gasped as he pulled the sign off Sarah's shoulders. "This is vengeance. If the purge is going to succeed, then it must be just. Only justice can cleanse the crimes of the past."

The fishermen looked nonplussed. Martin stared down at the strands of Sarah's hair glued to his hands by her blood. Goff asked, "What should we do with her?"

Grégoire panted and looked around. He handed the sign back to Martin.

"Rewrite that," he ordered. "Say: *Condemned for Horizontal Collaboration by Order of the Purge Commission*."

Goff disappeared to borrow paint from one of the neighboring houses and Grégoire took his sweat-stained handkerchief out of his jacket pocket and used it to scrub off some of the blood drying in rusty smudges on Sarah's cheeks. When Goff returned with the new sign, Grégoire placed it around Sarah's neck. He took a couple of paces back to better evaluate the scene. He squinted uneasily at the almost-bald woman sitting in front of him, her eyes screwed shut. Eventually, he nodded. "Okay," he said.

"How long do we leave her like that?" Martin wanted to know.

Grégoire pondered. "Leave her for an hour, then you can untie her."

A little over an hour later, as the sun slunk out of sight in the immensity of the western sky, Martin cut the ropes binding her wrists and ankles. They dragged her up and pulled her toward the entrance of her house. No one even checked on Otto, still slumped on the living room floor. Anneliese was nowhere to be seen.

Goff pulled Sarah by her blouse.

Along the street, the windows were now empty. The gardens were deserted.

When Sarah finally stumbled across the splintered threshold into her hall, no one was left to see her and she entered the silent house alone.

Lafourgue shakes his head. He says that Sarah never got over the purge. She became erratic and unstable. Terror had coiled in her nerves. When Otto recovered from his wounds he wanted to stay, convinced that the inhabitants of Sainte-Élisabeth had taken their revenge on him and would now leave him alone. Sarah made him go back to Germany, screaming at him or ignoring him totally until he had no choice but to pack up the few things he had and return to a land he could no longer recognize as the country of his birth.

Anne-Lise grew up in the shadow of Sarah's fear. Her mother used to drag her through the streets in haste, her eyes fixed furiously on the ground. Each time there was a knock on the door, a great pulse of adrenaline rushed through her body and she began to shake. Fear burned, tingled, and trembled in every inch of her body. Migraines felt like someone was drilling into her skull. Alcohol killed the feeling for a while, but these were infrequent highs followed by long hours of sickness, shaking, and exhaustion.

Lafourgue gazes upon the dark expanse of the sea. "Sarah is damaged," he tells me. "Scarred. Anne-Lise never cared at all about what happened. It was just provincial gossip to her. She wanted to go to Paris to get away from it. But more importantly, she wanted to get away from Sarah. As far away as possible from a woman destroyed by panic and who she could barely recognize as her mother."

Is that what Sarah became: someone whose traumatized brain was a laboratory of anguish, and who saw in her own daughter the evidence of a hideous mistake that had ruined her life forever?

I remain on the dock for a while longer, until Lafourgue finishes the bottle, stands up, and hurls it into the sea. I see it arc out into the night before it crashes against the lightless surface of the water.

I huddle in my greatcoat as I walk back home through unlit streets.

When I arrive the house is cold and quiet. A crisp brown envelope, delivered by hand, waits for me in the letter box. Inside, an official communiqué informs me that I shall be visited tomorrow morning by Capitaine Gallantin, who will discuss the "events in Algeria" before the preliminary hearing of the military tribunal on Friday. I am instructed that the capitaine is very much looking forward to my cooperation in this matter.

I don't want to go to bed. As soon as my eyes close, I feel once again the warmth of Amira's blood creeping along my legs and see her shocked, blank, staring eyes until I reach out and close them.

I lie down on the sofa, wrapped in my greatcoat, staring out into the darkness. I take the photo Sarah gave me out of my pocket and, in the faint glow of starlight, look at Anne-Lise and that pale half-smile flickering on her face as she dreamed of tomorrows that would come and save her, bathed in the glow of what must have felt like eternity.

DAY FOUR

The house buzzes with a quietness I can't bear. I turn on the radio and jolt slightly at the hiss of the announcer's voice. I need the noise. Any kind of words. The speaker seems elated at the news he is bringing.

"... *because we are now living through an almost unprecedented economic boom. This decade of ours has become the age of consumer goods. Millions of French households now enjoy such miracles of modernity as the refrigerator, the Citroën DS, or even the very radio which allows me to talk to you right now. And it is not only these feats of engineering which have made our lives better. We are cleaner than ever! Soap and shampoo are selling in quantities never before seen, and personal hygiene has become* ..."

I turn the noise off and wait until the sound of knocking at the door drags me from the hum of silence. Outside, clutched by the fingers of the mist, is a man in an army uniform. His dark, piercing eyes and hooked nose give him a predatory air. He frowns a little, showing an officer's instinctive contempt for my slept-in suit and unshaven face. Capitaine Gallantin's demeanor is coldly professional. Once inside, he places a perfectly ordered file in front of me.

"Perhaps we can start by examining the information you initially gave to the Algerian police about your duties at al-Mazra'a. Before the tribunal, you will need to carefully consider your testimony, and particularly those aspects of it that have been refuted by multiple other sources and could therefore make you liable to a charge of perjury, if not treason. You may still change any details of your statements or indeed ask for them not to be brought before the tribunal."

I read over the pages of neat typescript. The words are mine but they sound strange and disjointed. The phrases make sense but they don't seem to connect to any reality I can remember.

> My work at al-Mazra'a consisted mainly of interrogating suspected members of the FLN or ALN or their sympathizers. I took my orders directly from Lieutenant-Colonel Lambert, who was overseeing intelligence operations in the region. Lambert was especially focused on uncovering and eliminating supply routes for arms. When I arrived at al-Mazra'a in 1957, insurrectionary activity had been increasing dramatically for over a year, and better-armed and better-trained maquis were launching scorched-earth raids on villages with a colonial presence or pro-French sympathies. Recent explosive attacks on two French trains transporting matériel had elevated the stakes of the war and Lambert was determined to respond decisively.

The words sound oddly calm. Ordered. As if they'd been written by a simple observer who narrated objectively what he witnessed.

> My first suspect was a twenty-four-year-old medical student named Tarik. He had been sharing living quarters with two other students who helped to draft and print pamphlets making violent threats against Algerians who cooperated with

the French. There was no evidence to suggest that Tarik had any knowledge of the activities of his housemates. Lambert wanted to be sure.

When I came into the interrogation room, Tarik was tied to a chair and his skin was glistening with sweat. All over his body, black hairs stood on end. Was it cold down here in the silent earth? Was it the sweat drying on his exposed body? Or was it hypersensitivity? A chill of terror that made his whole body alert, throbbing with the fear of what was to come?

I looked into his deep black eyes rolling in their sockets. His jaw was clamped shut. I only stared at his face for a second or two but I felt sure he was here by mistake. After ten years in the police I could read the feint of guilt or the simmering of rage in the face of a suspect. Tarik had neither. There was just a blank, uncomprehending stare as if he simply couldn't grasp what was happening to him.

For about an hour I questioned him on his relationship to his two housemates. He seemed relieved to talk, gabbling faster and faster, desperate to add ever more detail to his account so that nothing could possibly remain hidden. At times I had to remind him to breathe, otherwise the flood of words would have choked him.

I reported to Lambert that there was no evidence of a connection between him and the FLN, but that I would investigate the house and gain background information on Tarik from the medical faculty. I was convinced, however, that such inquiries would prove unproductive.

Lambert stared at me coolly and said "Capitaine, once again I must remind you that this is a war. You cannot go and talk to a suspect's colleagues, because you are their enemy and they will refuse to speak to you. You do not have the time it would require to search his house and then follow up on whatever you find there. You need to obtain totally secure *information from this man within the next few hours. There is only one way you can do so."*

I tried to explain that I had questioned Tarik thoroughly, cross-checking his answers and returning to probe his statements from different angles, but Lambert cut me off with an impatient nod.

"Capitaine, you will not get information out of him by asking him subtle questions. How did you imagine that the service de renseignements would work? We don't worry about the standards of proof required for courtrooms. But we do need to know about armament networks and supply lines before more people are killed by terrorists incapable of understanding the principles of democracy."

There was a violent yet absolutely controlled fury about Lambert as he spoke. His blue eyes didn't blink and appeared frozen in his head. His untanned skin looked fragile. He stood up and walked to the door, each movement economical, contained, yet radiating power. He didn't need to beckon or to turn around. I followed him anyway. His boots echoed down the corridor and I trailed him silently.

In Tarik's cell, the light buzzed overhead. When he saw Lambert come in, his hands began to shake. Lambert said nothing. He simply walked to the back of the cell and turned on a tap above an old steel tub. He let the water run slowly. In the silence of the cell, the trickle of the water seemed to swell to a roar. Lambert stared off into space while the water flowed slowly in the quiet.

Then another sound started up. An uncontrolled, rapid clacking sound. Something brittle knocking together and grinding. Tarik's teeth.

When the tub was finally full, Lambert pivoted the chair around and, with Tarik's hands and feet still bound to the frame, pushed his head under the surface of the water. The tendons bulged in his wrists and neck as he held Tarik down. Tarik's arms and legs jerked against the bindings. The surface of the water was a churning mass of bubbles, swirling and bursting.

Just as Tarik's muscles began to slacken, Lambert pulled his head up out of the tub. As soon as Tarik sensed the air, his mouth sucked and gasped for oxygen. His lungs seemed to roar and his jaw pumped, trying to swallow all the air in the room. His diaphragm hammered in bursts and forced water out of his throat. His body shook with the retches. His eyes rolled wildly, pleading for someone to save him.

Lambert tightened his grip and pushed Tarik's head back down into the tub. He repeated this same action— gripping the head beneath the surface of the water until the body began to relax, then pulling it out into the air gasping, choking, vomiting water, and gulping oxygen—again and again for what must have been half an hour. Each time, Tarik's head seemed to stay down in the depths of the tub for longer and the seconds of frantic interlude grew fewer.

I could see that Tarik's body wasn't adapting, just getting weaker. With every passing minute, an apprehensive sickness crawled farther down inside me. Each time Tarik's head went under the water, I was sure that, this time, the breath would die within him. Just for a second, as his head was dragged back up into the air, I could feel my lungs stop too. Panic had infected every inch of Tarik, from his darting, incoherent gaze to his shaking, tensed legs and arms.

Finally, Lambert placed the chair back in the center of the room beneath the single bulb's glare. Tarik's eyes were a wall of silent screams. His lips started to move automatically, murmuring something in Arabic that even he didn't seem able to understand. Lambert had not spoken a single word to Tarik. He had not asked him about his connection to the leaflets or to the FLN, and when he had finished forcing Tarik's head down into the water, he simply stood there, quietly, as if he were waiting.

Eventually the ragged heaves in Tarik's chest subsided and, although his lips continued to trace out some noiseless incantation, his eyes appeared able to focus on and understand his surroundings. It looked as if he had returned to a state of sanity after the temporary madness of nearly drowning. Lambert nodded, opened the door to the cell, and walked out. His steps echoed down the corridor. I looked over at Tarik and saw that he was shivering.

A few moments later, it was not Lambert who returned but two young soldiers carrying an electric generator. They didn't move like Lambert, all ruthless, pared-down motion. They shuffled in. They didn't look at Tarik either. They began to set up the generator with mechanical motions, as if they were fixing a household appliance. Tarik's eyes were going wild. They were dilating and racing. His hands and feet were wan where he had cut off the circulation by straining against his bindings. For a second, his lips stopped moving. Then his face fragmented. He began to scream.

The next thing I can remember, I had left Tarik's cell and was striding rapidly along the corridor. In the distance behind me I could hear one long howl of wordless, terrified sound: a human voice that pain had turned into something inhuman. The noise swelled. It rushed closer and closer as my feet pounded the concrete faster and faster to get away from it, as if it were a tidal wave breaking at my back. I tried to outrun it but I knew it was too late. Even when I reached the outside, where the great sky receded infinitely above and where no sound from the warren would ever penetrate, I could still hear that same shriek. I stopped walking. It no longer made any sense to try to escape because that noise was now in my head. I could hear it reverberating in the recesses of my memory, burrowing down inside of me like a virus, infecting me, digging into the circuits of recollection from where I knew it could never be expunged.

I don't know how long I just stood there outside before Djamel's voice startled me back to consciousness.

"Chef. Chef. You need to come inside."

His eyes squinted up at me. I saw his face as a blur: the pinched nose and pointed chin, with a wispy beard tracing a line across it.

"Chef . . ."

He laid a hand on my wrist and pulled me after him. Djamel was a Harki, an Algerian who joined the French army to fight against independence. His father was French, and whenever the idea of independence was brought up, he thrust out his chest, his face reddened with emotion, and he cried out that Algeria would never be able to govern herself fairly or well. The French soldiers called him Jean-Michel. Once, I asked him what he would do if France withdrew from Algeria. Wouldn't the nationalists come looking for those who had thrown their lot in with the occupiers? He looked blank, then smiled at me, although his deep brown eyes were clouded.

"France will never leave," he said. "And if you did, then you would take me with you. We fought for you. You would not abandon us. It would be monstrous."

I followed Djamel hesitantly back down into the warren.

"Chef," he said, "Lambert wants you to come back inside. He says the suspect is ready to talk now."

Why not go back in? I couldn't outrun the sound of that voice that burst through the warren. It was a whisper embedded in my brain the way a bullet lodges in flesh. I followed Djamel's feet down into the dim corridors, through the glowing heat of the bulbs overhead. The door to Tarik's cell was open. The corridor was eerily quiet. There was just a soft yet persistent sound of scraping, an intermittent swish, as if someone were sweeping the floor inside. Then I caught a burning odor wafting faintly on the air trapped in the basement.

"Come on, chef," Djamel said. "Lambert won't wait long."

Tarik had been hung from the ceiling. His hands were tied behind his back, and the rope had been passed through a hook on the ceiling. The tendons running along his arms and shoulders bulged and strained, looking as if they might snap. His back arced, jerked desperately, trying to relieve the pressure his dangling body was exerting on his arms. That swishing, scrabbling noise was his feet. The tips of his toes, straining terrifically, could just make contact with the ground. Each time his nails managed to scrape the floor, the strain in his arms increased with the effort. It was tearing his muscles apart. But the urge was stronger than reason. Time and again he tensed his toes like an animal's claws and reached over and over for the floor that was always just out of reach.

Apart from a few breathless groans as his feet scrabbled for the ground, Tarik was now totally silent. His eyes were wide open yet utterly blank, as if he had been given a narcotic. The flesh around his nipples was blackened and gummy with blood. It no longer looked like human flesh at all, more like the mineral residue of fire. The head of his penis was fissured down the middle. I could see the tissue of the glans hanging in rubbery, torn clumps . . .

Gallantin taps the paper with his pen. "You seem at great pains to detail cases of alleged brutality, and to show your own disgust at what was happening. And yet we have no other reports of any such actions taking place. What's more, someone who spent as long as you did in the Resistance would have been used to such scenes. You lived with torture every day, even if only as an idea, a possibility. Why would these events have caused you such discomfort, even if they had taken place as you describe?"

Why? Perhaps because in the Resistance, we knew why people were suffering. It wasn't suffering itself that chased me out of the warren at al-Mazra'a. It was feeling that the brutality was meaningless. We were accomplishing nothing. The guilt spread like a sickness.

"Fine," Gallantin says, smiling wanly. "You don't have to answer the question." He gestures at my statement. "Finish reading it. You should think carefully about what you wish to present to the judge."

Djamel went up to where Tarik's body was dangling in the bulb's glare. He spoke to him softly and insistently for about five minutes. At that time, I couldn't understand much Arabic and I had to ask Djamel what he was saying. He looked subdued and he almost whispered.

"I told him: 'You need to talk. Do you understand? You need to start talking. If you don't talk, you'll die. Do you understand?'"

"What did he say?"

"He said he can't talk. He doesn't know anything. I told him: 'Listen, you have to find something to say. It's the only way you can get out. Otherwise, this will carry on until it kills you. So think!'"

For a while, Djamel and Tarik whispered in Arabic. Or rather, Djamel whispered urgently, cajoling Tarik, and great streams of words rattled off his tongue. He grabbed Tarik's sweat-soaked arm in a gesture of compassion. The Harkis came not like interrogators but like brothers.

Djamel appeared in the depths of Tarik's pain and spoke to him gently, but it didn't seem as if Tarik were paying any attention. His head lolled backward. His eyes were closed. His mouth twitched, although more in pain than from a desire to talk. Occasionally, whatever Djamel was saying penetrated the screen of his suffering and he jerked a little, his throat opened, and a few broken sounds were forced out.

Djamel eventually removed his hand from Tarik's shoulder. For some reason, I couldn't stop thinking that the flesh must be ice-cold in spite of the burning. Djamel nodded at me.

"Okay, he's given me something. We can go."

"Are you going to cut him down?"

Djamel grinned and a strange, sheepish expression came over his face. "No. Lambert is quite specific about it. Pain doesn't stop just because someone talks. It's always there."

"You should pay special attention to the following statement," Gallantin advises. "It will be contested vigorously and with abundant evidence."

The words stand clearly before my eyes. For the first time in weeks, I read something that seems to make sense. Something in which I have captured the murmur of the past:

I discovered that Lambert had refined and developed the techniques and apparatuses of torture with an almost scientific rigor. He insisted on the generalized application of pain almost independent of the processes of information-gathering. He used torture as a perpetual, capricious instrument to disorient and break detainees. He subjected suspects to agony for hours or even days without any attempt, initially, to interrogate them. If pain were applied solely in order to obtain information, and then suspended when information had been received, this created an evident and intelligible pattern that allowed detainees a measure of control over their situations. Lambert wanted to create a self-contained universe for detainees in which feeding or being starved, sleep or sleeplessness, and the application of torture or relief from it should form a complete system which exceeded entirely and at all times the detainees' ability to manipulate or master it. Suspects who could foresee when they would be tortured could make calculations about what information to give or to withhold, and when to do so, or about how long they could expect to keep particular secrets in exchange for other, less important details. Detainees were more inclined to resort to misinformation if they were kept in an environment that was amenable to logical analysis. At al-Mazra'a, Lambert had removed any sense of logic or control. It was almost literally a nightmare in which a profound, incomprehensible, and unending suffering held sway.

Lambert kept Tarik at al-Mazra'a for nine days. For much of that time he remained in the same position, his arms bound behind his back, hanging from the ceiling, just close enough to the floor to feel driven to reach out for it, but without being able to support his weight at all.

I tried to talk to Lambert about the information Tarik had given up. It seemed obvious that he had simply invented something in order to put an end to his torment and in the hope of saving his own life. Lambert barely listened. His eyes glimmered contempt. He continued to calibrate the maximum amount of suffering that he could inflict on Tarik, alternating periods of unendurable agony with respite so that physical inurement to pain and the psychological resistance that might emerge from too much unalleviated torture—the *sense of having withstood the worst—could never be attained.*

    Lambert was not at all concerned with the idea that Tarik's information could be false. He put unrelenting pressure upon all detainees, assuming that, as disorientation and weakness set in, misinformation would be contradicted and correct information would be corroborated by repetition. He created, in Tarik's broken mind, a perpetual need to provide intelligence. Tarik talked more and more. He babbled and begged and shouted into the stone walls around him when there was no interrogator in his cell. He sought through ever more detailed information to put an end to the insanity that was al-Mazra'a. He talked and talked. Names. Locations. Leads. He kept on talking. I could not believe this was intelligence. It was the terrified, temporary madness of a man in intolerable agony, desperate to end it however he could.

    Based on what he said, more suspects were brought into al-Mazra'a. The insanity spread from the detainees to the interrogators and out into the whole country.

Gallantin sits stiffly at the kitchen table. He shakes his head when I offer him coffee. He leans in toward me, and his eyes bore into mine.

"This, too," he says, "is highly contentious and will be refuted by extensive testimony. Allow me to read back to you what you wrote: *Truth didn't matter. What mattered was the means to propagate war. The notion of information-gathering enabled the widening of repression regardless of how it was carried out: True intelligence closed the net around insurrectionary groups. False intelligence allowed the war to break out of its confines as a military operation and for military power to be used as a tool of repression, terror, and even extermination on the population as a whole.* Again, I can only suggest that you consider the consequences of perjuring yourself before the tribunal."

His voice hums between us sharply as he continues reading: "*After nine days at al-Mazra'a, Tarik died of a heart attack. The last time I saw his body, it was lying beneath an unmarked sheet of tarpaulin in the grange. Other bundles were also there, wrapped tight to keep them from rotting in the heat. The next day, the body was gone.*"

Gallantin sighs. "When this comes to the tribunal, do you really want such highly problematic, patently untruthful assertions to be considered? Every piece of documentary evidence that exists will contradict your statements. You will not find a single soldier who served at al-Mazra'a who will corroborate your account of what happened there. You will therefore, if you persist in your story, appear not only as a delusional and dangerous traitor to your country, you will also be prosecuted for perjury and libel. It is my duty today to remind you that it is still not too late to retract the remarks you have made. I believe that this will allow the judge to look more clearly, and more *sympathetically*, at the circumstances surrounding the death of Amira Khadra. However she died—"

"She was shot in the head. No one denies that."

"Indeed." Impatience flickers in Gallantin's eyes. "But *how* she came to be shot, and under what circumstances, these are the true facts of the case and they remain to be established. She may well have been attempting to escape, for example, or resisting officers during detainment procedures. The judge will be acutely aware of how difficult life is for soldiers who bear the burden of the sacred mission to defend the nation. Do you not think that these are matters which the judge should consider in your case, rather than being required to work through your rather confusing account of the army's activities in Algeria?"

My silence floats between us. Suddenly, there is an urgency to Gallantin's tone.

"The girl was shot, as you say. And at the time she was shot, you alone were responsible for her. There is no way you can hope to escape prosecution for her death, if you insist upon bringing it before the court. All the testimony is unambiguous: she was with you when she died."

"I don't dispute it."

"What's more, your allegations have already been proven false. Here, for example," he turns to another page of the deposition, "you claim that Lambert's room was *covered with pictures of detainees which he had either taken himself or had had taken. In one that I remember vividly, an Algerian woman is standing between two French soldiers. A cord is passed around her neck like a leash put on a dog and one of the soldiers holds the other end. In the sepia tones of the photograph, the woman's naked body merges into the bronze hues of the dustlands behind her. Offset against the tawny expanse of desert and skin is the black triangle of her pubic hair. The woman and both soldiers all stare straight ahead into the camera, their faces rigid, blank, inscrutable.* You go on to describe other pictures of women stripped, tied up, forced into unseemly positions. Yet the military police have performed a thorough search of Lambert's quarters at al-Mazra'a and no such material was found. It has therefore been proven beyond doubt that your allegations are unfounded and, should you choose to pursue them before the judge on Friday, I am duty-bound to inform you that they will be interpreted as a deliberate attack upon the honor of the army and an attempt to subvert the mission to maintain order in Algeria. You will then be subject to the harshest prosecutions that can be brought against you and no mitigating circumstances or clemency can be considered. Do you understand?"

I nod slowly. These same words, or variations upon them, have been thrumming in my ears for weeks.

Once Gallantin has left, I wash some of the sleep out of my eyes. After being submerged again in the basements of al-Mazra'a, the shock of cold water feels pleasant. It jolts me, shaking off the tiredness and washing away the dead layers of the past.

I take Anne-Lise's photo out of my pocket. I return to that. Her gently condescending gaze. A girl living in a future that would exist only in her own mind.

Anne-Lise keeps me in the present. In three days' time, I will have to stand before the judge and sink back into the quicksand of memory. There are three days to find whoever killed her and left her body on the heather.

Three days to live with Anne-Lise, not with Amira.

I fix upon Anne-Lise's cool, untroubled eyes gazing out upon eternity.

The rue du Grand Champ is just another quiet Breton street: stone houses, blue shutters, the brown stalks of dead geraniums curled in window boxes, gray slate roofs. The Blanchards live in an old house with moss creeping across the facade. The stones of the building are huge, irregular masses somehow made to tessellate. Grass grows wild in the garden, great drooping clumps of it swelling out of the earth. Weeds sprout profusely between the flagstones of the path: dandelions, catnip, clover.

The old man who opens the door gapes at me. His eyes swim behind thick glasses. Wispy tufts of white hair are dotted across his scalp. I need to repeat to him several times that I would like to talk to Mathilde. Eventually he nods.

"Marthe, there's a man here from the police. He wants

to talk to Mathilde. She's done one of her stupid things again."

An old woman shuffles to the door, wiping her fingers on a filthy apron and shaking her head. Her tiny eyes strain to focus on me. "What's she done this time? Is it serious?"

"Madame Blanchard, she hasn't done anything. Please don't be anxious. She isn't in any trouble. I want to talk to her about Anne-Lise. Do you remember? She was Mathilde's friend. She died about a year ago."

"Well, well," Madame Blanchard mutters, "if she's done another one of her stupid things then I suppose you'd better speak to her. She's up in her room. Just go in. She won't answer if you knock anyway . . ."

She stumbles back into the kitchen emitting a chorus of lamentation while M. Blanchard points me in the direction of the stairs. I knock softly at the bedroom door and enter without waiting for an answer. Mathilde is fast asleep on the bed, her hair thrown around her head in a sprawling halo. One leg is bent beneath her. The other stretches out longingly. In spite of the darkness of her hair, her skin is pale. An infinitely fine dusting of dark hairs, running along her arms, trembles in the draft from the open door. Her skirt has ridden up to the top of her thighs, revealing smooth legs, finely muscled, tickled by goose bumps.

She screws her eyes tight shut, then squints up at me. She raises herself on all fours, rocking gently. Slowly, very slowly, she pulls her skirt back down and, tucking her legs under her, sits up on the bed and gazes vacantly at me.

"Who are you?"

"Le Garrec."

"Are you a cop?"

"No."

"Didn't think so."

"Why not?"

"*Why not?*" She seems to drift off into a daze. "Because you look scared. The cops never look scared."

The skin beneath her eyes is so purple it looks bruised. She sweeps her hair back from her face wearily and tries to focus again.

"So if you're not a cop, then what do you want?"

"I want to talk to you about Anne-Lise. I'm investigating her death."

She blinks. Once. Twice. Then two round tears well up in her eyes. She lets her head drop, as if it had been an unbearable effort to hold it up all this time. For a few minutes she sobs in complete silence, almost shivering, her face shaken by waves of sorrow. Her arms tremble and her stomach heaves. She struggles for breath. Sadness doesn't seem to be something that rises up inside of her; instead it breaks over her in great surges. It chokes her. Paralyzes her. Leaves her fighting for air and for control.

Slowly, the shaking stops. She wipes her eyes and takes a deep breath.

"Yeah," she says. "You can ask me about Anne-Lise. Whatever you want." She cradles her head in her hands and she looks suddenly younger, childlike. "Are you going to get him, whoever did that to her?"

"I don't know. I wish I could promise you that I will. It depends. The more you can tell me about her, though, the more likely it is that I can find her killer."

If there's anything there. If any connection exists or remains between her life and her death. Sometimes there is nothing. The vacuum of the past. All you can see are some distorted reflections on the surface. Any links remain drowned and out of sight.

Mathilde nods. "Just give me some time to get ready. I was out late last night. I need to . . ." Again, it is as if something in her brain cuts out for a moment. "I just need to wake up."

She wanders out, her bare feet padding softly on the wooden floor. Downstairs, I can hear the Blanchards clattering around in a chaos of dirty crockery and pans. In the bathroom the taps start to run. Looking around Mathilde's room, I am struck by an overpowering feeling of absence. There is nothing on the table or the walls: no pictures, no possessions. And what is here—some heavy brown curtains, nondescript pine furniture, a jarring floral bedspread—all seems so utterly alien to Mathilde, to her tired, soulful eyes, as if this cannot really be her room. She is a stranger here, just passing through. No sooner has she left than her presence is gone entirely from the room.

She returns looking pale, wrapped in a woolen cardigan, and lies down on the bed again. She gestures to me to sit beside her and closes her eyes.

"You surprised me before. I'm ready now. What do you want to know?"

"Why was Anne-Lise suffering so much, just after Christmas the year before she died?"

Mathilde shakes her head. "I don't know. She wouldn't say."

"Would Sasha know?"

She shakes her head again. "No. We talked about it sometimes. Before and . . . and after. He was sure that it was connected to her death."

"Where is he now?"

"I don't know. He comes and goes. When Anne-Lise was here he had a reason to stay. Not anymore." She enunciates slowly, murmuring each word faintly, almost uncertainly. She seems to need to concentrate in order to move her tongue and mouth when she speaks. A wild child, Sarah said. She looks exhausted and bloodless, drained by the comedown from whatever artificial paradise she was in last night.

"When you heard about what happened to Anne-Lise, what was your first reaction?"

"Shock, probably. You don't imagine something like that happening. She was the only one who made life in Sainte-Élisabeth bearable."

"How do you think it happened? Was it someone she knew or a stranger?"

"When they first . . ." Her throat contracts again and she gulps for air. "When they first told me she had been killed, I thought it must have been a stranger. But when I heard what he did to her . . . it seemed personal, I think." She shivers a little, pulling the cardigan more firmly around her shoulders.

"Think back to the last two or three weeks you saw her. Was there anything during that period that you remember as being different from normal? Think carefully, because it might be something very small, something you'd barely notice. She might have mentioned the name of somebody new, or her normal mood was changed somehow, or you noticed that she was dressing differently or changing her plans in an unusual way."

"I don't think so. After that Christmas she was so miserable. She couldn't concentrate, she got bad marks, she didn't want to do anything. She seemed to have no energy. Back then, something *hurt* her. But before she was killed, she seemed okay again. Not happy, I think, but more like her old self. Like she rediscovered who she was."

Could it be Anne-Lise's happiness, not her suffering, which is significant? Was she killed as a punishment for something she got over or forgot? Once you begin to listen to witnesses, the strange, fragmented, and contradictory past that they conjure up begins to teem with suggestions of things that may never have existed. Whatever was significant may have remained outside of their field of vision, or stood entirely unnoticed within it.

I ask Mathilde about "the spider" and the scrap of paper I found in Anne-Lise's room, but she just shakes her head. She stares for a while at the words and numbers.

"It sounds like a poem," she says. "I don't know what it means, though."

I ask her about Anne-Lise as she was, the living girl with a promising future: Mathilde's friend, not the victim of a tragedy that seemed so quickly forgotten. I let Mathilde talk, seeing Anne-Lise flicker before me in the warmth of recollection. Like Erwann, Mathilde conjures up her intelligence, her almost uncanny ability to follow the most difficult topics in math or philosophy without any apparent effort, while her classmates scribbled furiously, hoping to master the theme by writing down every word uttered about it, as others simply gave up, gazing in bemusement at the teacher. Anne-Lise glows a little brighter when Mathilde describes her together with Sasha: two small-town outcasts, one touched by the plague of Nazism and the other by the poverty and pogroms of the East. Mathilde describes Kurmakin as more artist than revolutionary: pale-skinned, contemplative, his eyes staring intensely from under waves of flowing hair. He also learned effortlessly but, unlike Anne-Lise, with an almost complete lack of interest in the process of getting a conventional education. He read Marx and wanted to change the world. After Anne-Lise was killed, the blaze that was within him seemed to smolder and die. He disappeared. Mathilde has no idea where he went. When she saw him again the fire was back but intensified a thousandfold, transformed into a raging, incandescent fury that seemed to be consuming him minute by minute.

I leave Mathilde lying on the bed, her legs curled under her. Her face is blanched, whether from drowning her nights in alcohol or her days in painful remembering. One more small-town outcast. I wonder if she too is infected, tainted by a stain that can't be expunged.

Downstairs, despite the clattering of dishes and pans, the Blanchards have made little impression on the piles of mess in the lounge and kitchen. They shuffle toward me.

"Do you need to take her away?" Monsieur Blanchard asks.

"No."

"Oh." He sounds surprised, even disappointed. "I hope she didn't give you any trouble."

Outside, rain clouds are clawing at the edge of the sky. Something Mathilde said stays with me, tickles at my nerves: Anne-Lise's words sound like a poem. In the Resistance, sections of poems were used to encrypt messages. I look again at Anne-Lise's note:

DEATH PAUSE PEACE LONG YOURS
5 14 4 21 9   23 18 17 2 20   4 1 12 13 1   13 21 8 19 ?

As I reenter the Blanchards' house, I realize I am almost running, stumbling back up the stairs and into Mathilde's room. She doesn't seem to have moved since I left her.

"Did you forget something?"

"Did Anne-Lise ever talk about the Resistance to you? About codes used in the Resistance?"

Mathilde shakes her head. "No. Or no, wait. She mentioned an English film she saw. I think it was about a girl who was killed in the Resistance. She was a spy and she got killed."

The question mark at the end looks careless, like the encryption was unfinished. I try to decrypt the first block by simply taking the letters in order: *HCTOS* . . . It looks wrong. Yet what if Anne-Lise knew *something* about encrypted poems, but not much. The first step would be to number the letters in order as they appear in the text:

D E A T H P A U S E P E A C E L O N G Y O U R S
5 6 1 21 11 16 2 22 19 7 17 8 3 4 9 12 14 13 10 24 15 23 18 20

I try the first block again, the *5 14 4 21 9*, as a simple substitution with no padding or further encryption: *DOCTE* . . . The full message now falls out: *DOCTEUR PASCAL NANTES*.

My voice rattles breathlessly.

"Mathilde, did Anne-Lise ever mention a Docteur Pascal to you? Or say anything about going to a doctor in Nantes?"

She shakes her head.

"Are you sure?"

"Sure."

"Can I use the telephone?"

Mathilde nods. The Blanchards don't even seem to notice me anymore. When I return to Mathilde's room, she looks up at me with something expectant in her eyes.

"Did you find out who Docteur Pascal is?"

"I didn't try. I think I already know."

"So who did you call?"

"An old police contact from when I worked in Paris. I want him to find out about the poem for me."

"Not the doctor?"

"I don't think Anne-Lise encrypted the message to hide the doctor's name. The encoding itself is nothing. It's not even finished. And if she'd wanted to keep the name a secret, she could simply have written it somewhere where no one would ever find it. She wasn't trying to conceal anything. She was putting things together in a way that made sense. It's more like symbolism than encryption. I need to know why she used this particular poem, and these particular words from it, to represent the doctor's name."

Mathilde hugs her knees and floats dreamily upon the bed while we wait. When the telephone rings, she follows me downstairs and inclines her head toward mine to listen into the receiver. I write down the text of the poem for her to see:

The life that I have
Is all that I have
And the life that I have
Is yours.

The love that I have
Of the life that I have
Is yours and yours and yours.

A sleep I shall have
A rest I shall have
Yet death will be but a pause.

For the peace of my years
In the long green grass
Will be yours and yours and yours.

The words fall uncannily into place. I can almost hear them before they are dictated to me. Docteur Pascal. *The life that I have.*

"Who was the poem for?"

The voice crackles on the other end of the line. It hums faintly, far away, an echo, disembodied noise. "It was given to an agent of the Resistance named Violette Szabo."

"What happened to her?"

"She was killed."

"By the Nazis?"

"She died in the Ravensbrück concentration camp."

I put the receiver down.

"What does it mean?" Mathilde asks.

"I think Anne-Lise had an abortion. That's why she needed the address of a particular doctor who lived far away. She read the poem like a dedication: *the life that I have is yours.* But she knew it had to end. I don't know if it was a reproach or just regret."

Mathilde nods. "It could be."

"She never mentioned anything about it?"

"No. But it would explain why she kind of fell apart that winter, the one before she died."

"Was she away for any days around that time?"

Mathilde shakes her head, not to say no, but because she can't remember. She wants to dredge up the past. She wasn't looking in the right direction and now it's gone, melted into forgetfulness just like Anne-Lise.

I decide to drive over to the lycée Jacques Cartier to catch Erwann before the end of the school day. Gusts of wind rattling off the sea beat against the car and the air is damp with the promise of unfallen rain. There is hardly another soul on the roads. The country seems to be in hibernation, hiding away from the brutality of the elements, the hedgerows and the fields and the relentless sea silhouetted grayly against the deeper gray sky.

Saint-Malo seems eternal. The great taupe rows of stones, the ordered lines of buildings, and the immensity of the walls, just rebuilt after pulverization by the Allies, project a sense of changelessness through the spasms of passing time. It is as if the years since my childhood have not elapsed and worn away so much with them. The light over the sea is electric, brooding; rocks jut out in jagged streaks from the beaches, breaking the surf in explosions of foam. The grand edifice of the town ramparts traces a perfectly crenellated line across the sky and forms a tranquil but implacable barrier to the waters tossing in the bays beneath.

It is late afternoon when I arrive at the lycée. The lights are burning inside. I walk around to find Erwann's classroom and see him lecturing animatedly to the pupils seated on wooden benches. He stares out at them intently, gesturing as if whatever he is saying is the key to understanding a mystery of the utmost importance. I can't hear his words, though I see his mouth moving silently through the windowpane. He is unshaven, and where the stubble prickles on his chin it is the same blanched gray as the hair around his temples. In spite of the erratic curls of hair, which from time to time he sweeps off his forehead, and his worn, patched jacket that suggests an indifference to day-to-day life, there is a furious concentration about him. He never saw philosophy as material for academic debate. He experienced it as a profound modulation of his perception of the world and, as such, of his own self. Time has drained some of the color from him, faded him, but his fervor for elucidating the mysteries of being appears undimmed.

When I appear at the door, he beckons me to come in and indicates a seat at the back of the room. In front of me, the students' heads incline curiously, trying to follow the permutations of the thought Erwann is elaborating. He seems to forget my presence almost immediately and continues his lesson.

"I was saying that because of the essentially *rational* character of Sartrean existentialism, emotion for Sartre is not a profound, almost sacred phenomenon from which truth or art can be mined. Remember, Sartre insists that my consciousness is totally transparent to itself at all times. He rejects Freud's notion of an unconscious, or a part of the mind that lies beyond rational understanding. I am, he says, *always* fully aware both of myself and of the world around me. I am always, therefore, responsible for what I do and for what I feel, and I choose the latter just as much as I choose the former. My emotions are not absolute and incontrovertible phenomena; they are *chosen* reactions to particular situations. My sadness, joy, or rage are all free choices which emanate from the perception of myself and my surroundings that I undertake to adopt."

He pauses for a moment, surveying the class in front of him, some of whom are scribbling urgently while others look up seeking further explanation.

"The danger comes when we convince ourselves that

our emotions are not choices, when, rather than seeing emotions as magical transformations of reality, we take that magic as the very stuff of reality itself. The desolation of unhappiness, the fires of rage, or the tender hues of love all exist only as illusions of our irrational perceptions. For Sartre, this is inauthentic being. In reality, rational understanding *always* remains, and it is this and not the sorcery of our feelings which must govern our actions . . ."

I close my eyes and focus on Erwann's voice, allowing it to transport me back to my own school days, before Algeria, before Amira's blood soaked my clothes and Tarik's inhuman voice wormed into my brain and fed upon me like a parasite. I search in memory for those endless afternoons listening to the drone of the teacher's voice, when deliverance meant nothing more than the bell to release us from class as we jostled and rushed for the exit, desperate to breathe the air outside and stretch our legs and hurry along in the remains of daylight.

These memories seem dim, as if they are not memories at all but images my mind has conjured to compensate for the loss of the past. They flicker gently, tiny fragments pieced together by desire, invented templates of an existence swallowed in the onrush of time.

A student raises her hand. Her skin is creamy. Her auburn hair bounces and catches the light. Her voice is melodic. "Is love an illusion then? Is it also inauthentic?"

Erwann seems to barely notice her. His entire attention is occupied by answering the question. "It is an illusion par excellence. It is a myth that we use to legitimize and to fantasize our existence. Love gives us a purpose and a destiny in life. It makes us feel that we need to be just the way we are. We deny our reality as contingent beings and try to fix ourselves forever in the luminous, undying gaze of adoration. What greater illusion could there be?"

After the bell goes, the class files out pensively and Erwann comes over to sit on the bench beside me. The smooth, sanded-down seats and scratched desks seem imbued with the infinite hours and labors of the past.

"Do you miss it?" Erwann asks. "Philosophy, I mean."

"It seems less and less important."

"I see. I suppose you're here about more pressing things. Like Anne-Lise. Tell me, have you found anything that might shed some light on what happened to her?"

"I don't know yet. I found many things, but I don't have a sense of where they lead." It's like trying to dive down to the bottom of a lake, paddling and choking among the murky, oppressive depths, and each time feeling yourself forced back upward into the light. "I know, for example, that there's something you didn't tell me about your relationship with Anne-Lise. You gave her things. Presents. Books."

He nods. "I knew you'd find out. Unlike that buffoon Lafourgue. He couldn't see the things that were right under his nose. How did you know?"

"Anne-Lise's room. There was a particularly fine edition of *Les Fleurs du mal*. I can't see a teenager spending her little money on that, so who might have given it to her? Her alcoholic mother, not educated past school level? Her revolutionary boyfriend? Or the same person who assigned her an essay on Baudelaire that she was never to finish: her teacher?"

"You're quite right. I did give her the book."

"No. You didn't just give her a book—you crossed a line. Your relations with her stopped being professional:

those of a teacher and student. You gave her a book of poems and asked her to think about love. You spoke just now about *adoration*. What else did that gesture mean?"

He nods very slowly and his brow furrows.

"Not only that. You knew you were crossing a line. That's why there's no dedication in the book, nothing that could link it back to you. You could have given her Descartes or Hegel if you'd just wanted to educate her, but you chose Baudelaire. You knew that there was something ambiguous in that choice. Erwann, look at me. Look up. Was it you who got Anne-Lise pregnant?"

I don't take my eyes off him for a second. I watch his eyes, his fingers, his throat, and his lips, his feet, his legs, analyzing every infinitesimal movement of his body to read his answers. Al-Mazra'a is back with me.

"No. It wasn't me."

Is he lying? He swallows faintly though his eyes don't waver. There's sadness in them. He's telling the truth.

"But you knew about the abortion?"

"Yes. Anyone could see that Anne-Lise was distraught that winter. She couldn't work. Her grades were falling disastrously. I couldn't just ignore it. She told me that she'd been pregnant. You're right, of course: I did care about her. But I certainly didn't get her pregnant. It was horrible to see her in that state. I was only glad that she felt able to confide in me."

"Do you know who the father was?"

"Kurmakin."

"Did she actually say that or did you just assume?"

"No, she told me, and I don't see why she'd lie. Unless . . ."

"Unless she was having an affair with someone she couldn't possibly name in front of her teacher. Did you know that she never spoke to Mathilde Blanchard about the abortion? Does that surprise you?"

"Not really. I know that Anne-Lise and Mathilde were close, at least in a certain way; but they were never equals. I'm sure Anne-Lise didn't talk to Mathilde about all kinds of things because she wouldn't have understood them. Mathilde is a funny girl. Very unstable. She could have gone much further in school but she dropped out a while ago. There was always a kind of perverseness about her: a refusal to conform, or a need to disappoint others' expectations. The Blanchards were at their wits' end with her. When she was at school, she was summoned to see the *proviseur* more than once for cruel or inappropriate behavior. She even had run-ins with the police on several occasions."

"What drew Anne-Lise to her? What made those two close?"

"That, I could not possibly say. I can only repeat that it baffled me. Perhaps Anne-Lise was attracted by someone so different from her, someone dark and troubled. It may have seemed romantic to her."

"I need to find Kurmakin and see if he can give me any more details about the abortion. Do you know where I can find him?"

"I have no idea. But perhaps Lafourgue can help you. Surveillance and spying are two of the rare arts he has probably mastered."

My remaining questions to Erwann draw only blanks. Like Mathilde, he cannot think of anything peculiar which happened during Anne-Lise's final weeks and he has no knowledge of where she was the night she died. He shakes his head when I ask him if he knows someone nicknamed "the spider," and when I leave he reaches out and puts a hand on my shoulder.

"When did you say the hearing is? Friday? My thoughts will be with you then."

I leave him sitting on the worn bench at the back of that room which he has tried for so many years to make vibrate with learning. He stares out blankly into space, perhaps seeing in the ghostly theater of his memories Anne-Lise's blond hair burnished by the light flooding in through the window. Perhaps he can see her slim white fingers clutching a pen as she feeds off his voice, and perhaps he feels as if the unfolding of identical days has suddenly ceased and the world hums with her curiosity and grace as she sits before him. When the image fades, he will see only an empty room darkening in the falling dusk.

There is no one left in the school corridors. My footfalls echo in the silence. On the ceiling, the paintwork cracks and flakes away, exposing the plaster beneath. On the walls, wooden panels bear engravings commemorating the achievements of long-departed students.

Grand Prix des Sciences Humaines
Blondet, Roger 1933
Boulanger, Claude 1934
Legrandin, Antoine 1935

Prix Albert Fénélon pour les Mathématiques
Caillot, Sarah 1943
Riffaut, Albert 1944
Kerbac, Julien 1945
Legendre, Edouard 1946

My feet have stopped still. The silence crowds in on

me. There is a tiny click in my head. I see once again two dull eyes, stubble-roughened cheeks, hair shaken this way and that, skin smudged with dirt. Lafourgue's case file. The drifter. The small-town ne'er-do-well whose desperation led him to expose himself to a peasant girl. The addled vagrant too dull-witted to have carried out such an ornate crime.

Julien Kerbac.

The best mathematician in the region's best school. My eyes rake the walls. What else can they tell me about a suspect I stupidly and carelessly ignored? Different names and prizes run past my gaze—classical translation, philosophy, historical learning—until something holds my attention and I can feel my heart lurch against my ribs.

Prix André Chartier pour les Sciences
Naturelles et la Dissection
Chapuisat, Jean 1943
Sabreur, Agnès 1944
Kerbac, Julien 1945

The light from the dim bulb swims in garish streaks in front of my eyes. My feet thump against the wooden floor as I hasten for the exit. Outside, it is dark. The nocturnal chill floods my lungs and jolts me into a state of alertness. It is too late by now to find Lafourgue and have him track down Kerbac and Kurmakin. Perhaps Lafourgue was right all along. I have been trying to reconstruct Anne-Lise's existence, convinced that the crime would flow out of who she was. Perhaps there was no real connection to her and the killer was just a dangerous drifter with a complex, tortured mind and memories of the dissection of animal corpses. Perhaps I was so quick to discount the possibility of him being a suspect simply because I needed to immerse myself in the long, patient work of salvaging the past. I needed to forget al-Maz-ra'a. Had that made me blind? Was I so desperate to lose myself in someone else's past that I could no longer look clearly at the events within it?

On the quiet roads back from Saint-Malo, as the car sways gently around the bends and the moon burns with a pale glow above, and then later, lying perfectly awake on the sofa at home staring out into the night, I keep see-ing those same dull eyes, the skin spattered with mud, and the gaping mouth. I count the hours until sunrise, when I can go out into the countryside and walk through the fields and paths paralyzed by winter, and I can roam the shadowlands where Kerbac lives and track him down and bring whatever secrets he may be hiding into the light.

DAY FIVE

In the slow emergence of a Breton dawn, I float in the endless star-studded nights of al-Mazra'a. In Algeria, fitful bursts of sleep seemed like wakefulness, so vivid were the images they conjured. The long hours of consciousness between were gray, exhausting, eternal.

Today I wake up choking. Amira's blood runs toward me in sluggish heaves but I don't move. I watch it flow gently until it bathes my knees. Its warmth is Amira's only caress. My skin crawls but still I don't get up.

Slowly, the pieces of the present start to flood back, filling my memory and calming my gasping lungs. The light filtering through the shutters is dismal. The nighttime cold has pinched and cracked my skin. I couldn't bring myself to light the fire. All the little gestures by which existence becomes routine, or even comfortable, seem wrong. The ice of the Breton winter has seeped through the windows and through the cracks in the walls and the wood and it has crept into my blood and my bones.

Kerbac. I remember. His hollow eyes were somewhere in the depths of my dreams.

The car shudders into life, trying to shake off the chill. The windshield is scarred with lines of frost. The tires slip and scrape on roads frozen like metal.

Lafourgue is seated at the counter of A l'abri des flots.

His thick, restless fingers tap at a glass of the alcohol he seems to live on. He stares at a newspaper. The bulk of his body and bullish head appear concentrated in the fixity of his eyes. He motions me to sit down.

"Drink?"

"Coffee."

"Well, what can I do for you?"

"Two things. Firstly, I need to find Julien Kerbac. Where is he likely to be? I'll need to pick him up."

"Kerbac." Lafourgue swills the name around his mouth. "On the road from Sainte-Élisabeth to Mal-à-venir, a couple of kilometers out, left-hand side, there's a disused barn. In the winter he usually bunks down there. Careful, though. He's wild. I'll send someone to go with you if you want."

"No thanks. Also, I need to talk to Sasha Kurmakin. No one seems to have any idea where he is but I suppose you'd be able to track him down. Can you?"

Lafourgue's eyes contract even farther, his pupils two tiny pinpricks glowing blackly in his skull. "I guess I can. But not before tomorrow. Will that do?" He reaches for his drink and swallows it. "Sure you don't want one? Okay. Have it your way. What about the case? Any progress in finding the killer? I don't suppose there's a lot left for you to go on now. Evidence perishes. People forget. The real information has long since vanished, if it was ever there. All you've got are the twisted memories, the obsessions, and the lies of the people who knew Anne-Lise."

I tell him about the abortion, the poem used to encode the doctor's name, the books Erwann gave Anne-Lise, and about Kerbac's past.

He nods in appreciation. "There might be more," he says. "The dossier that you saw doesn't contain all the information relevant to the case. It's just the official documentation, in case anybody's ever sniffing around, checking up on what we do. You know what officials are like. Always trying to pretend that you can do this job by following due procedure and believing in the *Déclaration des droits de l'homme*. But what you've seen isn't the real investigation. I guess I don't need to tell you that. You fought the Algerians over there, so you know what real police work is. Anyway, go and hunt Kerbac down and squeeze whatever you can out of him. When you come back, I'll dig out the real notes for you. You won't be able to use anything in them in a courtroom and I can't let you take them away, but you can read through them at my house if you want."

As I sit behind the wheel of the car, I have the impression that Lafourgue's tar-black pupils are still trained on me from inside. Something glittered in their depths when he spoke of the *real investigation*. I can feel the coffee jolt and kick in my veins. I start the engine and pull out into the quiet street. Tiredness falls away. Concentration takes over. My head buzzes and the caffeine vibrates in my heart as I turn away from Sainte-Élisabeth, pass the fields of dead grass, and head out toward the tiny, crabbed spire of the church at Mal-à-venir.

Cold has turned the trees to iron. On the horizon, their jagged silhouettes claw at the livid sky. Rains have scored channels into the mud of the fields, then the freeze has come to petrify them. How can Kerbac live among this? On the dead, waterlogged earth and under the wind tearing at his skin?

I pull the car in next to an old stone grange, exactly where Lafourgue said it would be. Whatever door was once there is long gone and the entrance gapes blackly. Underfoot, it is all mud and ice. My feet slip, then sink into the decaying ground. I listen for any noise that Kerbac might be making inside but there is only the howl of the wind and, beneath it, the weird stillness of winter— life shutting down, hibernating—and, in the distance, the hiss of the sea.

I can make nothing out amid the darkness as I peer inside. The feeble light at the entrance soon dissolves into the blackness. I call out from the door: "M. Kerbac, my name is le Garrec. I'm—I was—with the police. I'd like to talk to you about Anne-Lise Aurigny."

No answer. Only the faint reverberation of my voice and the whisper of the wind in the eaves. I walk farther in. I can no longer see my feet, but only hear the sucking sound where the mud pulls them in. The darkness seems to swell around me. I try again to listen for breathing or movement but there is only a kind of phenomenal stillness. I keep walking, still speaking softly, and as I approach the northwestern corner of the grange, it seems to me that I can hear wheezing in the dark. I stop and listen, unsure whether it is just my racing pulse and the waves of my own blood battering my ears. I hold my breath. I listen again and I am sure there is something crouching in the darkness, breathing quietly, waiting.

One more step.

There is a rush of air and the shadows leap in front of me. Something rock-hard crushes my cheekbone. The blackness tilts and wheels. White lights burst and flame in front of my retinas. I fall to the ground and lie cradled in the rotting earth. Silhouetted against the gray rectangle of the entrance, blurry in the haze of my failing sight, a shape flickers and vanishes into the light.

Kerbac.

I heave myself upright. Something burns the flesh on the right side of my head. Like a drill boring into the bone. The entrance to the grange lurches sickeningly as I try to focus on it. Lights explode and twinkle where I stare. I try to walk toward the door but it drifts to my left. Then I am kneeling down in the mud. I am drinking the fetid odor of the sodden ground. It clogs my nostrils and my throat. There is another searing burst of white heat before my eyes.

Then the darkness is absolute.

Something jolts in my brain and I gasp for air. This time, I manage to raise myself and reach the door. Across the fields, I can just glimpse the dim outline of Kerbac limping, shuffling, scurrying through the dead stalks of wheat, heading down toward the cliffs. I might be able to cut him off on the coast road.

Slumping into the car, I blink desperately at the road in front of me, willing it to remain still. It swims and whirls. The road and trees are one undifferentiated blur. They shimmer slowly, as if they are floating underwater. I feel like I'm drowning. The whole world around me is liquid. An unbearable pressure is crushing my head and roaring and rolling in my ears.

I drive slowly, trying to ignore the trembling, drowned road my eyes actually see and to just hold my arms straight. The crack of branches or hedgerows against the side of the car tells me I am about to plow into the fields, and I jerk the wheel back in the opposite direction.

By the time I reach the corniche my vision is clearing. The contours of things loom shockingly against the ashy air. Only my head still throbs, great heaves of pain building and bursting behind my eyes. I scan the heather to the south, forcing my eyes to focus on the line of trees where the fields end. Suddenly, about three hundred meters away, I see Kerbac's tattered silhouette burst through the trees and stagger into the heather. He can't move fast. His left leg drags heavily, as if half-paralyzed. With each pace he lurches unsteadily back onto his right foot. His hair is a tangle of filth and branches and his canvas trousers are ripped. He clutches at his threadbare jacket, trying to claw out of its remnants what little warmth he can.

I pull up level with him, stop the car, and begin to walk across the gorse toward him. He still hasn't seen me. He is looking over his shoulder, expecting his pursuer to come from the trees behind him, not from the sea. I move as quickly and as quietly as possible. Kerbac twists his head and darts anxious glances over his shoulder. *Wild*, Lafourgue said. But here he resembles the prey, not the hunter. I can see the bones jutting and bulging in his face. His skin is stretched tight, as if it's only just able to conceal his skeleton. His whole head resembles a skull: eyes bulging, cheekbones and chin almost piercing the frail skin.

When I am no more than twenty meters from him, he turns and sees me approaching. His mouth hangs open. He whirls around, disoriented for a second, then hurries back toward the trees. His bad leg jerks and twists beneath him. It takes me only a few seconds to catch him. As I draw level, he seems to give up. His body goes slack and he falls onto the winter heather. He lies there face-down, a wounded animal gasping for air and waiting to be hurt. His eyes and mouth are buried in the icy dirt. Beneath the rags of his jacket, his flanks heave and contract.

"M. Kerbac? M. Kerbac? I'm le Garrec. I just want to

talk to you. Why don't you get up? We can go and sit in my car where it's warm . . ."

I keep on talking to him gently for some time, trying to get him to loosen his grip on the petrified heather twigs. Finally he turns to look at me. Tangles of inflamed capillaries writhe in his eyes. He kneels down. He crouches.

Eventually we walk to the car. He sits in the front, gazing blankly out into the distance and the mist. His jaw hangs loose. Almost mechanically, his fingers rub against each other as if trying to keep warm. I examine my face in the rearview mirror. A large bruise has come up purple across the cheekbone. The skin is swollen and distended, pulling my features into an uneven grimace. In two days, when I come to the hearing, I will face the magistrate with this stain, this deformity, upon me. The thought makes me smile. As my lips move, a jolt of pain darts through my head. Looking at the welt—the tiny tears in the skin, the swollen ridge beneath the bruise—I would say that Kerbac hit me with a metal bar. Al-Mazra'a taught me a great deal about the architecture of scar tissue.

"M. Kerbac, I want to talk to you about the death of Anne-Lise Aurigny. Do you remember? She was killed back in February. Capitaine Lafourgue questioned you at the time."

The unsettling calm that has washed over Kerbac evaporates as soon as I mention Lafourgue's name. His eyes lurch and roll. His hands scrabble for the door handle and for freedom. I have to hold him down and, for a moment, I breathe in the odor of stale air and rotting earth that clings to him. His strength is already waning. The tendons in his arms and neck go slack once more. He sits still. His face turns numb and expressionless, as if he has immediately forgotten the fury that pulsed through his body just moments ago.

"M. Kerbac, do you remember Lafourgue questioning you about the murder of Anne-Lise? What did he ask you? Can you recall any of what you told him?"

"They said I did it. Said I killed . . . her . . . killed her . . ." His jaw moves slowly and uncomfortably, as if he has not spoken to anyone for so long that his muscles have forgotten how to form words. "They said I hurt her."

"Did you know Anne-Lise? Perhaps you saw her around sometimes? She was quite striking. She was the sort of girl you would remember. The sort of girl you could get attached to, even if you only saw her once, and from a long way off."

"Of course I . . . knew her." He speaks so softly that his voice sounds distant. "We were . . . very close . . . I would . . . never hurt her . . . though . . . whatever they say . . ."

"How were you close to Anne-Lise?" Something isn't right. I can feel the back of my neck prickling.

"We spent . . . a lot of time . . . together." He leans on the last word. Rolls it around in his mouth to see how it tastes. "We shared a lot . . . of interests and ideas . . . She was . . . everything to me . . . Why would I . . . hurt her?"

Nothing in Kerbac's face has changed. It is the same blank mask as before but there is something in the eyes, a sort of frantic attempt to focus, which is unsettling me.

"How did you meet her? . . . M. Kerbac, listen to me. How did you meet Anne-Lise?"

"We were in the same class." As he talks, his tongue seems to loosen. He recovers the power of speech.

"M. Kerbac, it isn't possible that you were in the same class as Anne-Lise. She was much younger than you. Think back—where else could you have met?"

He turns on me, his lips flecked with spittle and his

eyes ablaze and rolling back in his head. "Don't you think I know . . . where we met? The only person I . . . ever cared about." He almost screams it at me, but his voice cracks and breaks under the strain of forcing out the words, then fades to a wheeze. "And then you say . . . that I could kill her. When I would *never* hurt her. And I would . . . *always* protect her. And you say that I . . . would . . . rape her and kill her."

"M. Kerbac, Anne-Lise wasn't raped. What makes you think she was?"

He doesn't seem to hear. He keeps on channeling his failing strength into this one lament, not even directed at me, just sent out across the cliffs and over the sea and the horizon and into eternity. "How could you think that? She was more dear to me . . . than the air itself. When she died . . . all the light was squeezed out of the world. How could you think . . . I could ever live without her?"

Something isn't right. I can feel a tapping in my brain. I heard the same sound in al-Mazra'a when Lambert told me to shoot the prisoners kneeling before us. It was gentle but insistent, like the ticking of a bomb.

"M. Kerbac, no one is saying that you did anything wrong. Nobody is accusing you of anything. I'm sure you didn't mean to hurt her. But I want to find out the truth. Anne-Lise's mother and her friends need to know the truth."

Kerbac doesn't respond. He sits in silence, his eyes gazing into nothingness, his hands insistently, almost manically, rubbing together.

"Please just listen to me. Listen to the question. The girl who was raped and killed. The one you would never hurt. Tell me: what was her name?"

"Her name?"

"Yes."

He whispers it softly, cherishing the word for a second between his cracked lips: "Julie."

"And her surname?"

"Bergeret."

"She was raped and killed? Near here?"

He says nothing, but his head inclines fractionally forward.

"What year was this? What year did Julie Bergeret die?"

He turns away from me and his eyes blink rapidly. "What year? 1947. Don't you know? What are you doing here if you don't know?"

Another girl. Twelve years earlier. Another ghost of the heathlands.

"Was anyone ever convicted of the crime?"

He shakes his head slowly, as if doing so is painful.

"Who investigated the case?"

"Lafourgue. He was new back then."

"What did he find out?"

Kerbac turns abruptly to face me, his graying, grizzled hair suddenly terribly close to me. "He didn't find anything. He didn't try to find anything. He didn't even look."

"He investigated you, though. He thought you might be the killer."

He nods once, barely moving his head.

"Why? What made him think you were involved?"

Kerbac doesn't answer. The gray distance is reflected in the mirror of his eyes.

"Why did he investigate you?"

When his voice breaks out this time, it is cracked and strident: "Because he could. Because he could hurt me and he wanted to hurt me. That's all he did. He never even tried to find out who hurt Julie. He didn't care."

"M. Kerbac, listen to me. Earlier this year another girl was killed. Her name was Anne-Lise Aurigny. She was beaten, strangled, and mutilated. I know that Lafourgue also considered you a suspect in the case. Tell me, what contact did you have with Anne-Lise?"

Kerbac leans his head back against the freezing leather of the car seat. His breath floats against the window. He looks queasy for a moment, as if he might vomit. Then the sickness seems to pass and his eyes flicker oddly. He looks as if he is concentrating intently. "I never saw that girl. Never met her. I don't even know who she was. Lafourgue didn't find any connection between me and her. He didn't even pretend that he did. It was just another chance for him to . . . to . . ."

He fumbles for the door handle and, leaning out, retches into the roadside ditch. The force of it shakes his body in irregular spasms. His arms are emaciated but there's a wiry strength in his muscles where he grips the door and his body heaves. He spits, then leans back in the car, his face alarmingly pale, even gray in parts, as if the flesh is already dead and necrosis has set in.

"So you never even saw Anne-Lise?"

"Never." He mutters it between ragged bursts of breath.

"I'd like to ask you some questions about yourself, if you don't mind. I went to the lycée Cartier yesterday and I found out that you were an outstanding student. One of the best in the region. How did you come to live as a vagrant?"

Something glimmers in the corner of Kerbac's eyes. He blinks. "After . . ." I can see his throat begin to heave again. "After . . . After Julie—" He stops dead. He shakes his head slowly. I don't need him to say it.

"One final question. I know this could be painful for you to answer. Julie: how was she actually killed?"

I can see Kerbac's hands start to shake. The bones jut so visibly beneath the skin that it looks like an X-ray.

"She was strangled."

He declines my offer to drop him off somewhere. Instead, he gets out of the car and tramps slowly back across the heather, his left leg jerking and dragging behind him, until he is just a tiny hobbling silhouette that flickers and then is finally lost amid the trees.

By the time I return to A l'abri des flots there is a long line of empty glasses meandering across Lafourgue's table, yet he doesn't appear in the least drunk. His eyes are as cold and as steady as ever, the pupils two tiny black pinpricks in the whorls of the irises. He lifts a glass to me as if in salute.

"What did Kerbac give you, capitaine, apart from that rather extraordinary black eye?"

Involuntarily, my hand goes up to my face and I feel once again the torn and swollen flesh of my cheek. Lafourgue gestures and Sarah appears from behind the bar. She has a bowl of water and a cloth in her hand.

"Look up," she says. "Hold your head still." Her words are harsh but her hands are gentle. Her fingers are cool as she rubs the damp cloth across my cheek.

"He said something interesting. He talked about another girl, Julie Bergeret, who was killed around here twelve years ago. He told me that you investigated that case too. It sounds as if this girl died in similar circumstances to Anne-Lise."

Lafourgue's brow wrinkles a little. "I don't remember it all that well. Julie Bergeret—let me see. She was raped and strangled. The body was buried about five miles from here. Out in the woods at le Quéduc."

"Was she beaten or mutilated?"

"No. There was nothing strange about the crime. She'd been sexually assaulted and then murdered, probably to stop her talking. The killer buried the body. It was turned up a couple of weeks later by someone walking a dog through the woods. Nothing ritualistic or extraordinary."

"Tell me about Julie herself."

"She was a very average kid. Decent home. Quiet, unassuming girl."

"Did she stand out in any way?"

Sarah continues to massage my cheek with the damp cloth. The cold water sends little shivers of numbness through my skin.

"How do you mean?"

"Anne-Lise stood out. Everyone noticed her. Even people who didn't know her. What about Julie?"

"I don't think she stood out at all. Kind of the opposite. It was hard to investigate her death because everything in her life was so humdrum. She wasn't in any kind of trouble. No drugs. No dubious connections."

"Was she especially beautiful? Or clever?"

Lafourgue shakes his head. "And the family was reasonably well-off but not rich."

"So what leads did you have?"

"Just Kerbac. The two of them had a thing. It was pretty hard to see why. He was a strange kid. Reserved. Not easy to talk to."

"Clever, though. A stellar student. Like Anne-Lise."

"Perhaps."

"So what happened?"

"One day, Julie didn't come home from school. She wasn't the sort of kid to disappear without telling her parents, so they panicked immediately. *Everyone* knew there was something wrong. I can remember the mother in tears. She couldn't stop crying. She just kept on saying how Julie would never run away without telling her. And the father was standing around trying to look dignified and strong though we could see that he was breaking inside. Anyway, the parents ran around to see everyone they knew and a few coppers sniffed about and asked questions. Nobody had seen Julie and there was no trace of her anywhere. She'd vanished into thin air.

"Meanwhile, Kerbac was going to pieces. We brought him in for questioning two or three times, but each time it was like we couldn't get through to him. Like he didn't understand French anymore. He wasn't coherent when he talked. No one could really follow what he was saying. I think he actually managed to unnerve a couple of the boys who interviewed him."

"Was Julie at school with Kerbac? At Cartier?"

"No. She went to the lycée Balzac at le Quéduc."

"What happened when she was found?"

"That was about a fortnight later. We got reports of a corpse dug up in the woods. A girl. Found half-clothed with bruises around the neck. We knew right away it was her. She'd been buried, but not very well. It was winter and the ground was as hard as granite. The killer did his best, but he'd have needed a pneumatic drill to dig deep into the earth right then."

"What did you manage to discover about the crime?"

"There wasn't much that came out of the postmortem,

although because the ground was frozen the body was actually quite well preserved. The pathologist was sure that she had been strangled several hours after she was raped."

"So she was held somewhere."

"Seems like it."

"Like Anne-Lise."

"Although this crime seems much more routine: Violence. A period of uncertainty. Then the murder. An attempt to hide the crime."

"And you thought Kerbac had done it."

Lafourgue's thin lips stretch into a grin. "To be honest, I didn't know. There was a plausible story there. He loses his cool and forces himself on her, then kills her in panic and despair."

"But anyone else could have done the same. He doesn't strike me as someone who is scared of punishment."

Lafourgue nods. "He's scared of *himself*. You can feel it. He was a queer kid. He made people uneasy. He was the kind of boy people had doubts about. People would certainly buy him as the killer."

"So you pointed the finger in his direction."

"We had him in for questioning several times. Held him as long as we could. He paced around in his cell all night, and in the morning he flung himself at the door. When we pulled him out, he'd gashed his face open. To be honest, he looked like a killer. He behaved like a killer. Dangerous. Violent."

"Or simply *desperate*. A teenager deranged by grief and terror."

Without thinking, I reach up and feel the swollen skin on my own cheek. The contusion has receded where Sarah bathed it. Is that how the magistrate will see me on

Friday? Like the newspaper photograph of myself Aïcha showed me: a man whose face shouts out his guilt?

"Yet you couldn't prove anything."

"No. We ran some tests on hairs, fibers, the marks on the body, but there was nothing conclusive. Nothing that matched Kerbac or anyone else we looked at."

"So the body wasn't cleaned, like with Anne-Lise."

"No. The MO was very different."

"But the two girls were about the same age, and they were both attacked brutally first, then held, and killed or mutilated later."

Lafourgue shrugs. "There's probably another dozen crimes over the last ten years that are about that similar. Julie was strangled with her own belt, not by hand. And she was hidden. The killer tried to prevent the body from being discovered. Anne-Lise was left to be found."

She wasn't just turned into art; she was left on display. It was a sign of contempt. A killer who had already gotten away with at least one murder and saw no need, this time, to try to hide what he had done. The carefully chosen scene was a taunt.

I search for the words to make Lafourgue understand. "When he killed Julie, he didn't think clearly enough about how to remove all signs of the crime. He did something stupid: he tried to stop anyone finding the body. Afterward, he probably read the papers and knew that there were hairs and fibers and traces of his fingerprints on the body. It scared him. When he killed Anne-Lise, he didn't try to hide her because he knew how to efface all signs on her that could lead back to him. He learned from Julie. He refined what he did. When he killed Anne-Lise, he wasn't worried about getting caught."

"Let it go," Lafourgue replies. "Even if it is the same

killer, Julie Bergeret died over a decade ago. You'll never prove anything now. That case is always going to stay unsolved."

"What happened to Kerbac after the investigation?"

"He had some kind of breakdown. Didn't speak for months. He even spent a few months in an asylum—that big white house out on the edge of Corceret."

"And when he came out?"

Lafourgue shrugs again, but there's a glint of malice in his eyes.

When Kerbac came out, barely coherent, his face scarred, his hands shaking, everybody saw in him the image of a murderer. His wrecked body and vacant, tormented mind must have seemed like proof of his guilt. Maybe they were signs of guilt. Or maybe he started to believe they were. Maybe the gaps in his perception, where his mind turned blankly and his speech stalled, appeared in his recollections like moments where he lost control. His knowledge of his own actions, of his very self, perhaps slipped into the interstices of his conscious mind. In such moments he would be capable of doing anything and he might not even know. Even he could no longer be sure of what he had or hadn't done. Lafourgue said it: he was afraid of himself. His whole body was imprinted with terror. He lived in the shadows under the wild sky because he no longer knew how to live among other people.

"You said something before about the real case files. The unofficial ones. May I see them now?"

For a second, Lafourgue glares at me and it feels like being scalded. Then he nods. "Sure. After all, you couldn't spend two years in the *service de renseignements* in Algeria and not know what real police work is."

As he stands up to leave, his midriff collides with a table and sends empty glasses and cups skittering and shattering across the floor. He doesn't even look down. He just walks out toward his car, his feet crunching on the shards of glass, crushing them into the ground. I follow after him. From outside, I can see the server boy down on his hands and knees struggling to gather up the infinitesimal barbed fragments. In my mind's eye, I see the sharp filaments burrowing their way into his fingers and nestling in his flesh.

As the car jolts along the road past the church, its brown stones smudged purple in the winter air, snow begins to fall. The flakes waft, white and silent, through the distance and settle gently on the fences and the roofs and out on the heath where Anne-Lise lay. The bonnet of Lafourgue's car is dusted white. The great sheets of sky and earth seem to close in on us, shrinking the world to the few feet in front of the windshield that we can clearly see. Sainte-Élisabeth is deserted. Snow settles on the ground, covering everything, drowning each individual shape in its voiceless uniformity.

Lafourgue turns down the rue de la Haute Folie that meanders down toward the sea, and pulls into a driveway. The tires creak softly on the snow. The house is stone and freezing inside. A faint smell of damp fills the air. Lafourgue doesn't bother to wipe his feet. He just steps inside, leaving clumps of snow and grass in his wake. My eyes strain against the gloom of the hallway and my skin prickles in the chill. Lafourgue disappears down a staircase at the end of the corridor and I trail him into the basement.

There, hidden in the cold and forgetful earth, is a sort

of study lit by a bright, buzzing, uncovered bulb over-head. Lafourgue roots through his keys and pulls out a small silver one that he uses to open a filing cabinet standing by the far wall. He pulls out a drawer crammed with files and his heavy fingers flick through them until he alights upon the one he wants. He closes the filing cabinet carefully, locks it again, and drops the file on the desk directly beneath the glow of the light.

"Take your time with it," he says. "I'm not sure you'll get any further with it than we did, but who knows." He shrugs lazily. "You'll need to read it here. While you do, I'll go and make some inquiries about Kurmakin for you. I'll have a few of my men turn over some stones and see what comes crawling out. Do you need anything?"

I shake my head. Lafourgue leaves me alone in the oppressive cold of the basement. Buried in the earth. Like the warren at al-Mazra'a. Like Julie Bergeret.

Lafourgue's file bears no resemblance to a normal pro-cedural dossier. The whole thing is handwritten in tiny, cramped, yet impeccably formed letters. There is nothing that could pass for evidence, no crime scene photographs, no statements. There is just a series of notes and reports, interspersed occasionally with pictures clipped or stuck into the file. It starts with Kurmakin. Lafourgue's com-ments read as follows:

We know Kurmakin has links with at least two revolution-ary organizations:

Firstly, Aube: a group with only loose ties & probably posing no real threat. Members of the group fall into several quite common categories. 1) They are writers of tracts or pornography or poems which don't rhyme & they produce propaganda for the movement. 2) These are the intellectuals who carry copies of books by Bakunin or Trotsky & they justify why it is ok to blow up women & children in the name of revolution. 3) Homosexuals & pederasts who are the dregs of Christian society & are tolerated by the revolutionaries who think all attacks on the morals & standards of Western society are justified. 4) Junkies who cannot live among God-fearing people & their minds are rotted by the junk in their veins.

Some of them were once in the Resistance & they risked their lives for France. Now they sit around in basements full of smoke & shouting or they sit in dank cellars & read tracts calling for violence & for the overthrow of the system we live in. They shout their hatred for Christianity & for capitalism & for any other system that bans their perversions & shows them for what they are. They are themselves perverters of history. In their tracts they call their work a continuation of the Resistance. They claim to be fighting a war in the shadows, only the enemy is not the Boche, it is the government & democracy & the church in France.

They say that there is no authority & power is illegitimate. All methods to overthrow power are fair. I cannot see any action coming from them. It is just drinking & speeches & dreaming about a warped future that will never come. It is just depravity & nothing more. They are not even working class, they are the dregs of the degenerate bourgeoisie.

Secondly, MDCO (le mouvement pour la dictature de la classe ouvrière). This is a workers' movement but they are just would-be terrorists & ne'er-do-wells. They have also read some Lenin & Mao & the other poisons of the left & they are prepared to use violence. They roll up their shirt-sleeves & wipe the grease off their hands & talk a lot about ends & means & how this makes killing acceptable.

Last year they supported a strike in a textile factory in

Brest. They helped the workers to make picket lines & they
made signs saying, "A bas le patronat." Then they made Mo-
lotov cocktails & they threw them at the cars of the bosses.
One of the gas tanks caught fire & blew to high heaven. It
was just a strike & they turned it into a war. One of the
board members had his whole arm & back burned & had
to have skin grafted on where his flesh had seared & died.
The strikers were terrified & they turned on the MDCO &
blamed them for the attacks. Finally they all lost their nerve
& denounced each other & arrests were made & the factory
hired new workers.

Kurmakin's exact ties are not known but he has been
seen with members of both organizations. Written evidence
is hard to find. Both Aube and the MDCO call for an end to
Western Christian democracy & demand the use of violence.
This is a cutting from a tract published by Jacques Labrie in
Aube's newsletter.

A ripped, clumsily printed scrap of paper is clipped
into the file:

Violence is not a tool which enables revolution, but a necessary and indivisible aspect of the revolutionary process
right from its initial phase as resistance to prevailing ideol-
ogy. Only through an almost anarchic and indiscriminate
violence can the entrenched positions of liberal capitalism
be destroyed. The more absolute and radical the destruction,
the greater the chance that the following reconstruction will
wholly cast off the corruption of the past, thus preventing another bourgeois revolution from deceiving humanity.

Lafourgue's script continues underneath:

Hypothesis: Kurmakin is mature, in control, independent. He would not kill Anne-Lise out of jealousy. It is more likely that a revolutionary group or leader said he must kill her & called it a sort of initiation rite. This is common & it is a characteristic of the degenerates of the left. They use violent crime as a way to debase & control the minds of converts. They call it discipline. They encourage such acts. It is a way to erase the ideas of God & of order which are naturally implanted in the human brain. Kurmakin may have been made to kill & then mutilate Anne-Lise. This would prove his commitment to the cause. It would also change him & twist him & he would learn the kind of brutality which is needed to throw bombs at civilians & call it justice. Or he may have been told to kill her to free himself from anything that might weaken him. Anne-Lise was always in his thoughts & he could not tear himself away from her. He could not drag himself away from Sainte-Élisabeth. She was diverting his strength away from the revolution. This would explain the two phases of the crime. Firstly the murder itself, which was carried out in fury & also in despair. Then the calm hours after & the controlled way the body was dealt with (cleaned & wiped & dumped). Kurmakin may have been helped with this part of the crime.

27/02/59

We picked Kurmakin up & took him in for questioning right after Anne-Lise's funeral. Blanc & I waited in the church-yard in the rain. There were hordes there. It felt like the whole town had come. Most of them probably didn't know Anne-Lise at all. But they heard how she got ripped & killed & they came to gawk & to get excited by it. Whenever there is horror there is also a crowd.

When we arrived they were all standing around not

knowing what to do. There was a sea of people. They were all voyeurs in their decent Sunday suits & the women in their fine hats. Blanc said, "Look, it's a pack of vampires wanting to feast on Anne-Lise's blood. For a while it makes them feel like they are alive again."

Overhead it was dark. The mourners & the voyeurs kept looking up to the sky & prayed that the rain would hold off until she was in the ground. Then the clouds burst & the sky spat all over the hypocrites. Rain wet their suits & the brims of their hats sagged over their eyes. The women were shrieking & flapping to find their umbrellas. Some of them turned to go & their heels sank into the mud but they couldn't leave. There would never be another moment like this. They had to stay & see her body put in the grave.

Then the coffin came out of the church & it was cheap, simple wood. The gawkers were silent & there was something like embarrassment that she should lie for eternity in such a poor abode. The rain still came down & the sky spat on everyone there & on that Boche whore too & the people sighed as they put her carcass in the earth. Blanc & I shook our heads as we listened to Père Clavel's sermon. He stooped down by the grave & bent his head & tried to be solemn. He said that Anne-Lise had been blessed & luminous & chosen. He said that she had been too perfect for this earth & that she was with God. The drumming of the rain drowned out his words & all the time the derision of God poured upon him. Great rivulets of it flowed down. It plastered his gray hair onto his head & flooded his glasses. It poured down like an everlasting stream on the handful of mourners & the hordes of onlookers who were only there because it excited them to think of Anne-Lise screaming & cut.

We smiled at the words the father uttered & the gloss he tried to smear onto the life of a wayward slut. We watched the mourners crawl up in the half-night. The collaborator mother tried to pretend it was the muddy ground that made her slip & stumble & not the liters of wine she'd heaved into her gut. A hysterical little crowd of simultaneously menstruating would-be nymphets stood by the grave. They had trashy eyeliner on & powder that was dissolving into streaks on their puppy-fat faces. They stood there with their mouths open & their new black clothes sodden & clinging to them.

Then there was the revolutionary. He stood apart as if he was too grand to participate in it. After all, it was just small-town curiosity & grief. He was wearing a leather jacket & denim trousers out of contempt for the church. He stared with sadness at the cheap coffin & the cheap life within it that was an insult to the consecrated ground it was laid in. He stared around & tried to look pale & noble & the heavens spat their contempt down upon him.

The sorry parade straggled past the coffin. The mother reeled & swayed & the hips of the nymphets bounced. Each of them clutched at earth to throw on the coffin. The rain fell harder & harder & the sky rumbled at the blasphemy below. The earth that their fingers clasped was wet through & turned to mud & so what they threw down onto the coffin wasn't the sacred churchyard earth at all. It was the stinking mud that the German deserved to lie under until Judgment Day.

Blanc & I grabbed Kurmakin just as he was leaving the churchyard. Blanc twisted his arms behind his back & we knocked him down so he could taste the dirt that would be his lover's shroud for eternity.

When we arrived at the police station the mud had dried on him & he was caked in filth. He took a few knocks getting into & out of the car but he didn't whine. He muttered his dogma about repression & injustice & he took a few more knocks getting inside the station. Blanc said to him, "We can't put you in the cells covered in shit right up to your slanty eyes now, can we? Strip."

Of course the Communist refused & now it suited him to believe he had democratic rights. I left him with Blanc for a while and stood in the fresh air smoking a cigarette to clear the stench of decay from my nostrils. When I came back inside Kurmakin was curled up like a child on the cold floor. He was gasping for air. Blanc grinned at me. Kurmakin didn't look grand now. He was balled up like a whipped animal & the air was rasping in his lungs & it sounded like each breath hurt him.

"Is he ready to strip?" I asked Blanc.

He said, "When he's ready, he's ready. There's no rush."

I don't remember if it was the second or the third time I came back but there was Kurmakin & his hands were shaking like a homosexual I arrested once with a prostitute & who begged & begged, "I have children, I have children, don't tell my wife." He unzipped that James Dean jacket he'd put on to shame the church. When he was naked I could see the red welts where Blanc's fists had put color into his skin. He looked down the whole time. He tried to stand up & the muscles in his stomach heaved. Blanc smoked a cigarette.

Kurmakin was silent. He kept trying to stand up. Maybe he thought he could save some pride by refusing to stay down. Maybe he read somewhere that it's better to die on your feet than on your knees. Blanc knew better. A couple more blows to the ribs put him on the floor for good.

"Do you want to question him?" he asked.

I shook my head and said, "Put him in a cell."

Blanc took hold of Kurmakin's hair & started to walk. I saw his head jerk back & his feet scrabble on the ground as *he tried to keep up. I heard him go banging & sighing down the corridor. I went out for a smoke.*

Lafourgue's notes on Kurmakin stop here. If he questioned him, there is no record of it in the file. I turn to the next page and find a picture of Sarah. Her eyes are dead from exhaustion but there is a tiny, imploring flicker of terror in the taut lines of her face. Lafourgue's impeccable script continues as follows:

04/03/59

It is time to consider the idea that the drink-addled mother may even have been the one who choked her own progeny to death. This is a woman who prostituted herself to the Nazi plague-bringers in return for bread & liquor. She fornicated & funneled German goods into her mouth while the country starved. She would be capable of any monstrosity.

Blanc & I decided to hit her bar around midafternoon. The tables were full of fishermen celebrating the end of their work & having survived another day on the high seas. We waited for the number of drinkers to reach a peak so there would be a good audience. For a long time the collaborator has hidden in our midst & tried to pretend she is one of us. Today we overturned her rock & watched her squirm in the light.

She couldn't even keep her hands still as she poured me a drink. Her fingers shook & the bottle trembled & clinked against the glass. She dribbled spirits all over the bar. She mumbled something about being sorry. She mumbled something about how she couldn't get used to knowing that her daughter had been put in the earth.

Blanc came up next to me & tapped the bar. The collaborator fumbled for another glass & tried to pretend it was grief that made her hands shake & her words slur. She stammered at us, "Have you . . . ? Have you found . . . ?"

"We need to talk to you," Blanc said.

She mumbled, "I already . . . I already told you . . ."

Blanc said, "Maybe, but maybe not. So we're going to talk to you again. Properly this time. Move."

It was funny watching her try to understand what was happening. She blushed & stammered a few syllables but she couldn't find any real words.

"Are you too drunk already to even understand French?" I asked. I said it loud & there was suddenly silence in the bar. "We're going to take you with us. So move."

I reached over & grabbed the top of her arm where the skin was all soft & trembling & pulled her around the bar. I grabbed her arm tighter. It disgusted me. It was sinewy & wasted. I could feel the muscles twitching beneath my fingers. I gripped even harder. There was no noise in the bar. Everyone had turned around to watch what was happening.

Blanc grinned and said, "Sorry. We're going to have to take her away. She has some questions to answer in a murder case."

Sarah jerked & twisted herself free of my hand. She walked back over to the bar & took the two shots she'd poured for me & Blanc & downed them both. She smoothed the hair out of her face.

She said, "Fine, let's go. But get your goddamn hands off me. I'll walk myself."

"Be my guest," I said.

She marched out in front of us to the car & her feet slipped & shook & her drunken hips swayed this way & that.

05/03/59

We have watched the collaborator purge her toxic system for a full day & it has been instructive & satisfying. She has been quaking & shivering as the alcohol drains out of her blood. In her pain she has had to confront her own degeneracy. The sickness she feels is the one inside of her. She tried to sit calmly in her cell & leaned back against the stone wall. She looked like she was going to meditate.

It took just hours before she was curled on the floor & her sick & skeletal fingers clawed at her belly & her throat was bloated & throbbing & she retched & choked. She rocked & shook & fought herself in order not to cry out.

Weakness cannot be hidden. Sickness comes to the surface. She pretended to be strong for a few hours. Waves & waves of pain racked her corroded gut & her cries came wailing out of her cell. Her voice was all broken. She was calling for a drink.

Blanc went down with a bottle of Armagnac & downed a few swigs in front of her. He breathed heavily & smiled & let a look of bliss come across his face. He let the smell of the Armagnac float across into Sarah's cell. She was like a lab animal that starts salivating on cue. She rose up on her haunches & stared at the bottle held out in front of her. She stuck her claws out of her cage & her fingers grasped at the air. She begged.

Blanc took another swig and said, "Take something off. If you do, I'll let you have the rest of this."

She shook her head. She tried to say no. But already another wave of sickness hit her & it was her own moral sickness that was only now made clear to her. She didn't even seem to notice what she was doing. Her fingers were pulling at the buttons of her blouse. Blanc shook his head in disgust. She was so distracted she didn't even notice.

Blanc said, "Not that bit. No one wants to see your withered, bitten dugs. The skirt. Lose it."

She said no but her hands were already fumbling at the zipper & then there she was in her petticoat. She was shaking & humming & holding her arms out in front of her. Her legs were skinny & pale.

Blanc pulled hard on the bottle and said, "Jesus, didn't you learn your lesson after the war? Once a whore, always a whore, I guess. Hey, Lafourgue, do you want to see what she has rotting under that petticoat?"

I shook my head.

Blanc said, "Me neither." He walked off & Sarah just stood there. Her arms were still held out in front of her & her skirt was in a crumpled heap by her feet.

Lafourgue records any actual questioning only sketchily. He tries to ascertain whether there'd been any particular rancor or unhappiness between Sarah and Anne-Lise in the weeks leading up to the murder. Sarah confesses to anxieties about Anne-Lise's depression and says that she felt excluded from her daughter's life. Lafourgue doesn't note when Sarah was finally released.

As I leaf through the rest of the file I can see that Kerbac has also been detained, terrified, and taunted about the loss of Julie. In the quiet of Lafourgue's basement, the darkness suddenly seems immense. The bulb on the ceiling glows faintly. I think back to all the other files Lafourgue flicked past until he stopped on this one. How many more are simply records of bullying, humiliation, and violence? And yet, despite the venom, the entire procedure is implacable, ordered, carried out, and set down in a spirit of clear-eyed and unhurried calm.

I walk over to the filing cabinet. There must be hundreds of files in there. The light from the bulb seems to be growing watery. A damp chill floats on the air.

Amira was brought in by two French soldiers in sweat-stained uniforms. Her hands were tied behind her back and her face was smudged with dirt. I wondered if they had pressed her face down into the earth when they bound her hands or whether she had just been crying. The two soldiers didn't look at her. They dragged her down the west drive of al-Mazra'a beneath the radiance of the sunlight, which seemed to distend and swell the air. She let her feet dangle, making the soldiers work harder to drag her along. Her hair was uncovered— deep black, wavy, glistening in the midday heat. Her face was slender, curving gently around the cheekbones. Her eyes were almond-shaped. They stared outward but were somehow lifeless, empty behind the glittering deep-brown surface. The skin under her eyes was a tender purple like the skin of a baby.

Cold seems to be seeping in from the frozen ground. The filing cabinet is locked and Lafourgue has the keys with him. I shut the file on Anne-Lise. There is nothing useful in it. I sit with it on the table in front of me in the crackling glow of the bulb, waiting for Lafourgue to come back.

It must be late by the time he returns. Somehow, the twilight outside can be sensed. Lafourgue's boots squeak on the stairs and his voice thrums gently in the quiet.

"You'll get Kurmakin tomorrow. We'll pick him up and bring him in to the station. Take your time with him. Interrogate him how you like. You're a professional, so I don't need to tell you what to do."

"Thanks for letting me read the file." My throat feels tight. Desiccated.

"No problem." He gathers up the folder and looks through it carefully, perhaps to check that nothing is missing. He locks it away once again in the filing cabinet, then places the key back in his pocket.

"You know, I don't think most people understand why the police are there. Even some of the police don't understand. They seem to think that police work is about solving crimes, or bringing criminals to justice, or protecting people. People say that a lot, even though no one really believes it's true. Civilians can protect themselves and each other. And most criminals don't need to be caught. They give themselves up or they give themselves away. We don't need to do a lot. Some crimes don't even get noticed or reported. Others, like Anne-Lise, give you nothing to go on. There's no evidence and no traces. Sometimes we end up arresting the wrong person and we even know it, but we still need a conviction, so we get one. None of that has anything to do with justice or protection. So why are we here?"

Lafourgue's pupils are normally two tiny pinpricks, but in the dim glare of the bulb they have swollen. He looks different. More naive, perhaps. But crazier too. Like a sudden revelation has illuminated his mind.

"We're here to be the police. Not to perform the tasks that people think the police perform. Not the kind of tasks that can be summarized and assessed in terms of percentages and statistics. We're here to provide a police presence. Searches, arrests, the suppression of disorder, interrogation—these are the ways we make ourselves known to the population. We need to be visible to all people, not just to criminals. We create fear and repression in their minds. They are constantly aware of power and of the force it exerts on them. It makes them timid, contemplative, and cowardly. You must have seen it in Algeria, le Garrec. I read a great deal about the police—or the *service de renseignements*—out there. All we got was the sanitized version in the morning papers. But I could read between the lines. I'm sure you performed the tasks that were supposed to be your mission. Uncovering and disrupting arms supplies, monitoring terrorist groups, etcetera. But all of those things served a wider purpose. They allowed you to scare people. Not terrorists, ordinary people. People going about their daily business who might otherwise have started to believe in independence. Your real job was to be the police. To create terror and repression by your presence alone."

Lafourgue walks over to the filing cabinet and leans against it. "That's what the police really are. You see it clearly during an occupation. It's a form of the army used against the population at large. It's the tentacles of power made visible."

"If that's the case in Algeria, then it isn't working."

Lafourgue's voice is a faint murmur through the darkness: "Why not?"

"Repression didn't deter anyone. It nurtured nationalism. The more we deployed violence, the more the nationalists turned that same violence back on us. Our repression was the FLN's best recruiting tool."

"Then you didn't go far enough. Terror wasn't widespread enough."

"No. The army hasn't managed to constrain the Algerians because all it has done is magnify the very nature of our colonial presence. It shows us for what we are: in schools where we force Algerians to learn French and despise Arabic, in hospitals where they rot and die while we get the best treatment, or in segregated towns where the sewage pipes and clean streets are confined to the French quarters. All we've managed to do is make clear to all Algerians the violence inherent in every aspect of our dealings with them. It has made them desperate and furious. They see how we've embedded our own pathology in them. They don't know anymore what violence is theirs and what we have simply branded onto them and seared into their brains."

Lafourgue steps toward me and stares hard into my face. "Now isn't the time to back down. You need to stand by what you did. It was real policing. That's what I do here. That's what my files record. Actual police work. Exercising power and spreading terror. I don't know who killed Anne-Lise and I don't really care. The girl was a whore, and it is sometimes the fate of whores to end up as she did. The child was an abomination, like her mother. But I have used the case to fight the Communists and the collaborators and the degenerates."

He lays a hand on my shoulder. "I can see that they want to crucify you. That's politics. But what you did was right. Shall I drive you back to your car?"

I get up slowly and climb the stairs. My muscles ache from sitting for so long in the frozen basement.

I was told by Lambert that I was assigned to interrogate Amira. He informed me that she was an agent de liaison. *I asked him how we knew.*

"She's an Algerian. She's either a current agent de liaison *or a potential one. Either way, when you've finished interrogating her, she'll be neither. Get it done."*

He looked back down at his desk and began to write. With a single wave of his hand he indicated that the discussion was over.

Amira was down in the warren. She was probably shaking, chilled by icy sweats and rocked by sickness as she waited for the horror that was coming and that was me.

By the time I get back it is completely dark. Clouds and rain soak the atmosphere and make the blackness seem to float just overhead. There is no starlight, just the thick, waterlogged air.

As I pull into the driveway I can see that something is wrong. The door of the house gapes open before a gust of wind roars past and slams it against the frame. I switch off the headlights and the darkness is almost impenetrable. My eyes itch as they strain into the night.

For a while I stand by the door, listening into the house. I try to catch footsteps or rustling, any noise that would betray someone still inside. I can hear only silence above the distant whisper of the sea and the occasional crash of the door blown against the frame.

Something in my gut, some pulse of terror or adrenaline, surges as I step silently inside. Then, in the chill of the hallway, it subsides. That tingling alertness provoked by danger washes out of me. My muscles go slack. Weariness burns behind my eyes. The tension that has run static through my body for months suddenly ebbs away. Exhaustion soaks through me. I sink into it. Let the darkness bring what it will, whatever dangers it enfolds. For so long, fear seems to be the only thing that has bound me to life. It is all I can remember. My body suddenly rejects it. In the night, I am free of the persistent animal need to exist, even if only as flesh and nerves jolted by hunger and terror. No. Let it end now, whimpering and senseless in the dark. As well here as somewhere else. As well now as later when the only thing that separates the two is an endless series of minutes which rub and gnaw at the soul.

I go calmly to the light switch and turn it on. The glow is blinding. Books and papers are strewn on the floor. The table has been overturned. A smashed lamp rolls on the rug. Drawers and cupboards have been rifled through one by one, emptied, and their contents cast onto the ground.

There is still no noise in the house apart from the rustle of the sea wearing down the rocks, shrinking the land.

Who did this? Someone sent by the army, looking to remove any proof against Lambert which I might have hidden away? Or Anne-Lise's killer, who had blended back into the silence after the investigation foundered, but now, hearing of my inquiries, is alarmed enough to break cover and come and hunt down his pursuer?

I can feel the photograph of Anne-Lise pressed in my pocket. Would it matter if I discovered who killed her? She would still be just a corpse, putrefying matter in the cold ground, nothing more than cellular decomposition, a pure, organic thing dissolving, rotting, wasting back to the original nothingness.

I have to try to hold on to her. She is the only thing that keeps me from dissolving. She gives me shape. Without her, there are only the endless identical minutes passing by me, falling around me like snow, burying me, lying over me like a pall until I too fade and am forgotten.

There is still only silence in the rest of the house.

I clear some space on the sofa, pushing papers and books with cracked spines onto the floor. It seemed strange to come back home, to this preserved relic of a past that had long ago died in my memory. This chaos makes sense. This destruction. This living darkness in which an unknown person may remain, out in the distance, watching me, waiting for another opportunity to search for whatever he thought he could find here.

I turn off the light and lie down on the sofa. I listen to the door lurching and banging in the fury of the wind that whistles and swirls in the hallway and sounds like a lullaby.

DAY SIX

I am fully awake by the time dawn breaks with wintry slowness, filtering through the mist and damp and streaking the air gray. The light seems to trickle through the sky, struggling to exist at all, diluted and absorbed by clouds distended with rain and by the persistent night. I slept in my army greatcoat, but the air coming through the open door is heavy with the ice and chill of the sea and my muscles are stiff and my skin, stained by two years in the North African sun, looks jaundiced and pale.

Anne-Lise. Each time I sleep, the pieces of her begin to fragment. She seems farther away than ever when I awake. I spend my days reconstructing her last weeks and hours—the relationships that bound her, the infinitesimal details of her everyday world—only for it all to unravel in the indefinition of each new dawn. I try to gather up the shards of her life—her books, her friendships, her hopes—and piece them back into a whole. I try to remember how to look at them like a detective, how to analyze them, how to sift through them until, with the right turn of the kaleidoscope, something new, some luminous pattern, suddenly emerges from all the dashed and shattered parts. What have I missed? What meaning is imprinted on the most banal things that I have already seen or heard but let slip innocuously by?

This is how I want to think of Anne-Lise: In the faint traces of the past, she can be saved. Her death can be understood and stamped with justice.

But each morning, in the gummy no-man's-land between sleep and wakefulness, Anne-Lise slips away. Her past is distant and dead, and I feel only the uselessness of my desire to recover it. The only way back to Anne-Lise is the memory of those who knew her—and memory, with all its deviousness and its intelligence to protect us from what we know, is a deceitful guide. My own memory is devious. How can I stop myself from seeing in Anne-Lise another Amira, a victim who, this time perhaps, I can save?

The church at Sainte-Élisabeth stands at the hub of the town. All roads lead up to its brown stone walls and its spire dwarfs the houses around it and stretches up toward the platinum sheen of the sky. The early-morning light is murky and the church is almost dark inside, save for the flickering points of candlelight. The air is heavy. From my childhood, I can dimly remember ranks of old oak pews, the wood polished smooth over generations. They were plundered by the Nazis sometime during the war and now there are crudely carpentered boards nailed up in their place. I walk to the front bench and sit down on the rough wood. There is a tranquility here in the leaden air, something calm that tends toward the peaceful cessation of thought. I lean back and close my eyes. I want to force them open but exhaustion pulls on my muscles like lead weights. I can barely lift my head. I feel like I am tied to the bench as paralysis spreads through my nerves.

Then something jolts me awake. Out of the corner of

my eye, as it flickers half-open, I see the body of Christ bound to the cross hanging above the altar. For a second, it is Anne-Lise's pale flesh I see nailed to the wood, the torment of the body flaunted as an obscure yet majestic symbol. And whoever came to church and sat in the congregation and stared out at the martyred body of the Son of God could understand that gesture by which flesh became transubstantiated into art. In the mind of her killer, was Anne-Lise's torment also an apotheosis, a mark of love?

A gentle cough echoes behind me and Père Clavel appears in a woolen jumper, his eyes magnified behind the watery thickness of his glasses. He sits beside me on the front pew and lays one almost weightless hand on my arm.

"It's been a long time," he says. "I didn't think we would see you again. And if we did, I would have hoped for it to be in better circumstances."

"You remember me, then?"

"I remember that you weren't one for churches. Did Algeria make you change your mind?"

I shake my head. "I wanted to talk to you about Anne-Lise Aurigny. And about another girl, Julie Bergeret, who was killed in the winter of '47. Do you remember her too?"

"I have made it my business to know the people around here for forty years. I don't think I have forgotten any of them."

"Tell me about Anne-Lise. Was she someone you knew?"

"Only when she was younger. Sarah used to bring her to church when she was five or six. She didn't dare to go in herself but she'd leave Anne-Lise with me. She didn't want her daughter to grow up with a stigma upon her. She wanted Anne-Lise to learn about God and to be cleansed."

"How did Anne-Lise behave?"

"She wasn't the least bit interested. She was a re-markably stubborn, precociously self-assured little girl. She had an ability to totally ignore everything that she didn't agree with. She just used to sit down and gaze at the stained glass or through the open door. I soon gave up trying to teach her about the Bible."

"So you never got close to her."

"Not at first, but we were quite close for years. She didn't want to learn about the Bible but nor did her mother want to take her away from the church. Sarah wanted Anne-Lise to seem godly. She wanted her to be blessed, to protect her from the evil eyes that were all around. I think she also wanted some time for herself, in which she could drink quietly and without worrying about how to hide it from those inquisitive eyes that seemed to see everything and to see straight through it all at the same time. So Anne-Lise and I played chess. She was as inter-ested in those sixty-four black and white squares as she was utterly uninterested in the Scriptures. Sometimes we played games, and at other times we recreated great matches from the past. She used to stare at the board as I moved the pieces around to show her strategies. She soon played much better than me. I suppose she lost interest in me. I was, at best, a mediocre player."

"Why do you think she was killed?"

"I have no idea. There was certainly malice directed at the family, but I can't see any connection between ba-nal, small-town spite and the pathological violence of her death. I can make no sense of it at all. It is pure bestiality. Evil unchained."

"Someone told me that Anne-Lise may have been killed out of love. Could you believe that?"

He shakes his head. "No love could encompass such wickedness."

I point to the fallen head of the Christ, the torn flank, the nails hammered through the hands and feet. "What about love like that?"

"That was the most incomprehensible sacrifice."

"Perhaps Anne-Lise's killer thought the same."

Clavel shakes his head. "I don't believe such acts can ever be explained."

"What about Julie Bergeret? Do you think there could be any connection between the two killings?"

"They are a long time apart. What about all the years between?"

"I don't know. Did you think that Julien Kerbac killed Julie?"

"I'm not even sure whether Julien knows the answer to that question. As for myself, I have no idea. By now, I'm not sure anyone will ever know. Not in this world."

"What was Julie like?"

Clavel shakes his head gently. "It's going back a long way."

"Try. I need her to live again, just a little."

"I suppose, in many ways, she was quite nondescript. Soft-spoken, quiet brown eyes, and brown hair. She didn't want attention or say a great deal, she didn't stand out at school. She was the sort of girl you could easily overlook. And yet there was something about her that struck me when I was with her—you should remember that she went to church at le Quéduc, not here—and that was an almost radiant quality of goodness. It seemed to simply shine out of her: patience, tolerance, gentleness.

She cared for Julien, sheltered him from the harshness of a world he could never fathom. She let him breathe and be himself. When she died, nothing could hold him together anymore."

I leave Père Clavel enhaloed in candlelight and make two trips before heading off to find Lafourgue and, through him, Sasha Kurmakin. First I drive back to the lycée Cartier and, in their records, search for the year Erwann began to teach at the school. On a meticulously indexed card I find the date *September 1948*: the summer after Julie's death. Next I obtain from police records the date of de la Hallière's return to France. According to the files, he was back from North Africa in October '47, the last autumn when Julie was still alive: a quiet, virtuous, inconspicuous girl just months away from a nightmare that no one can now recall or understand.

When I arrive at the police station I am informed that Kurmakin has not yet been brought in. I decide to speak to Mathilde again. Something about her haunts me. I don't know if it's her hurt, dark eyes or her empty room. This morning I find her awake. Her skin is almost translucent and shot through with the blue marbling of her veins. She peers up at me dully but, unlike last time, she's not hungover. She just looks exhausted. Her soft brown eyes are red-rimmed and her hair is tangled and knotted. She runs her hands through it almost mechanically to smooth out kinks but she seems only to make the knots worse. She is dressed, but appears as if she hasn't been to bed at all. Her eyes stare at me, liquid, the pupils dilated and depthless.

"I guess you didn't get anywhere," she says. "Is that why you're back? To apologize to me and to say that you tried but you couldn't find out who killed Anne-Lise?"

"Can I sit down?"

She nods toward the foot of the bed. "Please." Her voice is husky, far away.

"I don't yet know if I've gotten anywhere or not. I found things out, but I don't know whether they'll lead anywhere until they do. Or they don't."

She shrugs. "You look even worse than last time." She tugs again at her hair. "Maybe I do too."

"I need to ask you about Lafourgue."

"Lafourgue?" Her voice hums gently. It seems almost tangible and, where it touches me, my skin prickles. I need her to talk to me. Her voice brushes up against me and melts against my skin. Her deep brown hair is thrown across her face and tumbles down her shoulders. She looks fragile.

"Did Anne-Lise have any connection with him before the killing? Did she know him at all? Did he seem interested in her?"

"Did he . . . ? Do you think he . . . ?" The words stick in her throat.

I want to tell her how I sat in his basement with the chill of night all around. I want to tell her what I read: how he carried out his police work with a kind of implacable ruthlessness that made me think of Anne-Lise's killer. I want to reach across to Mathilde and tell her that Lafourgue made no serious attempt to investigate Anne-Lise's death, and that she was not even the first girl to have been killed and the case remain unsolved under his command here. I want to tell Mathilde that Lafourgue despised Anne-Lise because of her origins and that, while my house was being ransacked last night, he was the only person who could have known that I wouldn't come back at any moment because I was in his basement. I want to say these things and to feel myself closer to Mathilde's translucent skin. I want to share with her the events of this case which have become the horizons and valleys of my world. I feel only my tongue lying heavy in my mouth. My palate is dry. I wait in silence for her to speak.

"I don't think he knew Anne-Lise especially," Mathilde says. "And I'm sure she had no interest in him at all. I do remember one time when he came into A l'abri des flots. His breath and clothes stank of alcohol but he seemed totally calm and controlled. He came over to where Anna and I were sitting. We were with some guys but I don't remember who they were. Some local guys. With Anna, there were always guys around. I don't know exactly what we were doing, nothing much, just talking, maybe sharing a cigarette. Then Lafourgue came over to the table. He didn't even look at the guys, just at us. He told them to get lost. He stared at us the whole time but everyone knew he was talking to the guys. They didn't bother to argue. They just got up and left. I think he just stood there for a while, not saying anything but not taking his eyes off Anna and me either. We could hear his breath going in and out and we just stared down at the table waiting for him to speak. Eventually he said something about . . . about dogs. How they give off a hormone that brings all the male dogs running. He said something about how we were like dogs, giving off some kind of . . . of smell . . . that would bring all the local boys running. Then he waited for ages again, not saying anything. I remember Anna's face was pink, I don't know if it was because she was furious or because she was ashamed. She was staring down at the table and her skin was burning. After a while he said something about how this was a Christian bar, not an Arab whorehouse. I think that was it. It's the only time I remember him ever speaking to Anne-Lise."

Mathilde looks unbearably sad as she speaks. It feels as if she is weighing up all the individual pieces of Anne-Lise's life and taking stock of their mediocrity: dreary conversations with local boys, the slow, repeated small-town evenings that she tolerated in the expectation of something better. Days that were supposed to be just a prelude, but that became all she would ever know.

"I don't think she ever spoke to him," Mathilde says. "Is that what you wanted to hear?" She smiles weakly. "It seems so long ago but it's not even a year."

Something glitters in the weird bareness of her room. On the floor at the bottom of the bed is a nine-branched candlestick. A menorah. The candles are blown out now but there are newly set beads of wax running down the sides. Nothing else in Mathilde's room seems to be hers. I remember her drained, hungover face when we first met. This sign of devoutness seems out of place.

"I didn't know you were Jewish."

"Neither did I."

"But your parents . . ."

Mathilde frowns in disappointment and I don't need to finish the sentence.

"They're not, are they?" Once again, I see the Blanchards shuffling around downstairs, half-deaf, lost to the world.

Mathilde shakes her head and the light glimmers on the loose filaments of her hair.

"The war?"

She nods. "I have no idea what happened to them. Deported, I guess. They"—she tilts her head to indicate downstairs where the Blanchards are probably bustling around in the kitchen—"were just acquaintances of ac-quaintances of acquaintances. Something like that. They don't really know where I came from."

"It was brave of them to take you in."

"Brave?" She is clearly surprised to hear the word spo-ken in connection with the scuttling, half-senile presences downstairs. "I guess so. I didn't really think about it."

"Did you ever search for your real parents?"

She shakes her head.

"Do you know that they're . . . that they didn't survive the war?"

"You mean that they're dead. I don't know. But I know that dozens and dozens of thousands of them went on trains to the East and that only a handful ever came back."

There is silence. *Tarik's inhuman voice is whispering into my ear. I can feel the gentle tide of Amira's blood beating against my knees.*

"Sasha told me that seventy-five thousand were taken and that two thousand returned," Mathilde says. "He knows all about what happened in the war. Anyway, if my parents were alive and they wanted to find me—if they were in a state to want to find me—then I don't sup-pose it would be too hard for them."

"Don't you even want to know who they were?"

She pauses. "Would it make any difference? Maybe there's a fortune with my name on it in the vault of the Rothschild Bank. Maybe I'm next in line for the title of some Eastern European nobility that the Communists abolished long ago. Probably my parents were just petty, frightened clerks who got crushed in the machinery when the Nazis came. I don't think it matters either way."

She stands up lazily and walks to the window where

the sky shines palely above the pulsing band of the ocean. "However it was before, this is my world now. Sainte-Élisabeth. This naked room in a house with two strangers. The church in the center of town. A l'abri des flots in the evenings. Fishermen who can't quite get the stink of guts off their fingers. Rain."

"You could leave."

"And go where? I'm not as clever as Anne-Lise. I can't go off and read philosophy in Paris. I could just take my chances and be one more wandering, homeless Jew."

The struggling light in the sky glints on Mathilde's skin, draining it of blood and emphasizing its pallor and its sheen. She clutches her cardigan around her skinny sides.

"And the menorah?"

She laughs faintly. "I bought it in a secondhand shop. I guess there were quite a few menorahs without owners after the war. I don't even know what to do with it. I just know that it's for the festival of light, in winter. I light the candles each evening and watch the flames dance and the wax melt. It's pretty. I wish I could say more about it, like what it's supposed to mean."

"You don't ever go to a synagogue, or see other Jews?"

"In Sainte-Élisabeth? And what do I have to worship? I didn't even know until I was fifteen what I was. I mean, what my parents were. I don't know if they worshipped or if they were just Jews by race. I think I always knew, though, that they"—another nod downstairs—"weren't my parents."

"How?"

"I don't know . . . You just know. Maybe lots of kids think that and it doesn't mean anything. I knew it was true. They always denied it when I asked but then one evening a couple of years ago—I can't even remember what we were arguing about—they gave in and told me that they'd agreed to take me in. They said it like it was a great revelation. I think they wanted me to be grateful or something."

"Were you?"

"I don't think so."

Although Mathilde answers my questions, she doesn't turn her gaze away from the window. She seems almost to be talking to herself.

"It was strange. I mean, when I found out. At first it was a relief. Like I'd been freed from a destiny that was choking me. I'd lived my whole life feeling I was someone else, or that I should be somewhere else, and then I found out that it was all true. Only . . ." She is silent for a long time and the quiet rolls around in this small, empty room. "Only what I found out is that whatever I am is completely lost. No parents. No stories. No people. A black hole."

"You could search—"

"Don't you understand? You can't just search out the past. Do you know what we're actually talking about here? The deportations. The death camps. It's the obliteration of an entire people. No records. No survivors. Nothing. It was supposed to be complete annihilation. There's nothing left for me to find. Maybe a couple of names on an official register somewhere. Dates and places. Pithiviers. Beaune-la-Rolande. Drancy. Auschwitz. None of that adds up to a past. That's why I bought the menorah. Not to try to rediscover some Jewish tradition that was never mine. To remind me of all the things I'll never know. I'm not trying to worship with it. I just keep it as a light in the night."

For a moment I can see Mathilde in her bare, dark room, listening to the clattering downstairs where two strangers bustle around in confusion. Outside, she hears the far-off roar of the sea, a whisper of infinity. At times, she must also hear the church bells tolling out the dull hours. By the window, gleaming frailly against the blackness, her menorah burns and glows, abiding in the gloom while she stares into the absolute darkness of her own past. Then another vision comes, eerily present for a moment: Anne-Lise's body lying across the heathland in the police photographs. The precise, almost ritual nature of the mutilation in her flank leers like a black hole in the fuzzy, blizzard-flecked tones of the picture. The flesh excised after death. The body laid on display like criminals on medieval gallows.

"Mathilde, how did it make you feel toward Anne-Lise when you learned that your parents were Jewish?"

"Anne-Lise?"

"With her being the child of a German."

"What difference would it make? She was who she was. Whoever her parents were couldn't change that."

"But some people did resent her. They saw in her the shadow of the occupier. You didn't?"

"She was my best friend. She was the only person I loved. I didn't ever even think about her being German. She was the same as me. She didn't know where she came from either. There were always people ready to accuse her because of it, but she didn't care. I don't think she even really noticed. Mostly people just let it drop because it had no effect on her. Sometimes it just made them furious, though."

"They resented her."

"I guess."

"Enough to hurt her?"

Mathilde's eyes are totally focused now, and utterly cold. She stares hard at me and her gaze yields nothing. "What are you saying?"

"Have you ever read *The Merchant of Venice*?"

She shakes her head slowly. "Why?"

"It's about Shylock, a Jewish usurer who lends money to Antonio, a Christian. When a tempest wrecks Antonio's ships and ruins him, he can't pay his debt back to Shylock. So the usurer demands to cut a pound of flesh out of Antonio in return. It's not so much compensation for the money Shylock has lost. It's an act of revenge upon a society which treats him like an outcast, a subspecies. I suppose you know that some hours after she was killed, Anne-Lise's murderer cut a piece of flesh out of her side . . ."

Mathilde closes her eyes. I see her shiver.

"By now, almost all of the evidence from the killing has gone. There was perhaps nothing even at the beginning. But there is still that one strange mutilation which may be the last, or the only, clear sign which explains why Anne-Lise was killed. I wonder if it might be a mark of revenge by someone persecuted during the war, or even after, who wanted to take a pound of flesh from Anne-Lise as a means of demanding atonement."

Mathilde sits completely still. She looks frozen. Her cheeks are sunken. "Are you saying that I—"

"I'm not talking about you. I just want you to understand that the meaning of the wound in Anne-Lise's side may perhaps be the only route that still leads back to whoever killed her."

She turns to the window and stares blindly into the great gray mass of clouds hanging above Sainte-Élisabeth.

"Mathilde, listen. Have you ever heard anything about

someone looking for revenge for the occupation? For the deportations? Anyone for whom Anne-Lise wasn't just a seventeen-year-old girl, but a symbol of evil?"

She still doesn't move. She gapes unblinkingly out into the swollen banks of storm clouds louring above the coast.

"Mathilde?"

She shakes her head. "I don't think so. I mean, I don't know. I never heard anything like that before. It sounds . . . horrible." Her voice is barely a whisper before it fades and dies.

The image won't leave my mind: persecuted Shylock ripping the satisfaction for his debt out of Antonio's living flank. Maybe Anne-Lise wasn't displayed as a piece of art, but as edification for the public. Was it a warning, like the hanged men dotting the boundaries of medieval towns, their flesh blackening in the sun, their eyes carrion for birds?

I leave Mathilde in her empty room, where only the menorah's gleam exists to remind her of the failure of memory. She is still standing by the window, her skin brushed by the sheen of light radiating faintly through the clouds, staring into the leaden sky that marks the boundary of her world, as another flurry of snow begins to drift gently down in white sheets.

Through the thick, reinforced glass window in the door to an interrogation room, I can see Sasha Kurmakin's silhouette. His right wrist is handcuffed to a metal chair and his left hand is sunk deep in his pocket. He leans back, appearing entirely relaxed, his deep blue eyes gazing into the middle distance. His hair falls gently around his face, a jet-black, liquid cascade.

"Told you we'd get him for you." Lafourgue's hand is like a rock on my shoulder. "We picked him up last night along with a few other unkempt revolutionaries. Take your time with him. We'll probably hold him for a few days anyway. There's enough evidence to drag out a possible conspiracy charge."

"Should I record the interview for you?"

"It never even took place. He resisted arrest too, so a few extra bumps and bruises aren't going to lead to any questions we don't know how to answer."

Inside, the room seems tiny. The windowless walls are oppressively near. Kurmakin doesn't even look up. Some of the Algerians were the same, trying to discipline their minds to disconnect from their surroundings. Others couldn't help themselves. They tried to stare down but their eyes turned toward whoever came in, and in those eyes was a look of mute, pleading terror. Kurmakin doesn't look scared at all. He must have passed through many police cells and interrogation rooms in the last months. He stares over at the far wall, his dreamy gaze floating freely. He's pale and looks weary. His eyes are gently bruised with tiredness and his skin is wan.

I offer him a cigarette and let him smoke for a while. His fingers tap the ash off with measured, refined gestures. He looks dreamily at the plumes of smoke wreathing in front of his face.

"Sasha, I'm Capitaine le Garrec. I'm the one who wanted to speak to you. I asked Lafourgue to bring you in."

"Le Garrec?" He rolls the words around softly in his mouth. "I know the name. It was in the papers. The soldier who got carried away and murdered an Arab girl he was only supposed to torture."

I hadn't intended to move, but suddenly my hand

is around Kurmakin's face. My fingers are digging into his flesh. His bones and teeth feel like they are about to splinter in my hand. I want to feel the crack of the jaw in my grip. I force his head upward to look at me.

"How many people do you think they murder in Algeria every day?" I keep hold of his face. The flesh warps and pales where my fingers bite into it. My voice is flat, or so it sounds to me. "Why do you think they would prosecute someone for doing exactly what the army does day in, day out? Are you really that stupid?"

I slowly let go of Kurmakin's jaw. I unclench my fingers. They feel alien, as if they'd been grafted on after an amputation. Kurmakin's cheeks are bloodless where my hand crushed his flesh. He looks up at me and there is something uncertain in his stare.

"That may be true." His left hand reaches up and gently massages the skin of his cheeks. "So why are they prosecuting you?"

"There'll be a hearing tomorrow. I'll try to explain it then. I can't say anything now."

He nods. "You never know who might be listening. The article said that you were in the Resistance. That before you became a Fascist yourself, you tried to fight fascism. Is that true?"

"Yes. At the time, I didn't see it as becoming a Fascist. I thought that somebody had to be there. The situation already existed, so someone had to act in it. Better me than someone who actually wanted to fight the war."

"And now?" He sounds a little incredulous.

"Now I think that the situation itself was just violence: colonialism, the nationalist rebellion, repression. That was the nature of it: pure violence; violence in its unreconstructed form. In that kind of situation, whatever you did, there was only ever going to be one outcome. I could have stayed in France and pretended it wasn't happening, but I don't think my hands would have been clean that way either."

For a while there is silence between us. Tobacco crackles and burns as Kurmakin pulls on another cigarette. Finally, he breaks the silence.

"So why did you want to talk to me?"

"It's about Anne-Lise."

He frowns slightly. Her name catches him off guard. Something trembles in his gut and that carefully cultivated blank mask he had presented for interrogation begins to crack. He blinks once, twice. "Isn't it too late now, for Anne-Lise?"

"I don't think so. Can I talk to you about her?"

"Are you investigating the murder?" His hand brushes his eyes.

"I'm trying to piece together the last few weeks before she died. I'm sorry, but I need to ask you some things which you might find painful. Did you know Anne-Lise was pregnant?"

"Pregnant? When she died?" His cheeks are suddenly flushed. He gasps slightly and his hands move to cover his face. The metal of the handcuffs clangs against the chair and his right hand falls back by his side.

"No, not when she was killed. But she was pregnant the winter before. You must have noticed her mood at the time."

"Of course, but . . ." He can't find an answer. He wasn't prepared to answer these questions. He looks away wordlessly.

"The reason for her depression last winter was that she was pregnant."

"Are you sure?"

"I have the name of the doctor who carried out the abortion. And she told her teacher, Dr. Ollivier. But no one else, or so it seems. She never told you?"

Kurmakin shakes his head almost imperceptibly.

"Was the child yours?"

"I don't know."

"Could it have been?"

He nods slowly.

"Did you ever think that . . . that Anne-Lise might have had a relationship with someone else?"

I can see fear shredding his gut now. "No." It comes out as a strangled whisper. He says it again, trying this time to inject some conviction into the word: "No."

"Do you want to take a break for a while?"

He inclines his head to say yes and the waves of his hair tumble down and obscure his face. I stand by the door, staring out into the gray corridors of the police station until Kurmakin's voice brings me back to the present.

"What did you hope to bring to Algeria? The values of capitalist democracy? Did you hope they might forget about their alienated and oppressed existence if they could afford a new refrigerator or a Western suit?"

"I don't think I thought enough about them at all. I was just looking for a way to sacrifice myself. Can you understand that? In the Resistance it was an idea we lived with every day. It can be hard to forget something like that and drift back into simple normality."

"Do you . . ." Kurmakin's voice breaks off. "Do you think she was . . . ?"

"Seeing someone else?"

"Yes. You can be honest with me."

"I don't know. There's no evidence at all that she was."

166 jr JAMES BRYDON

Involuntarily, Kurmakin lets out a flood of air as his body relaxes. "She was my life," he says quite calmly, as if he were stating his date of birth or the color of his jacket. "She was the one thing that shaped and lit up the time to come. Her face. Her hands. Her touch was gentle, like rain. I still can't accept that I will never watch her get older. Never watch the years make her weary and wise. She is fixed forever now. A girl who never grew up. I feel like I forget her a little more every day. I try to hold on to her— her hair, its scent, something sweet like cinnamon—but I feel like I'm making her up, not remembering. I think I know what she was like, but it's my rational mind telling me that, and so I invent scenes that correspond to what she should be. It's like my memory's degrading . . ."

"It's protecting you. There are some things you can't live with. Memory is clever. It makes you let things go."

"Do you know why she died?"

"Not yet. I have to ask you: did you ever have any idea why someone would have wanted to mutilate her?"

He simply blinks, seeming to find no other response.

"There was something ritual in the mutilation. Something that gave an enigmatic meaning to the act of killing. Did it make any sense to you?"

He shakes his head and his skin seems paler than ever.

"It must be something that explains the crime, but to whom? Perhaps not to those of us who simply look on, and for whom it seems grotesque and uncanny. Perhaps it explains the crime to the killer himself. Hours after Anne-Lise died, he marked her body to make sense of his own deed."

As Kurmakin tries to answer my questions, shaking his head, his skin sucked white as the blood rushes away from his face, he looks less and less like a militant and ever more like a teenager, drawn wide-eyed and trembling into an adult's nightmare. Getting arrested didn't faze him, but the memory of Anne-Lise is playing on his nerves and fraying his composure. Occasionally, without seeming to notice he is doing it, he tugs at the handcuffs binding him to the chair. Interrogation, for all its refinement and elaborate methods, is not a complex art. The mind becomes incapable of defending itself against perpetual attack. The body is transformed into a field of pain. Kurmakin bites his lip.

"What kind of relationship did Anne-Lise have with Erwann Ollivier?"

"He gave her lots of books to read. I think it was useful for getting into the École normale, but it was just the Western bourgeois canon. Individualist philosophy, Romantic poetry, the whole apparatus of psychology and emotion through which middle-class man creates his own self."

"Did the relationship go beyond that?"

He shakes his head.

"What about Christian de la Hallière? How close was Anne-Lise to him?"

"Close? I don't think they were close at all. She wanted to try to track down her father and she thought he could help. She was disgusted by the man himself."

"Did you ever get the impression that he might have misinterpreted Anne-Lise's motives and begun to form an attachment to her?"

"I don't know, but . . ." For a second, his eyes glaze over and he struggles to rip the words out of his throat. "There was one time, after she went to see him . . . after she came back . . . It was the only time I ever saw Anne-Lise scared."

"Do you remember when?"

"January, I think. About a month before she . . ."

"What happened? Did he threaten her?"

"I don't know what it was. All I know is that one day, after school, she went out to the château to meet him. I think she said he had some news about where Otto went after he left France. Anne-Lise and I had arranged to meet later, only when she got there, her eyes were . . . frantic. She kept looking around as if she thought she was being hunted. It was strange because Anne-Lise was never scared of anything. She grew up in a house choking on fear and it seemed to inure her to it. But that night she seemed scared."

"He terrified her?"

"She wouldn't talk about it. But it was strange, because the one thing that she did say is that he wasn't there."

"De la Hallière wasn't there?"

He nods.

"Do you think she was lying?"

"Anne-Lise didn't lie—" He breaks off, perhaps thinking of the pregnancy. "Maybe she didn't always tell me everything, but she wouldn't lie."

"So something else scared her, not de la Hallière?"

"I think so. Something at the château, but not him."

The strain of remembering is etched in the tense lines of his face. I'm not surprised he left Sainte-Élisabeth, where everything conjured Anne-Lise's shadow and forced him, through the long minutes of each day, to excavate his memories of her.

He blinks and shakes the tangled mass of his hair out of his face. His eyes are purple-rimmed but they burn tirelessly, sleeplessly. Something is driving all repose from him. Grief? Guilt?

Lafourgue peers approvingly through the glass at Kurmakin's crumpled silhouette as I leave the interrogation room.

"We'll probably hang on to him for a couple more days," he says.

As evening sets in, I drive out to the Château de la Hallière with tiredness inflaming my eyes and the road seeming to dip and sway in front of me. My head throbs where Kerbac caught me with the metal bar and sharp waves of pain pulse through my skull.

What was Anne-Lise afraid of, she who was never afraid?

My hands start to slip on the steering wheel. It feels as if my fingers have been wasted by dystrophy. Tomorrow, I shall sit before the judge and talk about Amira. Tonight, there is this one remaining thread running back into the past and connecting me to Anne-Lise. What scared her? Is Kurmakin even telling the truth? The ground seems to shake beneath me. The road floats hazily ahead, vaporized in the mirage of sleeplessness. I try to recollect the events of al-Mazra'a in preparation for the hearing but the words running through my mind dissolve into meaninglessness.

I park the car about two hundred meters away from the château, switch off the headlights, and wait. Dustings of snow caress the windshield, seeming not so much to fall as to condense in the frozen air. One light blazes in a downstairs window, but apart from that the building looks deserted, its gray mass hulking and rotting in the dusk.

After about twenty minutes the window goes dark and I see Aïcha's silhouette step out into the frozen air.

Her skin glows against the charcoal tones of the land-
scape. Shivering a little, wrapped in a black shawl, she
walks down the road toward Sainte-Élisabeth.

Now the château is dark. The snow-sodden, unmown
grass soaks my ankles as I walk around the back looking
for a way in. The wood of the window frames is disinte-
grating, falling away in damp splinters. I can see that one
of the latches is unattached and, by digging my nails into
the crack, I am able to pull the window open. The gap
is just large enough to crawl through and I find myself
in a dark hallway, breathing in the murky air of the château. The carpet underfoot is worn. An enormous painting hangs on the wall. In the half-light, I can just make
out the ancestral design of knights charging at hordes of
scimitar-waving Moors, bringing enlightenment to the
infidel lands in great tides of blood.

The size of the château makes it almost impossible
to search thoroughly. Where would Anne-Lise possibly
have been? I go through the cupboards one by one in the
grand reception room where de la Hallière sat, his chin
flecked with spittle as he exhumed and embellished his
memories of the Ostfront and the Division Charlemagne.
There are boxes of cigars. Bottles of whiskey, Calvados,
and rum coated in thick layers of dust. Old daguerreo-
types of girls standing around in knickerbockers. In one,
a girl is standing behind a shelf of apples, her breasts
interposed between the fruit.

I try to move silently and quickly, constantly listening
out for the rumble of a car engine, the whisper of voices,
or the sound of footsteps. The dark makes the search
difficult and slow. My hands are shaking slightly and
I keep fumbling with the objects I find as I go through
the rooms. I try to breathe slowly and run through in my

head the phrases I will need for tomorrow's inquiry. The more I try to construct sentences which express the reality of those final weeks at al-Mazra'a, the more the words seem incoherent and their meaning eroded and absurd. My head throbs heavily and my hands tremble and seem unresponsive to my will, as if paralysis is setting in.

The reception room reveals nothing. I try to return each object to where I found it but my unsteady fingers bump into things and knock them out of place. Where else could Anne-Lise have been? The bedroom? I guess it must be on the first floor, at the top of the wide wooden staircase with its sculptured columns and flourishes and heavy oak banisters. As night closes in outside, I can see less and less. The gloom blurs the château's bric-a-brac into indistinct shapes. The stairs creak beneath my feet. The wood sinks and groans. Up on the landing, doors lead off in all directions. Most of them open into rooms clearly not used for years, even decades. Tarpaulins, canvases, and sheets are draped over the bulky forms of rotting pieces of furniture. Cobwebs hang down from the ceiling like great folds of white muslin. Black mold bespatters walls rotten with damp. The air is so thick with dust that it clogs my throat. I feel like I'm underwater. Like I'm drowning. *I see Tarik's head forced down into the gluey depths of the tub. His muscles tense and knot frantically. His breath roars in his throat when Lambert pulls him out, as if his lungs are on fire.*

I can feel my airway contract. Panic shakes my limbs. I try to listen out for footsteps, an engine, voices. Still my hands shake. They rattle against the porcelain door handles as I enter each new room. It feels as if the wooden floorboards are sagging and swaying beneath my feet.

Finally, in the easternmost part of the château, I find

an inhabitable room with an old four-poster bed at its center. I try to move quickly. The familiar routine of searching a room should be an activity that my body re-members and can perform competently. My fingers are leaden. I work my way through cupboards, drawers, and bookcases. Everything moves agonizingly slowly. It is so dark that I need to peer closely at each object I find in or-der to examine it. I run through clothes, pockets, books. De la Hallière has an extensive collection of pornographic writing, from the Marquis de Sade to low-quality fanta-sies of rape and violence.

As I drag my fingers along the shelves, I feel some-thing sticking out of a copy of *Justine*. In the failing light, I can see merely that it is a bundle of photographs. The images are hidden by the dark, except for what looks like a naked body in a posture of crucifixion. I stumble to the window, my legs clumsy and numb. I try to pick out more details by starlight. The air in my lungs burns and dwin-dles. The pale glint from the sky outside shows me more: a woman, stripped, her arms outstretched and chained to a stone wall. Her hair falls in great luxurious waves around her shoulders. The skin around her flanks and stomach is torn. It looks as if she has been beaten with a whip or a cane. Something that would lacerate the flesh. Her skin glows, faintly radiant like the dying warmth of sunset. Her eyes are closed as if to blot out the stare of the photographer capturing her pain and humiliation.

Aïcha.

Even with her face half-hidden and her features only feebly picked out by the dead light of the stars, there is no doubting that it is her. Other pictures show her in similar poses: her arms tied to two thick metal rings, her skin martyrized before the photos immortalized these moments of her suffering. The surfaces of the pictures are dark; the images are drowned in shadows.

The blood pumps in my head. The gash on my cheek feels like a metal blade lodged in my face. My fingers tingle and are losing all sensation. My left arm is quivering slightly and an iciness runs along it from the shoulder to the fingertips.

The photos were taken inside. In a room with metal restraints. A dungeon. Somewhere hidden in the earth, where the screams would stay muffled. A place where someone could be kept for hours, even days. Anne-Lise. Perhaps she found the photographs showing the torture of Aïcha. It terrified her. If de la Hallière found out, it could have been reason enough to kill her. He took her down to the same chamber where Aïcha had been terrorized. In the last hours of her life, her world was nothing more than those four stone walls, the dirt floor, and the hopeless attempt to blot out pain.

Tomorrow I will return to al-Mazra'a. The basement warrens. The detainees living in those labyrinthine corridors and small cells and clinging to fragile memories. The bare bulbs gleaming overhead.

They stripped Amira too. When I went in to interrogate her, her hands were tied behind her back and her hair fell in great luxurious waves around her shoulders and tumbled jet-black over her breasts and her belly was stained with sweat and pumping hard, the muscles bunched and frantic, contracting and releasing, and her skin glowed in the nauseating light of the bulb faintly radiant with the dying warmth of a sunset. Her eyes were downcast; she couldn't look up and she had closed her eyes as if she wanted to blot out my stare capturing her pain and humiliation.

I push the photographs back into the book and try to restore everything in the bedroom to its original state.

My memory seems to be blanking out. There are great voids in my perception. I can't remember where any of the things I moved came from. I arrange the books, clothes, and papers I have disturbed into some semblance of order and pull the door shut behind me.

The corridors are almost completely dark by now. My feet feel out the way in front of me. The creaking of the wood resounds like gunshots in the quiet and makes my heart lurch in my chest. I manage to stumble down the stairs, my feet slipping on the threadbare carpet, all my senses straining into the blackness and the silence to pick up any indication that de la Hallière may be home.

Reaching the hall, my steps turn in the direction of the window and escape. But I can't go yet. I need to find de la Hallière's dungeon, whatever dark pit he kept Aïcha in, tearing her flesh and turning her pain into the polished surfaces of his photographs. I move through the ground floor of the château room by room, not daring to use a flashlight, feeling out the ground with my feet, stamping, hoping for a hollow echo to answer my search.

Ten minutes elapse in the darkness. Twenty. The night is absolute. There is barely even the faintest glimmer of moonlight creeping through the windows. Thirty minutes. As the time ticks past, my eyes are drawn ever more anxiously to the windows. I stare down the road to Sainte-Élisabeth, waiting for de la Hallière or Aïcha to return.

Forty minutes.

Nothing. No hollowness underfoot. No entrances that I can see. In my pocket is the crumpled photo of Anne-Lise. I try to remember her face. Kurmakin thought he forgot her more every day. His brain invented things to make up for the loss of the past. Aïcha's body, stripped, the skin broken, her eyes closed in terror, glimmers in my mind's eye.

Fifty minutes. Even the tiniest capillaries in my chest seem to have swollen. The air is being squeezed out of me. My lungs are distended. I can't get air into them.

Nothing.

Something that feels like tears is trying to well up behind my eyes but my whole body is desiccated. There is no liquid to expel.

There are no more rooms to search. I climb back through the window, and as I jump down, the wet grass caresses my ankles. I brush up against the château's walls as I stumble back around to the road in the dark.

Then my feet strike wood. I can feel something like a large board underneath the grass. I drop to my knees and scrabble with my hands. Wooden planks are set in the earth. The wood is thick, damp. Metal bars run across from end to end. Cold, eternal iron. On the right-hand side, my fingers pull at a catch. The metal bars are bolts.

Again and again, my eyes dart toward the indistinct curves of the road. I can almost hear the rumble of a car driving back from Sainte-Élisabeth but it is only the blood rushing through my head. The bones of my face throb and twitch. I pull back the bolts. The metal groans and shrieks in the night. I grope for a way to open the doors.

My hands fix on a metal ring.

The wood creaks and the door swings back. A hole gapes in the earth. The air coming out of it is damp and heavy. I can smell the faintest hint of blood on it. A mere trace that reminds me of the odor of the warren. The past lingers in the air. The little particles of degradation that have been stored down here are now seeping out, leaching into the night, settling in my mouth and on my tongue, laying their toxicity upon me.

My throat contracts violently. My breath burns in gasps. I crawl closer to the opening. I try to stare down into the blackness. Freezing air drifts upward, dusted with poison that floats around my face and settles on my skin. I move closer to the hole. I don't know why I don't stand up. I don't know why I am still on my hands and knees in the sodden grass. My hands are clutching the edge of the hole, but instead of pulling myself forward, I realize I am just clinging on; my hands are strangling the wooden frame, and splinters are needling my flesh and nestling in my fingers and I grip harder and harder, however sharply the wood tears into my skin I keep on holding tighter and tighter because it is the only thing to do.

It is the only way I can stop myself from falling.

The next thing I am aware of is sitting in my car, my head thrown back, gasping for air. Where am I? The woods and the somber outline of the château loom in the night. A wave of panic runs through me. It feels like a razor tearing at my gut. My skin prickles. There isn't enough air in the whole world.

Where am I?

Snatches come back to me. The hole in the ground. The fetid air from within floating up toward me. Air that was heavy with the sweat and blood of Aïcha. Perhaps with the terror of Anne-Lise's last hours too.

I can't remember anything else. How many minutes were swallowed by blackness? What happened? I need to go back to the château and go down into the dungeon and find out what is hidden there.

My legs won't move. They seem soft, as if the muscles

are wasted and the bones are decaying and can no longer support the flesh.

I realize that I cannot go back. Even to check whether or not I shut the wooden door. Nothing can make me step down into that lightless pit. My body simply will not let me.

I try to catch my breath and to regain some control. The vision out of my left eye is streaked with flashes of white light. I don't think I can move my fingers. I understand that this is the end. That I can go no further toward finding Anne-Lise's killer. There is no salvaging of the past. I no longer have the strength to investigate this case or any other. Tomorrow I will come before the judge. The stains of the past are inexpungible. The rankness of my memory will seep out as I talk and its poison will lie over everything like the chemical residue of a bomb.

I sit in the quiet for a time that seems endless. I focus on my own breathing. I gaze into the toneless immensity of the night. Feeling comes slowly back into my prickling fingers. I manage to turn the key in the ignition and pull the choke. The car rolls down toward the road. I hold my foot halfway down on the brake in case my muscles fail me again. I leave the headlights turned off. The car slinks silently past the château. I can feel the lacerations left by the wooden frame of the dungeon where my hands grip the cold steering wheel.

There is nothing more I can do. Tomorrow, before I have to drive to Paris, I will tell Lafourgue where he can find the pictures and the dungeon. I will leave him to arrest de la Hallière and bring to Sarah whatever peace she can find in the closure of the case.

My hands shake. I clutch the wheel. With the headlights off, the road in front of me is almost invisible.

DAY SEVEN

I fall asleep when it's nearly dawn and all my dreams are recollections of leaving for Algeria. It's summer, 1957. The Battle of Algiers is ending. In France, people talk about small handfuls of rebels and the need to maintain order. No one wants to say the word *war*. Rachel has just left me and I can still taste her skin on my tongue. Its mineral freshness makes me think of the sea-soaked breezes of my childhood in Sainte-Élisabeth. I can still feel her body beneath my hands. At night, my dreams are full of her tanned skin glowing in the dim light. I can still see the heat of her eyes smoldering in the shadows. I can still feel her in the bed next to me and I reach out for her, and only when my fingers close on nothingness and my arms remain empty do I awake and find myself alone.

Rachel. My work excited her, at first. Perhaps she thought it was a struggle against violence and degradation. She would sit up in the small hours, her eyes staring sleeplessly, wanting to hear about the cases I was working on. Over time, she began to realize that there are no boundaries. You don't fight depravity. It becomes your world. It molds you. It lives and breathes beside you, walks with you every day. It diffuses throughout the air you inhale. In the endless hours of police work, it becomes all that you know.

She started to go to bed earlier. She didn't wait to

hear about my work. She couldn't listen to it anymore.
She couldn't breathe the air that I existed in.

One day she was gone. There was just stillness in
the apartment, empty drawers and cupboards where her
things had been, and the faint trace of her perfume on the
pillow where she had lain.

After she left, I accepted Lesage's invitation to talk to
him about Algeria. I didn't understand why he needed
someone like me. He sat behind his desk, his one good eye
glittering savagely and his face tensed in fury. He told me
that more and more of the work carried out in Algeria was
actually police work, not military work. The fundamental
tasks in the process of pacification were making arrests,
carrying out searches, cultivating informers, collecting
and interpreting intelligence, and questioning suspects.
He insisted that the conflict would never be won by military force. The rebels were everywhere within the local
populations. Firepower couldn't eradicate them. Only
targeted arrests could diminish their number. The main
task of the *service de renseignements* would be to locate and
nullify the rebels with surgical precision. He told me that
this was the only way the conflict could end.

Even so, Kurmakin had insisted, *you must have known*.

I remember that, as I listened to Lesage, I could feel
something like the tickle of an insect's feet running down
the back of my neck. It was gentle but insistent, something fluttering in the back of my brain and casting a
shadow across my thoughts.

Lesage put it to me like this: Most of the troops who
were out in Algeria were conscripts. Kids. Eighteen,
nineteen, twenty years old. They were doing military
service. They weren't career soldiers. They were civilians
who'd put their youth on hold for two years to serve un-

der the flag. And every time they thought they were going to be liberated, their service was extended. Another two months. And two more. They were frustrated and scared. Many had seen their comrades wounded or killed by guerrilla rebels. And these were the people who were asked to deal with the indigenous population. To arrest and interrogate. Lesage kept saying that only professional police work carried out by the army in Algeria could reverse the escalation of the conflict that was ripping the country to pieces. He said that some aspects of the work would be abhorrent. He said that our sacrifice would save countless lives and prevent unimaginable suffering in the future.

"Do you understand?" His face was screwed up with stress.

Do I understand? On the eleventh of August, under a glittering azure sky, I board the boat for Algiers. It's heaving with young conscripts who are shoved down into the hold. They cling to their chairs while the boat pitches and lurches as we leave Marseille behind. Nobody sleeps. Waves batter the sides. As the boat rolls and tosses, nausea spreads among the men. Wine is served freely. It raises spirits for a while. Some talk loudly of "smashing the *fellagha*." Then the nausea closes in again in great surges. The conscripts clutch their chairs. Their faces are totally white.

A feeling of joy breaks out when we reach Algiers. As the boat draws near, the view takes my breath away. The bay sparkles, bobbing with ships. Wide roads lined with trees stretch out toward the heart of the city. Around the port, the buildings are elegant and European in style. The harbor is thronged with life. I see people in both djellabas and Western clothes dotted between the palm trees. Among the crowds, there are hugs and fond words. People are welcomed home. Despite the brightness of the sun, and the beauty of the white city, I shiver. I can't imagine a war raging behind such a perfect scene. It seems absurd to think of streets overseen by a military police force, boulevards littered with torn flesh and broken glass, each face a blank screen of enmity, and every piece of clothing camouflage for a bomb.

We are transported by train from Algiers. The conscripts are bundled into cattle trucks without seats or even straw to lie on. I am invited to sit in a passenger carriage at the front of the train. I had imagined Algeria as arid, with dusty tracts of desert stretching into the infinite distance. Instead, what I see is what we have come to defend: vast machine-driven acres of fertile cropland, the earth overflowing with fecundity, divided up into enormous sectors of capital and parceled out among the colonists. Tobacco leaves sway gently in the warm breeze. The wind brushes the train and its touch is hot, dry, and bitter. A half-track with a machine gun mounted on it runs along the railway in front of the locomotive to protect the convoy.

As the sun begins to fall from its zenith, toppling slowly toward the horizon and ushering in the chill of evening, I see a figure on horseback standing immobile amid the tobacco fields. Tall, sunburned, and corpulent, he holds a riding crop in his left hand, and his right rests next to a pistol holstered in his belt. A colonist. He nods as the train passes by, much as a medieval king might deign to acknowledge the troops he sent to battle or to slaughter for the glory of his empire. From out of one of the conscript trucks, someone shouts, *"Salaud de colon!"*

The officer sitting next to me grins. "Sometimes the

recruits turn up with Socialist convictions," he says. "But as soon as the *fels* launch an ambush, they'll be ready to massacre them sure enough. You're going to The Farm, aren't you?"

"The Farm?"

"Al-Mazra'a. That's what it means in Arabic: *The Farm*. That's what it was originally. And, in a sense, that's what it has remained."

I nod.

"It's good work that you people do up there. War isn't just about the front line. What you do saves lives."

I awake with these scenes running through my mind. I can almost taste the rough breeze wafting off the plantations, heavy with dust and pollen, burning my throat.

My watch says six thirty. I need to be in Paris this afternoon for the hearing but I have enough time to find Lafourgue before I leave.

I drink coffee and try to shave carefully, though my hand shakes as I clutch the razor. My skin looks dried-out and gray in the mirror. Purple lines ring my eyes. I look like a killer. Like that dead-eyed soldier in the local paper.

I finish shaving. The coffee gives a jolt of color to my cheeks as it hits my veins. I stare for a second into the pits of my own eyes. They are blank and impenetrable. Nothing is reflected there. Those are the eyes I will bring before the magistrate. Dull. Drained.

Too late.

Just before seven o'clock I am knocking on Lafourgue's door, banging the wood insistently for several minutes before he finally appears in a frayed dressing gown, gray stubble bristling on his cheeks, his eyes glowering furiously. He stares at me, looking nonplussed as I try to tell him about my visit to the Château de la Hallière. I explain about the photographs of Aïcha and where they can be found. There is something rapacious in his stare.

"It's not just the evidence of violence. It's also the setting. Inside. Hidden. The perfect place to keep someone a prisoner and then to deal with the body."

"Possibly."

"It's more than possible. I found it. De la Hallière's dungeon. The entrance is on the west side of the château hidden under grass and weeds. That's where he took the pictures of Aïcha and I'm sure it's where he kept Anne-Lise too."

I expect Lafourgue to look excited but he simply purses his lips. "It could be. What did you find inside? Was there anything that would connect Anne-Lise with de la Hallière?"

"I didn't have time to go in. I heard someone coming up the road. I had to leave. But you can go there today. Take a team to do a search and proper forensics. You'll find something that places Anne-Lise there, I'm sure of it."

He looks at me with that same mixture of uncertainty and rapacity. Something tempts him, and he knows that something isn't quite right. "Okay," he says. "I'll have a look. We'll see what we can turn up. Do you want to come?"

"I can't." It sounds like my voice is quavering but it might just be the throbbing pain in my head which, since yesterday, will not subside. "I have to drive to Paris today for the preliminary hearing."

Lafourgue smiles coldly. "Let's hope they make the right decision."

As I drive away I see his curious, predatory gaze following the car out of the gates and onto the icy road.

The roads are quiet. The whole world seems sunken in the lull of winter. The tires slip and screech on the frozen tarmac. I arrive at the Palais de Justice early and sit in the car, watching people strolling past, cocooned in their everyday activities. I listen to the sound of my own breath. I watch it tracing lacy whorls in the air until it is time to go in.

I haven't arranged for legal representation and so I am assigned a duty lawyer, a palpably nervous redhead who escorts me to the examining magistrate's office. The magistrate is seated behind a broad mahogany desk strewn with files. His hair falls in a thin veil over his forehead and his eyes focus intently on me. His face is pinched, the jut of the chin and hooked nose all sharp angles. There's something scrupulous yet unforgiving in his stare.

"Good afternoon, Capitaine le Garrec," he says by way of welcome. "Do please come in and sit down."

Gallantin, dressed in full military regalia, is already seated next to me along with a lawyer looking somber in black robes.

"I feel that it would be useful to have this confrontation," the magistrate says, "while we are trying to establish what, indeed, are the key facts of this case. I understand from Capitaine Gallantin that he believes the death of Amira Khadra may simply be an unfortunate but unavoidable consequence of the pacification operation carried out by the army in Algeria. I shall attempt to ascertain whether or not this hypothesis holds water. Let us begin with the established facts of the matter. On the morning of September 13, 1959, you brought Amira's body to a local police station, wrapped in tarpaulins . . ."

The blood creeps toward my knees. I don't look at Amira at all. I just see the swelling red stain spreading toward me. The filthiness of it is sickening. It crawls into my nostrils and seeps into my throat. I can't move. There is nowhere to go. I just watch the stain extending outward, easing toward me, until it bathes my knees. I can feel the warmth of it soaking my trousers, staining my skin, but I can't move.

I can't look up either. I can sense the monumental stillness of Amira's body but I dare not look at her. I don't know how much time passes before I slowly raise my eyes. The coat I wrapped her in is sodden with blood. Her neck is streaked. Gummy, spattered patterns run up her cheeks. Her eyes are open but are completely empty, just holes punched in her face. Another hole is punched in her temple. I try not to look at the place where the bullet has ripped away bone and brain and left her sprawled lifelessly on the ground. I reach out blindly and grope for her eyes. Her face is still warm beneath my fingers. I close her eyelids to wipe that terrible stare off her face forever, and her blood stains my skin and the heat of it burns its way into my body.

Eventually I manage to stand up. I pick Amira up in my arms and carry her to the hangar. Nobody stops me. Nobody says anything. She is obviously dead so there are no questions to be answered about where we are going. It isn't strange to see someone carrying a body out of the warren at The Farm. I lay her down on the concrete floor of the old grain store and try to look at her face once more, not because I want to, not because I think I can bear to, but because it will be the last time when someone who knows her will ever look at her. After this, she will be evidence at best; at worst, she will be just one more dead Arab. Through her closed eyes and her blood-spattered skin and her shattered skull, I try to find the traces of who she was. I search out the determined line of her jaw, the eloquence of her mouth, the fine, high lines of her cheekbones, the dark pools of her eyes. I pull her onto a tarpaulin and the coat I covered her with sticks to her flesh and her skin still glows warm as if the life has not yet entirely evaporated from her and I close the tarpaulin around her body and she is gone forever and I pick up the bundle that was Amira and take it outside to one of the jeeps standing in the dust and the sun.

"I'm just taking this one out to the sands," I say to the orderly, and I try to grin at him although it feels as if my face has been anesthetized.

"Bury it good and deep, sir. You don't want to find dogs gnawing at the legs tomorrow."

I drive down the long alley out of al-Mazra'a and the sun beats down on the jeep and I realize that Amira is already decomposing. The warmth is beginning to rot her flesh, making it disintegrate, turning her into pure, decaying organic matter, wasting her back to the original nothingness. I press harder on the accelerator and the jeep bounces and jolts along the dry road.

Gallantin's lawyer starts to say something about how there is no evidence of bodies being irregularly disposed of at al-Mazra'a, but the magistrate silences him.

"What exactly did you wish to accomplish by taking the body to the police?" he asks me. "You must have been aware that this would only draw attention to you. If you could have disposed of the body discreetly, as you suggest, why did you not do so?"

"I wanted the body to be examined."

"But the cause of death was clear and there has been no dispute about that from either side: Amira Khadra was killed by a gunshot wound to the head." He casts an inquiring glance at Gallantin and the lawyer, who nods his head in confirmation.

"It wasn't the cause of death I wanted to have examined. It was the state of the body."

"And why was that?"

I pull a creased A4 envelope out of the lining of my

greatcoat, where it has been sitting for weeks now. "Maybe it would be useful just to read the pathologist's report."

"Indeed?"

I hand the envelope over to the magistrate and he pulls out three yellowing sheets of paper scrawled over with black ink. He mutters as his eyes trace the faded sentences across the paper. *Single gunshot wound to the head . . . multiple cranial fractures . . . death certainly instantaneous . . .*

I point him down to the next part of the report, which he reads out slowly.

"*Aside from the fatal wound to the head, the body showed a large number of other nonfatal injuries of varying degrees of severity. These injuries had apparently been sustained over a period of several days prior to death. The soles of the feet, the abdomen, and the face all showed multiple contusions; flesh around the nipples was not only torn but singed, as if subjected to fire or to electric current; lesions around the vagina and anus indicated rape, possibly committed multiple times and by a variety of perpetrators.*" The magistrate looks up at me. "The woman . . ."

"Amira."

"Amira had been severely mistreated *before* her death. Is this especially significant to the matter we are here to investigate, which is how she died?"

"Yes."

"Who did this to her, Capitaine le Garrec?"

"Three privates in the French army. Privates Second-Class Guérin, Bernard, and Garnier, all acting under the command of Colonel Lambert."

Gallantin's lawyer starts to speak but the magistrate cuts him off again.

"I assure you, Maître Sablier, that you will have a chance to respond fully to the comments of M. le Garrec, but first of all I feel we should let him finish giving us his account of events so that you know exactly what it is you are trying to refute." He looks back at me. "Please continue. Who are these privates that you mention?"

"They're conscripts, part of the detail at one of the camps close to al-Mazra'a. I don't know exactly how they came to Lambert's attention, but he's always on the look-out for certain characteristics in soldiers. The ones who hate the *bougnoules*, drink too much, beat up Arabs on patrols, or burn down *mechtas* for no reason. Lambert likes to have some soldiers like that on The Farm. Sometimes he brings them in at night, perhaps when activity in the sector is low and soldiers find themselves with too much time on their hands. He uses them to work on the prisoners. They're not like professional interrogators. They're completely out of control. There's no purpose or pattern to what they do."

"I see. Is there any evidence, capitaine, of such practices taking place in Algeria?"

"If I might interject here," the lawyer says. Once again, the magistrate cuts him off.

"Capitaine?"

"The state of the woman's body is evidence of the treatment she received. That's why I took her to the police station: to get an objective record of the condition of her body before she died."

"Now, Maître Sablier," the magistrate says, "you may have your say."

"It should be noted that there is not a single testimony from any member of the *service de renseignements* or the army stationed at al-Mazra'a which corroborates the accusations made by M. le Garrec." The lawyer's voice is cold. "The three soldiers in question categorically deny having performed the acts they are alleged to have committed and they are upheld in their testimonies by their superior officers, including career soldiers with highly distinguished service records. There is no evidence at all in support of M. le Garrec's claims that the suffering that this woman underwent was carried out by army personnel. The more likely explanation would be that these wounds were caused prior to her arrest by members of the FLN, whose brutality is notorious, as some sort of punishment."

"Capitaine?" The magistrate peers back at me.

"Look at the timescale indicated on the pathologist's report." I point and the magistrate reads out loud.

"All of the wounds which the body has sustained were caused within two to three days of death, judging by their condition."

I take out a second envelope from my greatcoat in which there is a single photograph. "This is a picture of the record of detentions at al-Mazra'a, showing who was brought in and when. Here you can see the entry for Amira Khadra, dated September 10. She died on September 13, having suffered three days' worth of torture. For the entirety of that time, as the detention log proves, she was imprisoned by the *service de renseignements*. For the three days in which she was brutalized, she was at the mercy of the French army, not the FLN. In her final hours, she was just another one of the animals kept on The Farm."

"That certainly doesn't prove that these three men are guilty of the offenses," says Sablier. "Nor, even if they were, that they were acting on the orders of anyone else, least of all Colonel Lambert. You yourself were at al-Mazra'a during those three days, and you were principally responsible for the detention of Amira Khadra. These injuries could very well have been caused by *you*. That would certainly explain your determination to smear the army of the Republic in this respect."

"That, maître," the magistrate says firmly, "is quite enough speculation. Save your hypotheses and your oratory for when you have a jury that might prove susceptible to them. Nevertheless," and here his hooded, intense eyes are trained upon me again, "we certainly do need to establish, and in a manner founded upon clear evidence, what happened to this young woman during her detention. Perhaps, capitaine, you can explain to me in your own words what you remember happening at al-Mazra'a."

The first time I go to see Amira she has been put in room 15. The bulb buzzes and blinks overhead. Nauseating shadows are flung across the chipped plaster of the walls and the stained concrete floor. Amira is dressed like a European. She's wearing khaki trousers and a gray shirt unbuttoned at the neck. Her dark hair hangs in rigid, polished curls around her face. Her skin glistens, burnished by a sheen of sweat. Beneath one eye is a bright, glowing welt. Her cheek is beginning to swell and force her right eye into a slit. She sees my eyes drawn to the wound and seems to shrug, as if it's nothing. She must already be preparing herself for what's to come, knowing it will be unimaginably worse than a simple blow to the face.

In the Resistance, I spent a long time thinking about this moment, trying to prepare myself to deal with it. Lesage managed it. He didn't talk even when they gouged out his eye. I was never in this position. I never found out if I could be silent or not.

I see Amira preparing herself. She must have been trained to do that. She has thought about this moment before. That means she is involved. She hasn't been brought here by mistake.

She is guilty, according to what the French colonists call law. And now she is going to confront the darkness that she has pictured many times in her own mind. She is going to find out whether she can be silent.

I ask her in Arabic how she is and she laughs and replies in perfect French.

"Is concern for my well-being really why you're here?"

"I'm here to find out what you know. What you can tell me."

"And if I don't feel very talkative?"

She tries to make it sound nonchalant but I can hear the tremor in her throat. Her skin is smooth and unlined. It glows with life. She must be about nineteen or twenty. I sit down beside her and offer her water to drink.

"Officer," she says, and I realize she is afraid of the quiet, as if she can feel it thrumming emptily in her head, waiting to be filled with her nightmares, "why are you doing this?"

"Doing what?"

She sips at the water and I can see her hand shake.

"Killing people to protect your colonial empire. Do you know what they teach us in school? That France is the mother of civilization. She brought technology and medicine to Algeria to save us. Does it look like that to you?"

I shake my head. She looks surprised, as if she'd expected an argument or an outburst of fury. She looks like a bright student preparing for a debate. This is probably the world she has always known: classrooms, libraries, lecture halls—implicit monuments to the ideals of progress and reason. Now there is only The Farm. She will find out here exactly what her education and its Enlightenment values amount to, living in a world without logic or reason, buried in the silence of the earth.

"Let me be absolutely clear," the magistrate says. "Did you yourself have any role in, or did you personally witness, the bodily harm that was done to Amira Khadra?"

"No."

"Then how can you be sure that the incidents took place as you describe, and that the parties whom you allege to be the perpetrators are, in fact, guilty?"

I talk to Amira for about two hours on that first day. I don't find out any precise information about her work as an agent de liaison.

I can't bring myself to ask her. I have known from the first minutes I spent with her that she is involved with the nationalist cause. She follows it because it chimes with the ideas of freedom and human dignity that France is supposed to embody. I find out that she grew up in Algiers and that she used to watch the European ladies in the streets when she was a little girl and it made her feel dirty. I find out that the FLN scares her because of their radical beliefs. I imagine that if she supports them it is because she sees it as the only way that the colonists will be forced off Algerian soil, and she wants to live in a country where girls don't grow up hating the color of their own skin or the sound of their own language.

I leave her in the early evening and write up a report for Lambert saying that she has some very minimal knowledge of fellagha activity through anecdotal means, but that she plays no role herself within the organization of the FLN. It is the best I can do. Lambert will be more inclined to interrogate her himself if I deny all possible links with the rebels. My report is intended to play for time.

"What did you imagine would be the consequence of this initial interrogation?" The magistrate's face is hawk-like and he looks intent on ripping the truth out of me.

"I thought it would get Amira a few days of peace. I asked to be able to check out some details of her story."

"And that was the tenth?"

"Yes."

"When did you next see her?"

"The next time I saw her was the afternoon of the twelfth. I'd cross-checked intelligence about some of her supposed associates, and I wanted to go over the facts with her. I was dragging the investigation out, thinking that it could go on for several days as long as it looked like there was some progress."

In the warren there are no times of day. Outside, the afternoon heat is starting to gutter in the fading daylight. In Amira's cell there is

just the bulb's eternal glare. Her face is badly swollen. I step back in
shock when I see her. I struggle to pick out the features that had been
so clear two days ago. She can't move her jaw to speak. Something
is flickering in her eyes. I stare into them. The flickering is nothing
rational. It's like a spasm, a madness playing on her nerves and eating
away at her control. Her gaze darts past me and through me.

I hold her head very gently. I feel her rock in my arms. I keep
talking to her, murmuring softly and insistently, as if I too have become afraid of silence. Eventually she stops twitching. Her jaw moves
very slowly. Her face distorts in pain with the effort.

"Did you . . . come . . . to see?"

"No. I didn't know . . . I didn't know . . ."

She closes her eyes. It doesn't matter to her. It only matters to
me. She doesn't need to hear one more colonist trying to keep his conscience clean. Her hair is matted with sweat and blood. The waves
have become clumps. Thick, shapeless tangles.

"None of this provides us with an answer to the question," the magistrate says. "How do you know the names
of the men who did that to her?"

I want to ask her what happened but the question is absurd.
The answer is written into her fissured, discolored skin. Al-Mazra'a
is brutal, but there is something sadistic in the way she has been attacked. Something deviant. As if this is a personal message from
Lambert.

I don't know what to say to her so I ask her if she knows who
came.

She nods. She tried not to look at their faces. It was too much to
meet their eyes looking into hers. She couldn't watch them watching
her, remembering her pain, carrying those moments out of the warren and back into the world in their memories. She stared away. She
stared down at their sweat-stained green shirts. She stared at the tags
where their names and ranks were written. She looked at the letters
and the numbers and that was all she saw.

194 of JAMES BRYDON

"M. le juge," Gallantin interjects, "the capitaine's remarks cannot but place in doubt his allegiance to France. He appears to be almost admitting to collusion with the enemy."

The magistrate nods, noting the objection without passing any judgment upon it, and gestures toward me.

Amira seems to grow tired. Her head nods on her breast as if sleep is washing over her. Then she starts awake and her eyes roll in fear. She whispers, "Can you . . . get . . . me out?"

Not alive. Lambert will never let me leave with her.

"Maybe. I don't know." It was all I could say.

I glance around at the people in the magistrate's office. My red-faced lawyer is adhering to his promise of silence as long as what I say doesn't harm my defense. Gallantin's predatory stare challenges mine. The magistrate's eyes are keen and calm.

"I didn't think about allegiance. With hindsight, I don't think that France would be well served by"—suddenly my voice seems to echo around the empty corners of the room—"by torturing a girl barely past school age."

"That," Gallantin's lawyer replies, "is an allegation which you have made, but which remains without the least substantiating evidence."

The magistrate sighs. "Maître, we are aware of that. There is no need to repeat it each time Capitaine le Garrec speaks."

I only vaguely hear what they are saying. My voice continues. It sounds hollow as I talk over the top of them. The mechanical buzz of it is directed at no one in particular.

"When I look at those days in September, or even my whole time in Algeria, I think I have become a coward. I don't know how or when, but it must have happened. I could see how much pain and danger Amira was in. I could see that moment in her eyes when choking fear rotted the rational brain within her. The world made no sense to her. She had lost her grip. Yet I did nothing. I wrote reports. I tried to see Lambert again. I even sent a dispatch to Lesage asking for more authority to control the interrogation of suspects. Useless, time-wasting activity. The actions of a desperate, beaten, bureaucratic man. And all that time I left Amira alone. And so I can say that whatever else I was during my time in Algeria, more than anything else I was a fool and a coward . . ."

Gallantin nods and starts to open his mouth to speak, but the magistrate cuts him off abruptly.

"Capitaine, in the darkest hours of France's recent history, you exposed yourself to great danger to protect her honor. No one in this room who did not heed that call, as you did, to struggle for liberation, has the right to call your courage into question. We shall not do so. When did you next see Amira Khadra?"

"When I next saw her, I knew it was over."

She was slumped on the chair she had been tied to. She had been stripped and her skin looked wan in the glare of the bulb overhead. Her hands and feet were swollen. They were so purple that the color of the fingers seemed to blend in with the crimson nail polish she was wearing. There was piss and shit and blood on the chair and the floor beneath her. It had stained her skin and the wood she sat on. I thought I should look away. I shouldn't see her, because even just looking was violating her. I covered her with a coat. As I put it around her shoulders, I felt the glacial, sweat-soaked expanse of her skin. My fingers trembled.

Her eyes were glazed. She didn't know that I was there. She had fled from her pain into some internal realm and she couldn't get back. I had to try to find her again. I spoke to her softly. I can't remember a single one of the words. It was just noise. My mouth was parched and I could barely tear my tongue from my palate. I stared into her glazed eyes and hoped to see something stir in their depths. There was nothing: only the tiny, distorted shadows I cast with my hands as I moved to touch her. I sat with her for a while and tried to keep talking. I held her head in my hands. I have no idea how much time passed, but after a while the weight of her head made my fingers feel leaden.

In the isolation of her cell, my voice was the only thing living. I told her that she was fighting for the freedom of her country. I said that her struggle was meaningful and that the lives destroyed by it were not lost in vain. I wanted her to hear that there was a purpose to what was happening to her. I wanted to piece back together the ties that bound her to the world beyond the walls of the warren.

She couldn't hear anything I said. She had retreated from a world that had hurt her in ways she couldn't understand. I had to keep speaking. It had become an incantation. It dulled my own thinking and feeling. I insisted that she had served her cause with courage and would continue to do so. I stared down and saw the cracked nail polish on her bluish fingers and heard, reverberating in my memory, her bright, educated words. My mind was suddenly full of images of the women of the fellagha, robed all in black, hunched over their cooking pots and washboards and surrounded by the uncannily quiet children of the poor and hungry.

I kept talking but all I could think was that there was nowhere for Amira. Not this European abomination in which she was merely a sideshow absurdity, a Hellenized native. But nor could she exist in the world that was coming to Algeria when the colonists had been driven out and the FLN took power.

My voice dried up. I couldn't say anything to her. I just let her head roll between my hands, and her skin seemed both chilled and feverish to the touch, as if the dead air in the basements of al-Mazra'a had sucked all the heat out of it, but underneath a devouring, quenchless fire was raging.

The magistrate's voice seems to travel across a great distance to reach me: "Assuming, capitaine, that your version of events is accurate—and we shall let M. Gallantin have his say in this matter in good time—could you perhaps explain to me how you were able to stay with the girl for so long?"

"I tried to tend to her. I gave instructions that I should be left alone with her for the time being so that I could get her in a suitable state for further interrogation. I remember screaming at Djamel and some of the French soldiers. I don't know what the words were. They didn't even matter. It was the noise and the fury that mattered. I think I was trying to say that Amira was an important source of information and now she was in no state to be able to answer my questions. All I remember is the expressions on their faces. There were little twitches of shock. Djamel's eyes were wide and a tic fluttered in his cheek. I don't know if they were scared *of* me or *for* me. I must have seemed frantic."

I shut myself back in with Amira and I tried to find the words again that were like a lullaby, a spell to stave off the dark. I said that the war would end. That peace comes when war ends, not just another different, unending war. My throat was raw where I had been shouting and the air was dry and thick with dust and I could barely breathe.

Once again I was alone with Amira and I just sat cradling her head, trying to bring her back from wherever she had escaped to, sunken in herself and far from The Farm. I had no sense of time. I couldn't move and the light was unchanging. Lambert annihilated time in the warren. It seemed never to pass at all. Then came the stifling fear that days, even months, were slipping away while you rotted down here in the dark. I felt my fingers lock and go numb. My joints began to ache but I didn't dare to move away from Amira. I didn't dare to let her go.

I think hours must have passed. Outside it would have been deep in the middle of the night. In the basement of the warren the night didn't end. I saw Amira's eyelids flutter and she coughed. Slowly and painfully, she blinked. Something glowed briefly in her eyes.

I pulled my coat tight around her shoulders. I tried to take her hand but she flinched and started as if I had attached another electrode to her skin. Her teeth clacked together. She stared up foggily and her eyes swam in the murk. She seemed to strain to make them fix on me. When she spoke it was in Arabic so broken and faint that I could hardly hear, and her voice seemed to drown in her throat.

"End it now."

Those were the three words she said to me. I heard them clearly even though I could barely make out her voice. I tried to keep talking to her. I touched her cheek and forced words out of myself, trying to reach whatever fragment of her conscious mind had surfaced long enough to whisper that one sentence to me. It didn't matter what I said. Amira wasn't listening. She just jerked her head slightly, almost mechanically, as if shaking off a twinge of pain, and then she said it again.

"End it now."

I kept hold of her head. I was too scared to move. I could hardly even breathe. I don't know how long I remained frozen like that, pretending that if I remained perfectly still I wouldn't have to listen to the words Amira had spoken and the one lucid, earnest wish she had dragged out of the blackness. I listened to the throbbing of footsteps in the corridors and the hum of the lightbulb above us. I felt Amira's head jerk and twitch between my hands. I couldn't tell whether she was shaking from the pain in her body or the shock of memory now that the mist in her consciousness was dissipating and she was returning to The Farm.

My fingers were totally numb by the time she opened her eyelids again. Her eyes were burning. She stared up at me and seemed almost to nod her head. Her mouth was swollen and she struggled to form the words with her half-paralyzed jaw.

"*Why are you waiting . . . ?*"

"*I can't,*" *I tried to tell her.* "*I can't.*" *She didn't seem to be listening but I felt her head twitch again. I could sense that it was already over. After three days in al-Mazra'a, she would never again be whatever she had been before. They had made her into something else. Amira was gone.*

I unclipped my gun and pressed it into her hands. Her skin was rubbery where the circulation had been cut off for hours. I tried to close her fingers around the butt but she couldn't grip it. Her hand lay limply in mine and I stared down at the weird bluish skin that looked as if the whole hand were bruised. Her fingers were lifeless. Her voice was soft and still and it floated on the rattle of her breath.

"*You . . .*" *Then, after a long pause, she found one single word, the last one she ever spoke.* "*Please.*"

Her head fell back. Her hair was stuck to her face in grimy, bloody streaks. That was all there was. The Farm took her out of the world and enclosed her within its walls. Her universe became the disintegration of her own body and the limits of its pain.

I held her. The minutes drained into hours and the sounds in the corridors stilled and eventually I felt that, somewhere above ground, the sun must be coming up, glinting red on the vast horizon.

I saw Amira's cracked nail polish for the last time. I took my hands away from her face and found that her blood had tattooed my fingers. I picked up the gun that she wasn't able to hold and placed it against her temple where the pulse of life still beat faintly within her, inside her head where her memories and her self abided too, as frail and indomitable as that pulse, and I shot her.

There is a strange silence in the magistrate's office. Then the voice of Maître Sablier starts up again, saying something about how I have even confessed to giving a weapon to a detainee, an act close to treason. My court-appointed lawyer now breaks his own silence, his querulous voice cutting across Sablier's outrage and asking for time to consult with me before the hearing goes any further.

The magistrate simply lifts his hand to call for silence. "I think that Capitaine le Garrec has been admirably lucid," he remarks. "I can see no reason for us to start bandying about absurdities such as treason or asking him to reconsider his testimony. I should like to ask you a question, however, capitaine. Do you feel that the circumstances you describe, and the conditions in al-Mazra'a, mitigate or justify the shooting of the girl, to which you have in fact confessed?"

"No."

"And yet you have described those things in great detail. You have wanted us to hear about them."

"Not to exonerate myself, M. le juge. I am guilty of her death. Amira was right. I couldn't avoid it. Whatever I did, I was always guilty. That was in the nature of things in Algeria."

"But you could have tried to help the girl recover."

"For what? The rest of her life was just however long she could stand being tortured in al-Mazra'a. There was no other way out. She made a decision. She told me what she wanted."

"You could have disagreed."

"Like a proper colonist. Isn't that our pathology? We build a hell for the natives and then think we know better than them how to exist in it. She knew what she was saying. She chose how things would end."

"But she was barely conscious, her mind addled by pain. She had no idea what she was saying."

"She knew how it ended. Under a tarpaulin in the grange. One way or another. This was the way she chose."

"And yet you still consider yourself guilty of her murder."

My lawyer starts to tell me that I should on no account answer the question before we have consulted.

"I can't answer the question. I don't know anymore what words like *guilty* and *murder* mean. Not the way they're being used in this room, or anywhere in this Palais de Justice. In any case, I didn't come here today to ask for mercy. I came so that people could hear the truth. I wanted the truth to be written down somewhere official, where it might remain. That is all."

The magistrate nods. "Nevertheless, the decision about whether or not a crime has been committed—and who may or may not be guilty—remains one which I must take. And we shall now see what the capitaine and the eager Maître Sablier have to say from their side. They have certainly been anxious enough to advance their version of events, and now they shall have the chance . . ."

I don't take in a single word that is spoken after I finish giving my own testimony. I sit through the rest of the hearing in a kind of daze. At times, the magistrate asks me whether I want to counter anything Gallantin or Sablier has said but I just shake my head. I feel a sort of light-headed relief, like after vomiting. The discussions must take hours but I can only remember a few minutes of them by the time I get out of the Palais de Justice. I stand on the stone steps facing the city, rocked by the wind, and my senses seem sharper than they have for days. My vision is clearer. The tiredness that has clogged my brain and my retinas for as long as I can remember seems to ebb away. I gulp in the gray city air and let the cold pinch me back to wakefulness. My red-faced lawyer stands behind me, squinting youthfully at me and weighing up his words as he shakes his head.

"Why did you tell the magistrate that you shot the girl? Isn't it going to be very easy to condemn you now?"

"Perhaps."

"Is that what you want?"

"I don't care too much either way. Something that I think is true has been committed to the records today. And now, if the judge decides that there's a case against me, he knows what will come out. It won't be easy for the army, even if a lot of people will refute what I say. There's enough evidence to make things complicated, and to attract attention."

"It won't be easy for you either."

I leave him standing on the stairway with his brow knotted in confusion. He stares after me with something like despair in his eyes.

By the time I am approaching Sainte-Élisabeth it has begun to snow again. The air is aflutter with white. The flakes smother the earth, settling in sheets and veiling the ground beneath. The clouds are a violent gray, presaging a storm drifting in from the sea.

Images flash in front of my eyes so vividly that I lose sight of the road winding past the cliffs and into town: fields alive with corn; green stalks of maize towering above me; the hum of insects on the pollen-thick air. The colors of childhood float eerily against the desolate winter air.

Each step back toward the past only makes it recede further and augments its strangeness.

Snow continues to fall in the quiet afternoon and lies voicelessly upon the ground.

Once again, I think of Rachel. Four a.m. in our Paris apartment. Her sleepless eyes are glazed and bloodshot.

She stares at me as I come through the door but she is too tired or too numb to find any words.

"I thought you would have gone to bed," I say.

Her bloodless lips are tight with anger. "What was it this time?" she asks.

What was it? It was what it always is. Nothing. Everything. Life.

I'd had Babette sitting in my office, her body shaken by sobs and welts and cuts running down her back. She was a prostitute in her late thirties and nearing the end of the line. She was never an informant but she'd sometimes share information with me that she'd picked up on the streets. Jean-Jacques, her pimp, had beaten her with his belt for refusing to turn a trick with a client who'd wanted to tie her up. She didn't know why she'd refused. She just panicked and so Jean-Jacques taught her a lesson. One minute she told me she hated him and the next she said she deserved it and he'd done the right thing.

I'd asked around and had a tip-off that Jean-Jacques had been spotted in a bar in Pigalle. We scoured the area until nearly midnight. At about one, we picked him up in a back room playing cards. We took him to the police station and questioned him for two hours about a stabbing in Belleville from a week before. He was drunk and tired. We told him there were witnesses who put him at the scene of the crime. He got so agitated about fighting the murder charge that he admitted to having beaten Babette.

I just remember Rachel's tired brown eyes like two deep pools swallowing all the light. "That's it? That's why you're home at four in the morning? Because a whore got beaten? That's all?" Her voice cracks and fades away.

She left soon after. I came home late and now there was only silence and shadow in the apartment. The rooms were empty and cold. For a while, I even missed the noise and the blame. Then the quiet became all I knew, all I could remember.

At the police station I find Lafourgue in a noncommittal mood. De la Hallière has been brought in and is sitting calmly behind a table in one of the interview rooms. His long fingers stroke the end of a cigarette and he stares at a wall. A faint smirk of satisfaction plays across his face.

Lafourgue looks at me intently and shakes his head. "I think you'd better come out to the château with me. I want to show you what we found out there. You can tell me what you make of it."

He is silent in the car as we drive. I wonder if he has found anything to prove that de la Hallière kept Anne-Lise there. He shows me up to the bedroom I searched last night and asks me if this is the room I meant.

I nod.

He walks over to the bookshelves and pulls out the copy of *Justine*. He leafs through the pages and lets the pictures fall into his hands.

"Here you are. Are these the ones you were talking about?"

I look down. In my hand are some old photographs of a naked Arab woman standing in front of a wall. She peers vacantly in front of her. She looks a little embarrassed. She doesn't look scared. She stretches out her arms but they aren't bound. Her skin isn't torn.

She isn't Aïcha.

I start to shake my head. My fingers rifle through the little pile of pictures. They all show the same woman. In some she is naked. In others she wears frills or furs.

She often looks blank. In one picture, dressed as a maid, she tries to pout as she pretends to reach up to do some dusting and her lacy skirt rides up to show her buttocks.

Aïcha isn't anywhere in the whole set of images. It's barely even pornography.

I start to shake my head again and I look up at Lafourgue, who just shrugs.

"Let's go and look at the dungeon," he offers.

In the daylight, I can see a simple wooden door and steps leading down.

"After you," Lafourgue gestures.

I walk down the stairs. There is just a faint smell of damp. The wood creaks a little beneath my feet. The floor at the bottom is earth. I step slowly into the darkness. I reach out my hands. I touch wood. A great wooden rack.

I squint into the dark. My hands rub up against smooth, glassy curves. Nestled between the wooden slats are rows and rows of bottles.

Lafourgue is suddenly right beside me. "It's just a wine cellar," he says. "Nothing that looks like a dungeon at all. Was this all you found or was there something else?"

I can't find any words. I can hear Lafourgue's voice buzzing and echoing in my ears.

"I don't know . . . I thought that . . ."

He rests a hand on my shoulder. "Look, you were under real strain with the hearing today. Sometimes this job gets to you at the best of times. It isn't hard to start seeing ghosts. But they're not there. Anyway, if this is all we've got, there's nothing we can hold de la Hallière with. I'll have to let him go."

"I'm sorry," I say. "I don't know why I thought . . . I'm not sure what happened." I walk back up the wooden staircase and out into the daylight. It seems immense, blinding. I try to think back to last night. What I sensed in the musty air rising from the cellar was the faint odor of my own past. The underground cells of al-Mazra'a. A dead girl, her blood leaching out into the dark. For a moment, it was enough to make me almost mad.

The road home winds in front of me, a white streak in the white immensity of the snow. It glows on the ground and irradiates the night. Now that my head has cleared, I can see how little I have really discovered about Anne-Lise. The fragments of her past have led nowhere. I have stumbled through the investigation, constantly confusing Anne-Lise and Amira in my mind, worming ever deeper into the endless well of my own guilt.

And all the while, Anne-Lise slipped away.

DAY EIGHT

I watch through the window as the first light of dawn begins to diffuse through the night. My mind is endued with the same clarity as yesterday after the hearing. My thoughts are restless, grasping for something I can't quite find. The unease it provokes drives me out of the house and sets me pacing the coastal paths between expanses of heather shrouded in snow while the pale sunrise flickers fitfully on the horizon. In the damp breath of the mist, I am the only thing living.

For the first time in weeks, I can see clearly, without my eyelids feeling leaden and the world swimming queasily in front of me. The single thing about Anne-Lise's death which could still lead back to her killer is the mutilation. Why hack the flesh out of her side? Perhaps it is now too late to find the answer. Time has cast its shadow on the past, effacing it from memory and then from existence, just as the bed of heather on which Anne-Lise's corpse lay has been erased by the glowing silence of the snow. Whatever my mind is groping for can no longer be found. There is nothing more to do here.

I touch Anne-Lise's picture in my pocket and determine to return it to her mother.

Sarah answers the door with a flash of expectation in her eyes. Her throat is tight as she speaks. "I heard about them arresting that Nazi yesterday. Does that mean . . . ? Was it him who . . . ?"

I shake my head gently. "We don't know yet. The police are looking into it, but there's no sign that he did."

Something heaves in Sarah's throat. "Right," she says. "Did you . . . then . . . Did you come to look for evidence again?"

There is hope in her eyes. I nod. I can't say that I came to bring the photograph back. She points me up the stairs. A week ago, this was where I began, in Anne-Lise's room, weirdly preserved in this one meaningless moment that became frozen forever. I sit down on the bed and feel the springs creak beneath me. Anne-Lise must have heard that same noise each night when she lay down to sleep. I wonder what dreams came to her in the isolation and the silence. I reach over idly to the shelves and flick through some of her books, scanning the words her eyes have scanned, watching the fine, precise lines of her handwriting where a passage captured her attention. She had labored long over the following lines from Rilke:

> Sing nicht, sing nicht, du fremder Mann:
> Es wird mein Leben sein.
> Du singst mein Glück und meine Müh,
> mein Lied singst du und dann:
> Mein Schicksal singst du viel zu früh,
> so daß ich, wie ich blüh und blüh,—
> es nie mehr leben kann.

> Er sang. Und dann verklang sein Schritt,—
> er mußte weiterziehn;
> und sang mein Leid, das ich nie litt,
> und sang mein Glück, das mir entglitt,

und nahm mich mit und nahm mich mit—
und keiner weiß wohin . . .

What did it mean to her, that strange evocation of the passing singer in the tongue of her absent father? How did she understand his uncanny intimacy with the girl and the enchantment he held for her? And where did she think he carried her away to in the end, never to be found again? I pull out the volume of Baudelaire that Erwann gave her. I wonder what she found in that darkness. The gilded paper glows beneath my fingers. The smell of the leather is fresh and sweet. At the top of one of the pages, a hand other than Anne-Lise's has written:

But oh, self-traitor, I do bring
The spider love, which transubstantiates all,
And can convert manna to gall. (Donne)

I read the words without breathing. *The spider love. J'ai peur de l'araignée.* I read the poem underneath, "A Celle qui est trop gaie," and when I reach the last three verses it feels like my heart has stopped.

Ainsi je voudrais, une nuit,
Quand l'heure des voluptés sonne,
Vers les trésors de ta personne,
Comme un lâche, ramper sans bruit,

Pour châtier ta chair joyeuse,
Pour meurtrir ton sein pardonné,
Et faire à ton flanc étonné
Une blessure large et creuse,

Et, vertigineuse douceur!
À travers ces lèvres nouvelles,
Plus éclatantes et plus belles,
T'infuser mon venin, ma soeur!

It feels like a flood is washing over me. *And make in your astonished flank / a wide and hollow wound.* I look again at the handwriting at the top of the page. Precise, flowing, elegant.

Erwann.

It must be him. He bought her the book. He quoted poetry about love.

He scared her.

I place the book carefully back on the shelf. My feet cannot get down the stairs quickly enough. I am out of the door before Sarah can say a single word to me.

The car crunches through the snow. The whiteness seems immense. I can barely see the road as everything blurs into one unified and glowing expanse. My breath shines against the distance. The weak daylight falters against the glassy, dark mass of the sea, which stretches like a planetary wasteland toward the horizon. The roads are silent and empty as if everything living is cowering away, hiding from the winter.

By the time I reach Erwann's house I feel calmer. I try to forget about the Château de la Hallière and the panic that gripped me in the cellar. That madness has left me. I can see the lines of the trees and the snowcapped roofs clearly now. I knock firmly on Erwann's door. I knock again. The cold has frozen the wood to iron. No one answers. Inside, the house is dark.

I turn the handle and push. It is just frustrated instinct rather than hope, but to my surprise, the door opens. I step inside. The air in the hallway seems thick with dust. I wonder whether this is where Anne-Lise died, choking, with this fusty stench in her throat.

I call out. No answer. There is only a peculiar quiet disturbed by the murmurs in my own mind.

I go through to the lounge and sit down at the desk, opening the drawers one by one to find a sample of Erwann's handwriting. I pull out a leather-bound journal. Across each page, flowing, precise characters stretch out in immaculate rows. It is the same hand as in Anne-Lise's book. Each entry here has the date traced perfectly above it. They go back months, to well before Anne-Lise's death. My hands are shaking as I turn the pages, looking for her name.

10/09/58

A potentially interesting occurrence has punctuated the dreariness of yet another rentrée. For once, something threatens to enliven the impression of repetition which attends the beginning of each new year. This is the time when the revelation of futility is most acute. I contemplate the prospect of the next ten months spent iterating the same ideas that I have uttered so many times before and that each year the pupils are less and less able to comprehend. I read voraciously in the weeks before term begins, trying to find purpose in the rediscovery of Kant and Plato. This year, for the most part, it is the eternal return of the same. Rows of vacant eyes stare at me during lessons. I read essays of almost infantile incoherence with a sense of rage that blends quickly into despair.

Yet something is different. I have inherited the Aurigny girl and her eyes are alert and they seem to bore into me as I speak. Already I can sense burning within her some great longing for knowledge, a genuine and almost literal thirst to read, to understand, and thus to better grasp existence.

She has a reputation for being clever, but despite the fact that she commented lucidly on Hegel today, I have seen no evidence yet of any special ability. She also has a reputation for loose morals. Although this seems to rest upon hearsay and jealousy, when I observed her today in her tiny tartan skirt and with her bare legs pressed on the school bench, she looked very much the part. And yet it is certainly not this which made me pay attention to her, while her classmates are still to emerge from faceless anonymity. Of them I saw nothing but fragments of petulant or eager expressions. As they spoke, I heard nothing other than the predictable croak of their voices. They wield no power at all over my memory, whereas the Aurigny girl, I cannot deny it, exerts a sort of traction over my recollection and draws my mind ever back to her.

What is it about her that makes it appear as if, in the dullness of the classroom and the numbing abjection of the adolescent mind, Anne-Lise Aurigny somehow shines? For nearly two decades, all there has been is the trivial, half-understood philosophizing and the self-discovery of teenagers filling the air around me. The Aurigny girl is different. She seems to disregard her audience, not to feign indifference or superiority, but because she sounds as if she is genuinely thinking when she speaks. She carefully works out the permutations of an argument or a theory rather than trying to display herself to others. Never mind that her grasp of Hegel is subtle and that she has mastered the terminology in German! (Although it did afford me a certain pleasure, watching her cradle in her marbled lips such words as "Weltgeist" and "Erhebungseffekt"!) This, though, is little more than a titillation, a trivial enlivenment of the taedium vitae.

It does not explain the constant return of my thoughts to this one girl.

No, what arrests my attention, what drags my eyes back to her time and time again, wrenching my mind from philosophical abstraction, is the naked yearning that is almost palpable within her. It seems as if an abateless desire for knowledge flames inside her. This drive, this longing to apprehend the arcana of existence, this Wissensdurst . . . this is what separates her from the dismal multitude and drags my attention toward her with the gravitational pull of a collapsing star.

The light outside is watery and thin. An eerie sheen reflects off the snow.

I flick through the pages of the journal looking for Anne-Lise's name. I can hear the breath wheezing in my lungs and my fingers skitter and tremble as they turn the pages.

25/09/58

Already it has become clear that the intellectual capacities of the Aurigny creature far outstrip those of her classmates (although such an achievement in itself would not merit any special attentiveness on my part). Today I questioned her on Nietzsche and I made her stand up, since the experience of intellectual interrogation is doubtless best accompanied by physical discomfort. I want my pupils to be aware of the uselessness of the body as the mind gropes ever upward. They can thereby not only understand but actually incarnate the age-old dichotomy between spirit and flesh!

Nothing could shatter her calm. She rose languidly. Her skin was soft jasmine and her hair was a torrent. As she raised herself, I saw the little wriggle of her hips and the rise and fall

of her breasts beneath some clingy item that is no doubt pop-
ular in women's magazines dealing with matters of fashion.
She stood before me. Her eyes were soft and bright and her
body was held hard and still. The contrast, the chiaroscuro,
was quite exquisite! That indomitable posture she struck was
so gloriously offset by the softness and the yielding contours of
her body! I drank in the joys of her proximity to me. I felt like
Donatello staring at a naked shepherd boy before him and
preparing to transform that vision into art.

For a while I asked her nothing. I just let her stand like
that, majestic and unfazed. Waiting did not perturb her, but
not because she exuded the cheap defiance of other teenagers.
She disdains the leering mask behind which their ignorance
seeks refuge. With Anne-Lise there is a control, a mastery
of thought which leads to a concomitant mastery of action.
She stood perfectly still, waiting for me to speak. I simply let
the silence flow on, savoring the way this moment had been
framed: the statuesque girl who had to stand at my bidding
and await my pleasure.

Finally, I asked her about On the Genealogy of Morals.
How does Nietzsche define interpretation in the work?

"As domination," she said, "overpowering, reinscribing.
The meaning of anything is what is forced upon it by power.
What we see and understand are the effects of power and
domination."

What, then, of the search for truth?

"It is the ultimate expression of slave morality. All forms
of seeing and knowing are perspectival and not absolute. Ob-
jectivity is a myth. The search for truth is a lie; worse, it is a
cocoon. We shelter our weakness in it. Knowledge is inter-
pretation and all interpretation is an act of violence."

So how can we escape from the myth of truth?

"Art. The knowing lies of art free us from the false belief

in truth. Art wears its falseness openly. Here we find aware-
ness of untruth and pleasure in it."

14/10/58

Today Anne-Lise came to speak to me at the end of school.
I had not expected it. The final lesson of the day had been
an ordeal of drudgery as the winter night set in and lulled
everyone to sleep. I looked out upon a sea of drooping eyelids. When the bell rang it was a deliverance, especially for
me. Anne-Lise lingered after the others had filed out, fin-
gering her books slowly, pretending to organize her papers. I
watched her and I too pretended to gather up my papers and
books long after the stupefied horde had disappeared. They
straggled out, desperate to return to their identical lives with
their transient fashions and friendships and gossip forgotten
as soon as it is uttered.

I knew that Anne-Lise wanted to talk to me; however, as
she pawed awkwardly at her bag and shuffled her feet, I began to realize that she did not simply want to talk. She wanted
to tell me something that made her nervous. She chewed her
lip and it was almost painful. I could feel my skin tingle as I
saw her teeth sinking into the flesh around her mouth, and in
spite of the numbing wave of heat flooding from the radiator,
I shivered.

She finally moved toward me. She started to say something about wanting to study philosophy but doubting her
capacity to succeed. She looked down at the floor while she
spoke and knotted her fingers together. She looked as if she
were confessing a crime to me and I said something noncommittal about how she seemed troubled and waited for her to
speak again.

There was trust in the way she regarded me. Her eyes
were soft and they washed over me. It felt like radiation. It

contaminated me. I could feel the cells, the molecules, the minuscule fragments of my being mutating and metastasizing. I looked for one more second into the vacuum of Anne-Lise's brown eyes and then I had to turn away.

She moved to speak and I saw only her hair. I felt its scent collect around my face, clog my nose, slip at first gently into my throat, and invade my lungs. When she spoke her voice was naked, stripped of all defiance and indifference.

She told me that she felt like she was abandoning her mother. The guilt of it kept her awake at night, but no amount of guilt would stop her leaving Sainte-Élisabeth. She asked me, "How can you stand living here? Knowing this is all you do." She kept on speaking, saying that guilt made her afraid but that it was easier to live with guilt than with regret. Her mother had lived with both her whole life, but it was regret that had twisted and shriveled her. She would accept any guilt rather than live like that.

She asked me to give her extra work to help her pass the entrance exams. I don't remember what words crossed my lips. I only know from her bright, open stare and the tiny flicker of joy that ran across her mouth that I must have agreed. She made some rapturous sound, not even a word, and she turned back. I looked up and saw her float back over to her books. This time she picked them up quickly. She glanced back at me as she walked out. There was trust in her eyes and I shuddered when I saw it. After she left I sat down slowly and tried to collect my own papers but I found I could no longer move.

I waited there, in the classroom. Outside it was night. I should have left long ago but I could still smell her in the air. Her sweetness lingered in the dusk. It felt like a hand pressed over my nose and mouth that was slowly, gently choking me.

15/12/58

There is something in the mythical darkness of Germany that draws Anne-Lise. It magnetizes her and holds her enraptured. Perhaps it is a corresponding darkness in herself, although there is no trace of it in the elegance of her everyday movements. Perhaps it is the darkness of her own past—her father, the Nazi, his origins shrouded in uncertainty—that draws her into the glorified violence of Nietzsche and the desolate woodlands where Goethe's Erlkönig tempts and touches and murders children. As she quotes the lines, her body shudders and her voice lingers, half in love, half in horror, over the words:

> "Ich liebe dich, mich reizt deine schöne Gestalt;
> Und bist du nicht willig, so brauch' ich Gewalt."
> Mein Vater, mein Vater, jetzt faßt er mich an!
> Erlkönig hat mir ein Leids getan.

The term is ending and I shall not see Anne-Lise again until I have passed through what seems like an unending corridor of days. I want to look forward to the peace of the holidays; the long hours in pleasant isolation; the chance to work and read. Yet when I think of Anne-Lise I see my house not as quiet, but as empty. The minutes stretch in front of me in a monotonous parade. What felt like peace feels like isolation. The world is elsewhere, in homes where people huddle together, wrapped in the glow of firelight and their own warmth.

I wonder how I will get through not the days, but the hours, the minutes, the seconds, the infinite, fragmenting moments that separate me from January and from her. Loneliness preys upon me and plays tricks on my mind. I feel as if

I am aging, inexorably graying, withering, imprisoned in the decay of my body. My life is a failure and a waste, a succession of squandered, lonely moments. No one will grieve when I die.

Without her, I lie awake in the darkness and think about the void of my past. It has brought me to this moment unmarried and unpublished, an unnecessary and soon-to-be-extinguished pulse of cells, blood, yearning, hatred, and words. A human life like any other. A trivial thing imbued with the notion of greatness. An ant that learned to read and write.

Anne-Lise, I count the hours and seconds until I shall see you again. I shall unwither and grow in the glow of your light.

Shafts of weak sunlight fall through the window and illuminate the desk in front of me. As we move into the final weeks of Anne-Lise's life, I read faster and more breathlessly.

16/01/59

Gloomy shadows were lengthening and gathering outside. Inside, I sat with Anne-Lise in the glare of the strip lights. Her face was pale and bloodless. Her skin was almost translucent. Beneath her eyes were two blue semicircles. Her hands twisted together. Reaching out compulsively, she pulled and knotted her hair. I sat across from her behind my desk, my eyes fixed on her. She looked downward, staring at her books, shaking her head.

She had not done the reading I had given her: Plato's Symposium, parts of Sartre's L'Être et le néant and Baudelaire's Les Fleurs du mal. I wanted her to research the representation of love. She looked downcast and distracted. I hardly recognized her.

I could hear my own voice talking, trying patiently to explain to her what each work was about. Although she nodded from time to time I could see that she was deaf to my words. Occasionally she looked up, as if trying to engage with the subject. Yet as I attempted to meet her eyes, I realized that she was staring past my shoulder. Again and again, whatever was behind me drew her gaze and held it rapt. My words fell on her deafness. Slowly, I turned and peered into the dim square of the window. Was it merely the outside that attracted her? Escape? Freedom?

And then, as my eyes adjusted to the twilight, I made out a figure waiting in it. I could glimpse the face glowing ghostly in the dark, which swallowed up the hair, the body, merged with them into one great expanse of blackness.

An immigrant's face with Slavic almond eyes.

Kurmakin. He waited for her in the cold evening and her eyes crept toward him. To me, she could only mumble half-remembered fragments of dead texts. He pulled her into his orbit.

I told her to go. She said sorry. I didn't see the expression on her face because I couldn't look at her. Her voice was strained. I heard the door close behind her and then I saw her silhouette outside next to his, both blurred by the dusk, two frail shadows about to disappear into the night.

23/01/59

Four o'clock in the morning. Sleep will not come and so I sit here at my desk hunched over the paper. My cold fingers clutch the pen that jumps despite my attempts to control it. I can hear my breath and my pulse beating in my ears.

She has not been in school for three days now. Each morning I feel my heart squeezed with terror, waiting to see whether the chattering tide of pupils will carry her in. I look *for her pale skin amid the flippant smiles and the weary eyes. The disappointment when she does not appear is an almost physical pain, a kind of malignant growth that swells in my chest and sets my nerves on fire. I try to concentrate on what I have to teach, but it is a useless effort. I can feel my thoughts breaking apart, my mouth straining to form words, my speech slurring into nonsense. My eyes turn toward the window and scan the distance. I look to pick her out amid the mists and the rain, even though I know she will not be there.*

I turn my head and look out upon rows of baffled faces. I try to force the pieces of my mind back together. I want to carry on but the memory of her is like radiation scarring and devastating everything within me.

In the quietness of the night, shivering at my desk, I wonder what the difference is between loneliness and isolation. I always saw the latter as a precondition of serious thought: a necessary distance from the chatter of the world.

In the sleepless hours of the morning I can no more think than stop my bloodless hands from shaking with cold. The silence around me feels not like a cocoon but like the emptiness that waits for us all in death.

26/01/59

Anne-Lise has returned! A little quieter than before. A little paler. Her skin has been drained of some of its brightness. Its golden tone has faded gray. Her deep brown eyes seem wider, as if the flesh of her face has somehow melted away. I did not know how to speak to her but she seemed anxious not to waste any time. She came up to my desk at the end of the lesson, almost shyly, crossing and uncrossing her arms. She swayed slightly on her hips and chewed at her bottom lip.

"Dr. Ollivier, I'm sorry for my absence this last week. I wasn't well . . . and . . . I couldn't read."

I *perhaps nodded. I still couldn't look at her. What illness could have eaten away her flesh like that?*

"But I want to continue now. If that's okay with you. I hope that you want to continue too."

The nerves in my skin are dancing. She hopes that I too want to continue. That I want to . . .

Now it is February. The last days and hours Anne-Lise will ever know.

13/02/59

What am I to make of the strange contradictions that inhabit this child? For days she had attacked books with a kind of fervor. She was desperate to compensate for the time she had lost, weakened by whatever it was that hollowed out her cheeks and made her eyes shine even more wildly than before. It seemed as if she had forgotten her illness. More than ever, she wished to exist solely in the élan of pure thought. She seemed alive once more with that intensity of intelligence and feeling that makes the rest of the world fade into insignificance and draws me irresistibly toward her.

And then today her face suddenly decomposed. There was water running down her cheeks and some primitive sounds, like choking or vomiting, came out of her. She said, "I'm sorry, I'm so sorry, I can't do this now," and she grabbed her books and turned away from me.

As she reached the door she stopped. "Dr. Ollivier, can I talk to you?" She said it almost inaudibly. "Not now, not today. But . . . I need to talk to you. Is that okay?"

I said nothing. I nodded but I kept my eyes trained on the books in front of me on the desk. Whatever had eaten Anne-Lise's flesh had smashed into her like a train and broken her into pieces. The girl who had tormented my dreams for so

222 Ł JAMES BRYDON

*long was gone, she didn't exist anymore, and I couldn't bear
to look at the wreckage.*

This is the final entry. Three days before Anne-Lise's
mutilated body was laid to rest on the heathland above
the wild glitter of the waves. I lay the journal back down
on the table. I can feel the cold that Erwann spoke of.

After some time, I don't know if it is minutes or hours,
I hear the creak of the door. Footsteps sound in the hall.
Erwann enters and starts to say something. Then he sees
the diary open in front of me. His brows contract. Something quivers in his face and his eyes sweep the room.

"You killed Anne-Lise," I say.

Once again, he looks as if he might say something. A
flicker crosses his face like a smile. His eyes flit from side
to side, desperate, cornered.

He walks over to the bookshelves and picks up a large
stone paperweight in his left hand. Then, turning, still
holding the rock in his bunched fist, he walks toward me.

Through the wire-latticed glass of the interrogation room
door, we watch Erwann sitting on a gray metal chair. He
rests his head on his hands, which clutch at the graying
strands of hair dotting his temples. He has not spoken for
hours now. Instead, he rubs his eyes, or simply stares at
the dull walls, his mouth clamped shut.

"Are you sure it's him?" Lafourgue asks.

"It's him."

Lafourgue shrugs. Only yesterday I told him it was de
la Hallière. Why believe me now?

"What have you got, apart from the diary?"

"Nothing."

"And it doesn't prove anything at all, except that he

fantasized about teenage girls. That's not a crime. We might be able to shame him with it, but not convict him of anything."

Lafourgue is right. And yet I saw that darting flicker in Erwann's eyes: part prey, part predator. He started to come at me with the paperweight and then, suddenly, his fingers loosened and he simply placed it on the table in front of me. He seemed totally calm. Eerily cold. "And? What are you going to do about that idea?" he asked.

"I want you to come to the police station with me to talk about Anne-Lise."

"Do I have to?" A faint smile emerged from the corners of his mouth.

"No . . . You know that I don't have any police powers."

"I see." He sauntered back over to the bookcase and peered at the volumes arrayed there. "But if I don't come, I imagine that you will simply go to Lafourgue and then I shall have to suffer the indignity of being questioned by someone of vastly inferior intelligence."

"Yes."

"In that case, I would prefer to come with you."

He didn't utter a single word as I drove, but it seemed as if that icy calm were beginning to ebb away from him. His breaths grew heavier in his chest. He twisted his fingers and gazed hard into the distant whiteness where the indefinition of fog blurred into the spectral shapes of snow-bound trees, hedges, and fields.

Now, in the interrogation chambers, he simply sits still, silhouetted by the gray walls, waiting.

"We have absolutely nothing on him," says Lafourgue.

"Right. And he knows that. For a moment, when he saw me reading the journal, he was afraid. There was a moment of panic. Then his intelligence reasserted itself.

That same glacial intelligence that knew how to erase all traces of the crime from the body. He knew there was no proof. He knows it now."

"So why's he here?"

"Because he wants to hear what I know. And what I can guess."

Lafourgue seems unconvinced. "What do you want to do?"

"Can I talk to him?"

"Only if he wants to. I can't detain him. Let me ask."

I watch Lafourgue's lips moving through the glass and Erwann nods slightly. Lafourgue comes out and holds the door open for me. I sit down across from Erwann.

"Lafourgue says we can talk."

He doesn't respond.

"Let's start with what we know. You loved Anne-Lise. There's no point in denying that. It's imprinted in every word you wrote in your journal. The whole world came alive when she was near you. When she wasn't there, you felt confined. Trapped. Closed within the desolate boundaries of yourself. That oscillation terrified you— between a kind of delirious, unstable joy and a barren, desperate isolation, a loneliness so extreme that it made your whole life seem meaningless. You felt you could only live again in the glow of Anne-Lise's presence.

"That was love, as you experienced it. Anne-Lise *terrorized* you. Oh, she illuminated your days. But when you woke up with shivers and night sweats and faced the interminable parade of identical minutes until the dawn, then you understood the power she had over you. She was your torturer. In your seemingly eternal separation from her, you must have hated her every bit as much as you loved her. She reduced you to such misery, abased you, annihilated your self, made you believe that everything you were and had ever done was worthless because you couldn't inspire her to love you.

"You tried to talk to her about it. Not directly. That was why you gave her philosophy and literature about love. It was the closest you could come to acknowledging the pain and the rage inside you. You needed to hear the word *love* on her lips, even if she couldn't say it about you. It eased the pressure a little. Afforded you a tingle of pleasure. Made you able to exist for one more day, hoping and hopeless.

"So it went for weeks. Months. Then Anne-Lise disappeared for a few days and came back looking as if something had eaten away the flesh of her face. You didn't know what it was, this thing that had corroded her. Cheapened her.

"She wanted to come and talk to you about it. She told you that three days before somebody beat her until she was unrecognizable, then strangled her, mutilated her body, and left it framed by the majesty of the sea like some work of art."

Suddenly, Erwann pushes his chair back from the table and doubles over, clutching his stomach. He retches. The spasm shakes his whole body. A stream of bile spews in an arc from between his lips. His chest heaves painfully. For about a minute he can't move, can't control his own body, which twitches furiously and spills its waste onto the tiled floor of the interrogation room.

Before I can move there are policemen in the room with us. One of them helps Erwann to his feet and steadies him. "We'll have to take you to another room," he says.

Erwann, his face ashen, simply nods.

"Do you want some water?"

Again, Erwann can only nod. He shuffles into the corridor, and once we are settled in another identical-looking room, he sips intermittently at a plastic cup.

"I'm sorry," he says to me, "about before. That was . . . abject."

"Can we continue?"

He is silent.

"I know what Anne-Lise told you. She came to you looking for understanding. She couldn't talk to her mother. Her friends were too young. She respected you. She thought that you wouldn't judge her with small-town morality. And so she sought you out to tell you that she had been pregnant with Sasha Kurmakin's baby and that she'd had an abortion. The guilt was chewing at her insides. Eating her flesh, you said. That cellular pulse inside her had been a life and she had destroyed it. It would have stopped her going to Paris to study. She knew that Sasha would never have wanted to be tied down. Every logical instinct screamed at her that she couldn't have a baby. So she put an end to the existence of that tiny, unformed life in her womb.

"She came to talk to you about guilt but you couldn't hear what she was saying. You saw only Kurmakin's pale hands clutching the hidden reaches of her flesh."

For a second Erwann's eyes meet mine, then he looks away. Something in the depths of his gaze troubles me. I don't know what happened after this. The diary ends. The evidence has all disappeared. Only Erwann now knows and he has twisted everything in his own mind. He has invented some things and forgotten others. He has deformed whatever fragments of the past remain with him until they've become something that he can live with day by day.

"From this point on, I'll have to guess. I don't know exactly what happened. I think Anne-Lise said that she needed to talk to you. She asked if she could come and see you. You didn't know why she was suffering. Perhaps you hoped that it was for you. Some desperate, illogical longing rumbled in the pit of your stomach. You thought it was her desire for you that had martyrized her flesh. Hope blinded you. You set a date: the sixteenth of February. You told her to come to your house.

"What did you do before she arrived? Were you nervous, checking your clothes, your skin, your smell? Did you think about how long it had been since you'd kissed a woman, and suddenly you were aware of the awkwardness of your hands, your words, your tongue? Perhaps you drank a little, choked back a few mouthfuls of something chemical, anesthetic, something that made your hands lie still but your head swim. The minutes must have trickled by painfully. An agony of waiting, and still she didn't come.

"I see you by the window, staring out, willing her to appear, wondering if she could have changed her mind. Has she slipped away from you, vanished and left you alone?

"Then you hear the tap of her fingers on the door. You feel like you might cry, either out of joy or despair, you can't even tell the difference anymore. You wonder where she'll sit. How close to you. But before you can speak, she has sat down at the other end of the lounge, far away from you. She looks drained. Apologetic. Something isn't right.

"You offer her a drink. Alcohol isn't subtle but it is magical. It seems to pull her toward you. You take another drink. The blood drums against your temples. It feels like having your head pushed down beneath the waves. The half-lit room shudders like a drowned city.

"Anne-Lise opens her mouth and starts to speak. She looks up at you. She *trusts* you. She thinks that you will speak to her with dispassionate wisdom. You won't say that she's a whore who killed her own baby. She tells you that she was pregnant. She says that the baby was Sasha's and she glances down as she says it. You can't see her eyes. She says she didn't know what to do. She would have disappointed him either way. She would have ruined her own life. There was no good way out.

"She had a scan and she saw a fuzzy, shapeless blob on the screen no more than a few millimeters in size, pulsing with life.

"She put an end to it. And now those gray clouds of growing cells haunt her sleep. That pulse ticks in her ears.

"You saw Kurmakin's body pressed against Anne-Lise. Her fingers reaching out to hold him. Her legs spread wide. Her head thrown back as she floated on his scent. Her hair a corona. Her skin damp with sweat. Her breath in ragged gasps from the pit of her belly. The pale kinks of her ribs crushed against him. A rhapsody by starlight.

"The police photos of the injuries to Anne-Lise's face are stuck in my mind. The way her eyes were destroyed. Her gaze must have been unbearable to you. What did you see in the depths of her stare? Her indifference to you? Your own powerlessness? You felt everything in the room lurch away from you and rush toward her.

"You walked to the bookshelves and picked up something heavy, perhaps a stone paperweight, and beat her face to a pulp. That skin that made yours tingle, that breathed poison at you, came apart beneath your hands. You made her unrecognizable.

"You waited. Did you realize what you had done? Then you choked her. You wanted one final act of intimacy with her so you used your hands. Anne-Lise breathed her last in your embrace. She died on your living room floor. She must have screamed. Your blows blinded her. She faced her last moments in the dark, terrified, writhing, her broken skin pressed against your hands.

"I don't think you can remember it now. Your mind turned blank. When you came to, you found her lying on the floor beside you. Your fingers must have been aching and bruised.

"Did you know she was dead? Did you touch her? Caress her body for the first and only time? Did you panic?

"I don't think you did, not even for a minute. Everything you did then was calm and methodical. Perhaps you had learned from what happened to Julie Bergeret. You remembered your hasty attempts to hide her body. This time, you would not need to skulk. You washed the body inch by inch. Destroyed or disposed of the clothes. Then you saw the corpse that you had made of Anne-Lise. The battered face. The bruised neck. Another commonplace, trivial crime. Love that turned to jealousy and then to rage. A soap opera of trite rejection. A footnote in the local newspapers. The momentary blind rage of an aging man.

"You didn't see it like that. You thought of Baudelaire and of love. You cut the flesh out of Anne-Lise's side as if you were living a great moment of ecstatic nihilism. Perhaps you were also thinking of the abortion: the living flesh taken out of her belly; the obscenity of her impregnation and the termination of that tiny life.

"I wonder if it hurt you, or even disgusted you, to hack at the flesh you had so adored. You saw the wound hanging open in her flank. There wasn't any blood. The heart had already died.

"You didn't mutilate Anne-Lise's body out of hatred but out of love. You wanted to give a sense to the crime. It was an act of interpretation. You wanted to say *why* Anne-Lise died, that she wasn't just the victim of helpless rage.

"In the cold and the silence of a winter's night, you carried Anne-Lise's body to the heather and laid it there, naked, exposed, one hand grasping at the brown shoots and the other resting chastely upon her breast. You left her in that posture that seemed to summarize and eternalize the contradictions of her life. In death, you made her tormented existence into art."

For a long time Erwann sits perfectly still, rigid, his greenish-gray eyes blankly reflecting the light.

"Was it like that? Say it."

He shakes his head.

"Say it. You need to say it."

Once again he shakes his head. He blinks, as if confused for a moment. Then he smiles. There's something like relief in the twitch of his lips. He looks weary, though. The skin around his eyes is a maze of wrinkles.

"Is that all?" he asks.

I nod.

"Am I free to go?"

He picks himself up slowly, swaying slightly. His tanned skin looks gray in the dullness of the strip light above us. He walks slowly out of the room, and in my mind I follow his halting steps along the corridor and past the front desk. Nobody stops him. He walks out untouched into the light.

* * *

Lafourgue touches my shoulder. "You can't sit in this room all evening."

I feel his grip beneath my shoulder, lifting me out of the chair.

"What did you think would happen?" he asks.

"He needed me to know. To understand. That's why he begged me to investigate the case. So that the poison of it wouldn't only be inside him. He could have gotten away with it. The case was dead and nobody would have picked it up. He knew that. But he felt the memory of it corroding him. He thought that I could explain to him what he did. That's why he cut Anne-Lise's flesh, and that's why he needed me to investigate long after the case was cold: to understand and interpret what he did."

"I had some forensic work done in his house while you were questioning him. We didn't find anything yet, although some of the samples will take time. You understand that we had to let him go."

"I know. There was nothing to keep him with. No traces. No witnesses. No confession. It's over."

Lafourgue purses his lips. His shrewd eyes narrow. "Okay. Then it's over. For now. But we know how to put pressure on people. We'll keep track of him. Follow him. Put a man behind him, someone in his peripheral vision. We'll be like his conscience, his memory. We won't let him rest or sleep. Then we'll see what comes out."

My body feels numb as I step slowly out into the chill of evening. For some reason, I don't want to take the car. I need to try to calm my muscles. The frozen air tastes clean, disinfected.

In my mind I see only Anne-Lise's sightless eyes gaping, her hands scrabbling, her final moments consumed by wordless terror.

I see Erwann's face twisting and distorting as his guts heave and he spews his bile across the interrogation room floor.

Abject, he said.

The heathland is one immensity of white glowing spectrally, staining the sky with its brightness. I still have the picture of Anne-Lise in my pocket. I can't bring it out to look at. My fingers are bent with cold, as if they've iced up, become pure bone. And the light that radiates from Anne-Lise is unbearable. Cancerous.

Three words throb in my mind: *Do you know? Do you know?* I thought I knew before. I was convinced that de la Hallière had killed her in his basement. I have become more like a schizophrenic than an investigator. The hum of the past is a constant distortion in my head. I can't hear my own thoughts. I hear only the whispers of words long forgotten, fluttering like bats' wings, murmuring in the dark, brushing the inside of my skull.

Do you know? Do you know? Do you know?

EPILOGUE
DAY NINE

Morning

Loud and insistent knocking wakes me up from a deep sleep. As my brain gropes for reality, I am aware of something clinging to me, a cloying embrace that only slowly loosens its grip on my lungs and heart. Fear. I can't remember what I was dreaming, but the feeling wears out my nerves and digs deep into my brain.

As I stumble to the door, I am convinced that it will be Erwann. The wish to see him is overpowering.

It is Lafourgue who stands in the mist, his face impassive, and says, "Erwann Ollivier's body was found this morning smashed on the rocks of the La Fosse beach. We don't know if he jumped, fell, or was pushed. Some kids found his body around seven a.m.—or rather, what was left afterward. Most of its left side was obliterated when it hit the rocks. The drop is over fifty meters. The rest of the body was pounded by the tide all night. The flesh was green and swollen. It was him, though, there's no doubt about it. I think it will go down as suicide."

Lafourgue speaks laconically and I hear once again the promise he made yesterday: *We'll be like his conscience.* Was this what he meant?

"We never got a confession from him and we couldn't find anything at his house either. I suppose that means that the Aurigny case is never going to be officially closed."

Not closed, just left abandoned until her death sinks into amnesia. Finally, like Julie Bergeret, she will exist only in the memories of a few paranoid, addled drifters who carry their visions of her out into the blind and indifferent world.

Did Erwann jump? I saw him walk out into the light yesterday but perhaps he felt the darkness hemming him in. Perhaps he had lived through these last months waiting only for the moment when he could pass his burden on to someone else. He needed another person to know what he knew. Someone else had to carry it, like a malignant strand of DNA buried deep in the body. Once the transmission was complete, he could walk slowly to the cliff top and feel the fury of the wind lashing his face. He could see the leaden mass of the sea and do the one thing he had dreamed of for so long: walk into the void.

He didn't just want to kill himself. He wanted to annihilate himself. To return his flesh and bones to the churning and indistinguishable pulse of matter that is nature. He wanted to pretend he had never existed. It took courage, to step off the end of the world like that. He must have felt gravity wrench him through the air. Did he feel the impact? Was there a moment of atrocious pain? Or did oblivion come at once as the rocks smashed his unquiet skull and pulverized his body? Is this what he finally wanted? To disappear? To leave the world as if he had never been in it?

Or was this his final revenge? Leaving us amid a mocking, unending silence, an emptiness in which only the drone of that eternal question recurs with the furious monotony of the waves battering his body to nothingness and the rocks to sand: *Do you know? Do you know? Do you know?*

"Do you want to see the body?" Lafourgue asks.

The skin sodden, bloated, broken. Water rotting the flesh before bacteria could break it down. Moldering flotsam strewn on the beach.

I shake my head. Lafourgue turns to go.

"Hey, Jacques, I forgot to ask. Are you done with the car now? If so, I'll take it back to the station."

I stare up at Lafourgue's blank, gray eyes and at the blank, gray air behind him glinting through the mist. "No. I have an idea. There's something I need to check. And then there's one last thing I need to do."

The road to le Quéduc winds through rows of trees and over icy stone bridges. The town is sleepy. Old ladies with shopping bags shuffle outside the bakery. Passersby stare down at the pavement, trying not to lose their footing on the frosty concrete. The lycée Balzac is a small stone building with bright yellow shutters drawn back from its windows. Pupils sits in groups outside, smoking cigarettes and huddling into their jackets. I park outside and make inquiries at reception. I can feel my body shaking. I am so impatient that I can barely get the words out.

I lie. I say that I am a police officer and that I am investigating a violent crime. I explain that the case may be connected to the murder of Julie Bergeret. I ask to see the school's personnel records going back to the end of the war.

I need to see Erwann's name on the list. Where was he before September 1948? I am now convinced that he was right here, at the lycée Balzac, where one of his students, Julie Bergeret, through what Père Clavel called her luminous goodness, drew his attention. It was the fact that he noticed her, picked up some glowing signal from her, that led to her strangled corpse being dug out of the hard ground in the winter of 1947. If Erwann taught here before working at the lycée Cartier, then I can finally answer that question that throbs in my head. It wouldn't be enough to get a conviction, or to close the case file. But it would quiet the murmur in my mind. I could let Anne-Lise go.

I trawl through the records very carefully. Name by name. Year by year. Erwann has to be there. In dull brown ink on yellowing paper, I have to find his name.

The years trickle past. There is nothing. My heart is thumping. I try to breathe steadily and I begin again. Earlier this time. I go right back to 1940. I read and reread each piece of paper but still Erwann does not appear.

I ask to speak to the *proviseur*. He beckons me to sit down but my legs are twitching too much to be still. I ask him whether the records are complete. I ask him whether there is any memory of Erwann being at the school. He says not. I ask him to make some further enquiries. To check. I need to be sure.

He nods and withdraws. There is something uneasy in his glance but I am too impatient to inquire into what is bothering him. I simply need the answer to this one question and then whatever else happens will no longer matter.

After a while he returns and assures me, calmly but with a clear note of finality in his voice, that he has spoken to various teachers who have been at the school for decades and there is no possibility that a Dr. Erwann Ollivier has ever taught here. He wishes me the very best of luck with my investigation and stands politely and holds the door to his study open for me.

Outside, the winter sun strews sparkling jewels through the air. The pupils have all gone inside to begin their lessons. I am alone in the courtyard, staring up at the clouds dispersing above.

Nothing connects Erwann to Julie Bergeret. And what about Anne-Lise? He loved her and it tormented him. She haunted his dreams and his waking hours. Sickness wracked his body when he thought about her death. But was it guilt or simply despair? Did he murder Anne-Lise, or had he lost the only thing that brought light into his life?

Perhaps my accusation seemed like an unbearable betrayal. Did remorse kill Erwann, or my need to offer justice to Anne-Lise and so to atone for Amira?

His silence now is absolute.

The sea beats its tattoo against the rocks, monotonous, eternal: *Do you know? Do you know?*

The creek by the Château de la Hallière has frozen over and the ground is bone-hard. The car's engine purrs softly as I pull in by the trees, then all is quiet as I turn the ignition off and wait. I sit there with my eyes on the road, staring as the glare of low-slung winter sun sparkles on the horizon and makes the vast expanse of snow dissolve into myriad individual crystals. The mist wafts slowly, obdurately, across the estuary. Birds mill about, squawking and wheeling in the weak blaze of light.

I remain motionless for a long time, my eyes straining against the sharp sunlight to see both the château and the road. Hours go by. The sun starts to fade. The mists thicken and wreathe the car. The world is all whiteness.

Finally, I see what I have been waiting for. A shadow

moves amid the fog, coming out of the château, tripping lightly down the path, toward the road to town.

Aïcha.

Even in the murk, I can see the shimmer of gold around her wrists and neck. I watch the bounce and the rocking of her gait. I watch her silhouette diminish in the distance before I put the car into gear. I take the hill down to Sainte-Élisabeth gently, letting the car roll forward under the influence of gravity until I am right behind her. She waves a hand at me without turning around, to signal that I can pass.

I pull up next to her and wind the window down. "Aïcha, do you remember me?"

She nods. She is a riot of color. Her golden-brown skin. Turquoise lids above her black-rimmed eyes. The crimson flashes of her nails. I speak to her in Arabic.

"I'm leaving Sainte-Élisabeth. Today. Now. I'll take you with me, if you want. I can drop you off wherever you want to go. I don't mind where. I'm not going anywhere special. Or you can stay with me for a while, if you want, while you figure out where it is you'd like to go. That's okay too."

Aïcha looks puzzled. "Where would I go?"

"You can decide that later."

"You should leave me alone now." She reverts back to French. "Christian wouldn't like you talking to me like this." She gnaws at her lower lip and turns away from me. I watch her steps dwindling into the distance.

Then she glances down at the empty grocery bags in her hands. She drops the bags into the snow, turns around slowly, and walks back up to the car. She taps my window with one scarlet nail. She speaks Arabic again. The words sound gentle.

"It's just a ride out of here? You'll take me wherever I want to go?"

"Wherever you want."

"Then I'll come."

As she sits down on the leather seat beside me, I breathe the sweetness of her perfume right down into my lungs. I can feel the breath suddenly tighten in my chest. I think about picking up some things from the house but I don't ever want to go back there again. I hope that Robert or Madame Gallier will fix the door, which is hanging off its hinges and flapping madly in the madness of the wind.

I let the car start to roll slowly down the hill toward Sainte-Élisabeth, and as we reach the edge of town, I turn into the corniche. We trundle unhurriedly along the icy, empty route and on our left the heather lies hooded and buried in the snow and on our right gusts rip inland from across the sea. Beneath my hands the steering wheel jerks when the tires struggle to grip the ice. I turn away from the metallic mass of the sky. I try to blot out the sweet scent of Aïcha's skin and the thump of breath quickening in my lungs and I grip the wheel tightly and concentrate on holding the car steady on the snaking, deserted winter road.